# Triple
# Homicide

Also by Charles Hynes

*Incident at Howard Beach: The Case for Murder*

# Triple Homicide

CHARLES HYNES

Thomas Dunne Books | St. Martin's Press
New York

This is a work of fiction. All of the characters, organizations, and events portrayed in this novel are either products of the author's imagination or are used fictitiously.

THOMAS DUNNE BOOKS.
An imprint of St. Martin's Press.



www.thomasdunnebooks.com
www.stmartins.com

Library of Congress Cataloging-in-Publication Data

Hynes, Charles J.
Triple homicide / Charles Hynes.
p. cm.
ISBN-13: 978-0-312-33860-2
ISBN-10: 0-312-33860-0
1. Police—New York (State)—New York—Fiction. 2. New York (N.Y.)—Fiction.
I. Title.
PS3608.Y58 T75 2007
813'.6—dc22

2006053303

First Edition: June 2007

10 9 8 7 6 5 4 3 2 1

For my wife and best friend, Patricia, for your
constant encouragement and support.

To the men and women of the New York City
Police Department whose courage, integrity, and
strength have made New York City safe for
the people they selflessly protect.

# acknowledgments

I want to especially acknowledge those who helped me make this book possible:

Sean Desmond, formerly of Thomas Dunne Books, St. Martin's Press, and my original editor, who provided great editing skill and creative ideas, turning this book from what I hoped was an interesting story to what we both believe is an exciting mystery novel.

To Howard Kaminsky for your encouragement and help in finding a publisher.

To New York State Supreme Court Justice, Honorable Edwin Torres.

Peter Israel for your ideas.

To Thomas Dunne for believing in the worth of this project.

Special thanks to Catherine Schauf and Maureen Kravitz.

Thank you to Anne Swern and Mortimer Matz.

To Honorable Robert G. M. Keating, dean of the New York Judicial Institute, Harvey L. Greenberg, and Joanna Zmijewski with gratitude.

Finally, to James E. Kohler, Esq., deceased, a great trial lawyer whose ideas contributed so much to this book.

# Triple Homicide

# prologue

The story that I am about to tell is mostly true. I have changed the names of the characters out of my concern for their privacy. Much of this tale was told to me by an extraordinary journalist who was perhaps the last of those insightful observers and courtroom commentators working in New York City up until the 1970s. Those in that elite club included Jimmy Cannon, from the *New York Post*, Scotty Reston and Russell Baker, both of the *New York Times*, and, of course, the great Murray Kempton, who for years wrote for the *New York Post* and who ended his distinguished career as a columnist for the New York City and Long Island newspaper *Newsday*.

I'll call my guy Morty, not his real name, because that's what he wanted. "If," he once said to me, "you ever get around to writing about this, leave me out." Then he added, "Ya see, if I wrote it, it would sound so far-fetched that no one would believe it, and I got a reputation to keep. You, on the other hand—you're a fuckin' lawyer, so it doesn't matter if anyone believes you!"

For years, Morty covered the New York City Criminal Court in Brooklyn for a great parochial newspaper, the *Brooklyn Eagle*. It was during the late 1950s and early '60s, and it was a glorious time to be a reporter. In those days there were ten major daily newspapers; the *News* and *Mirror* (many people thought that they were one newspaper, as in "da *News 'n' Mirror*"), the *Post,* the *Times,* the *New York World Telegram and Sun,* the *Herald Tribune*, the *Journal American,* the *Staten Island Advance,* the *Long Island Press,* and, of course, the small but mighty *Brooklyn Eagle.* Just as so many great trial lawyers learned their basic skills and honed them early in their careers in the local criminal courtrooms, working for the Legal Aid Society or the district attorney's office, these same venues provided exceptional training for young journalists. And just as the lawyers cut their teeth on this invaluable experience and began to develop their technique through the sheer volume of cases available to them, so, too, did Morty and his peers learn their trade. They learned the critical need to make a deadline in order to get a story printed, how to cultivate sources, and how to find ways to get tips and scoop the competition. For these police reporters, particularly the young ones, the criminal court was unvarnished high drama, with its share of heroes and villains, joy and tragedy, chaos and pathos. Morty never permitted himself to lose his enthusiasm for covering the courtroom scene. He called the court at 120 Schermerhorn Street in Brooklyn "the Hall of Hell." The hall, actually called the Criminal Court for the City of New York, is a huge ten-story building whose facade was constructed of gray sandstone blocks. It houses a dozen courtrooms, judges' chambers, clerks' offices, a large complaint room, where criminal charges are first docketed, and offices for the assistant district attorneys and for the lawyers from the Legal Aid Society, an organization known elsewhere in the country as the office of the public defender. The building, which occupies nearly three-quarters of a full city block, is filled each day with hundreds of police officers, hundreds more victims and defendants, and an equivalent number of tragic stories.

I first met Morty in 1963 when I worked as a criminal defense attorney for the Legal Aid Society at the Criminal Court. Our meeting was one of instant and mutual dislike. I was representing a federal agent, charged in a series of brutal sodomy attacks on seven children in separate incidents. None of the children was older than nine. While each act was particularly vicious, performed at gunpoint, there was a serious question whether any of the children had correctly identified the assailant. The children separately described the assailant as much heavier and considerably taller than the defendant. The only accuracy of the identification was that both the assailant and the defendant had facial hair, although even that similarity created difficulty for the prosecution because the hair color described by each victim ranged from bright red to jet black. The agent, a childhood friend of mine whom I had not seen in years, was in the lockup—the holding cells located in the basement of the courthouse. He spotted me while I was interviewing one of my clients. This subterranean cellblock could have been designed by Dante. It was poorly lit and permeated with the ubiquitous stench of urine and body odor, which clung to the walls and the clothing of everyone who passed through the holding area. In sum, it was a dungeon, which echoed with the ceaseless ramblings of the detainees packed together in several adjoining cells, creating a loud, frightening din. It most certainly was a terrorizing experience for a federal cop from the other side of the criminal justice system.

Special Agent Frank O'Sullivan of the Federal Bureau of Investigation was dressed in a blue golf shirt and tan slacks with worn brown penny loafers. His smoker's face was prematurely aged with deep lines, and his hair was an odd mix of white and gray with clumps of each in no particular pattern. His slumping shoulders made him appear even shorter than his five feet six inches. He was leaning against the bars of his cell when he first spotted me. He was sadly self-conscious of the dried tears that streaked his cheeks, and through a voice breaking with fear, he begged me to represent him at his arraignment on the criminal charges. An arraignment is part of the initial court proceeding where a person charged with a crime is formally told the specifics of the charges. He told me that his lawyer was delayed and he had been told by the correction officer in charge of the detention area that his case would not be called until his lawyer appeared. I telephoned my boss and got permission to represent O'Sullivan for the arraignment. I was directed to make it clear to the judge that the Legal Aid Society was appearing on O'Sullivan's behalf only for the arraignment.

When the case was called, the courtroom was filled with the anxious and angry parents of the seven little victims, several dozen police officers and court officers, and seemingly every reporter in New York City. This only served to piss off the local police reporters, Morty in particular, making them all the more ravenous for inside news in order to show up "those people from the City," as the regulars referred to their invading colleagues. Of course, the children were kept in another room, protected by a detail of police officers and watched over by several social workers from the citywide trauma unit of the Victims Services Agency.

The court officer motioned to O'Sullivan, who was seated in a holding area in the courtroom, and directed him to come forward as he called the docket number and the name of the case, which included the name of the defendant. This particular announcement has a daunting effect on the defendant because it proclaims the awesome power of the state, "The People of the State of New York against. . . ." Then, turning to me, he directed, "Please give your notice of appearance." A notice of appearance is one of the court system's numerous anachronisms. It means simply that the attorney must give his or her name, address, and affiliation for the stenographic record of the proceeding, which is preserved for future review—for example, to show that a defendant was properly advised of the charges brought by the prosecutor. I replied, "Charles J. Hynes, associate attorney, the Legal Aid Society, representing the defendant."

"Does he have a name?" was Judge Cromwell's curt inquiry.

"Yes, of course he does, Your Honor, and it was just announced by the court officer, when the case was called." Judge Cromwell, a huge man whose distended belly and florid face were the marks of the final stages of a diseased liver, the result of decades of gluttonous boozing, immediately took offense. In a booming voice for all to hear, particularly the families of the victims, but especially the assembled media, he demanded, "Why is the Legal Aid Society representing this federal agent, who surely has the resources to retain private counsel?" Nothing I could say by way of explanation would keep the judge, one of the worst political hacks we had to deal with, from getting his moment in the sun. Judge Cromwell closed his tirade against the Legal Aid Society in general and me in particular with "Bail is set in each of the seven cases at one million dollars. Each," he added, not sure that he was fully understood. Then he ended with this:

"If this defendant, a federal agent"—and here, in a loud and melodramatic voice, he pronounced and spelled O'Sullivan's full name—"Francis Emmett O'Sullivan can put up seven million dollars to secure his return to court when necessary, then perhaps you, Mr. Hynes, and your organization, which exists to represent indigent criminals—"

"Defendants," I shouted, interrupting the judge.

"Don't you dare interrupt me or I shall set bail on you!" he screamed, with such intensity that it was accompanied with a noisy belch and the unmistakable odor of rye whiskey, part of his breakfast routine, assaulting everyone within five feet of the judge's bench. He kept his menacing stare fixed on me for almost a full minute. Then he continued.

"Very well, if he makes bail I assume he will pay for his own lawyer." My poor friend Agent O'Sullivan was too shaken to attempt to reply to any of this as he was led away in handcuffs. He looked plaintively in my direction and shrugged his shoulders. As he was being led away, handcuffed behind his back, to the detention cell, I mouthed, "Don't worry," and then I raced from the courtroom. It took less than an hour for me to prepare and serve a writ of habeas corpus on the New York City Department of Corrections, which was holding O'Sullivan.

A writ of habeas corpus is an ancient legal remedy that is a birthright of every American citizen and is one of the foundations of our protection against the vast power of government. The writ is an order issued by a judge directed to the custodian of a person held in confinement. The opening words of the document demand, "Habeas corpus ad subjiciendum"—or, in substance, "You shall have the body brought before me immediately!" Like so many other rights available to American citizens, it has its roots in English law. It is perhaps the most celebrated writ in English law and is revered universally as the "great writ of liberty."

New York State Supreme Court Justice Peter King, who heard my application for the writ and who promptly granted it, at first laughed. Then, when he realized that Judge Cromwell was involved, he shook his head and said, "That asshole!"

I rushed back to the courtroom with the writ. It was there that I first encountered Morty. In fact, I ran smack into him, just as he stepped in front of me and in one breath snarled, "I'm Morty —— of the *Brooklyn Daily Eagle*. How do you get off representing this bum, anyway?" Morty was not much more than five feet tall with a rasping voice, the result of too many years of inhaling Camel cigarettes. He reeked of nicotine. His face was framed by an odd-looking porkpie hat, and he had a huge yellow pencil resting on his right ear. He was wearing a cheap cardigan sweater, dark gray trousers, and a loud red-and-white-striped shirt; it appeared to me that he chose his outfit for what he believed was the appropriate dress of his trade. I recalled that most of the other reporters in the press section of the courtroom wore similar attire. Morty repeated as if I hadn't heard him the first time, "What the fuck gives you the right to use taxpayer money to represent a bum like this?" After my ugly encounter with Judge Cromwell and his absurd brand of justice, I was in no mood for Morty or anyone else, so I pushed him aside and tried to ignore his shouts and complaints that I should be arrested for assault as I made my way to my office. Morty's persistent telephone calls to my office, eleven of them, I left unreturned.

Later, after the writ was granted and Agent O'Sullivan was released without any bail set, Morty accosted me again. I ignored him and resisted a powerful temptation to take his head off.

As the years passed I went on to different jobs, mostly in government, but with some time spent in the private practice of law as a criminal defense attorney. I began to notice Morty's byline on a number of significant crime stories. While I didn't forget our first unpleasant encounter, I admired his writing style. It was clear, thoughtful, and comprehensive, and it contained no personal judgments. Soon he had a column in a major New York City tabloid three times a week, and I became an avid reader and very soon an admiring fan.

In 1985, our paths crossed again. In June that year, New York Governor Mario M. Cuomo appointed me the corruption special prosecutor for New York City. One of the first calls I received was from Morty, who asked to meet with me. He made a luncheon reservation at Forlini's Italian restaurant on Baxter Street in lower Manhattan, not far from the federal and state courthouses and a favorite hangout of prosecutors, defense attorneys, and judges.

The restaurant is divided into two rooms. The main room, entered from Baxter Street, and its attached rear room have an identical placement of booths along the wall on the right side as you go in. Both in the middle and on the left side of each room, there are neatly arranged tables properly spaced for privacy. The booths in both rooms each have a small plaque affixed to the wall, identifying a famous customer, usually a judge, such as New York Supreme Court Justice Edwin Torres, the author of *Carlito's Way*. Justice Torres is famous for a line in a sentencing speech he gave to some incorrigible drug seller: "Listen to me, pal. With the sentence I'm about to give you, your parole officer hasn't been born yet!"

One of the booths bears a plaque dedicated to the current district attorney of New York County, Robert M. Morgenthau, the well-respected dean of the state's district attorneys. Another honors John Fontaine Keenan, a federal judge, formerly the brilliant chief of the Homicide Bureau in the office of the legendary Frank S. Hogan, a feared and respected predecessor of Morgenthau in the DA's office.

The lighting in Forlini's rear room is subdued, so it appears to be a more confidential setting than the brightly lighted entry room. In truth there is really no difference. It just seems more private, although the occupants of the booths, seating four, are often seen leaning over, in secret huddles. Naturally the front room is usually occupied by people who want to be seen. It is generally filled with lively conversation and a great deal of laughter, interrupted by new important arrivals.

The bar at Forlini's could easily be a setting for one of Damon Runyon's stories. It is the venue where the various levels of the court system meet with little thought to class distinction. Court officers, defense attorneys, police officers, prosecutors, and judges freely mix in a convivial setting, gathered around a very long bar. The open kitchen sends waves of tantalizing garlicky smells throughout the bar. The bar is dark, and when you enter through its separate Baxter Street door, the patrons look more like shadows until your eyes adjust.

The bar area is filled at lunch hour, and some of its regulars remain late into the evening. It is mostly dominated by loud conversation, and the din it creates ironically offers more protection for confidential conversation than the rear room.

Appropriately Morty and I met in the rear chamber to discuss our mutual fascination with public corruption and, in particular, police corruption. Before we got to that subject Morty opened with, "So kid, what ever happened to that fed child molester you represented, watshisname O'Reilly or . . . ?"

"O'Sullivan," I corrected him. "It was a tragedy seemingly without an end in sight. You may not remember the details but Frank O'Sullivan was accused by seven little girls, none older than nine years, of separate or unconnected sodomy assaults in different neighborhoods throughout Brooklyn. He was arrested despite the fact that the only evidence was the eyewitness identification by the children, each of whom offered a contradictory recollection of his facial hair. The hair color given to the police by the kids immediately after each assault ranged from bright red to jet black, nevertheless the nature of the brutal attacks, which were identical, was so horrific that the district attorney refused to dismiss even though O'Sullivan's facial hair was distinctly blond. He concluded that the discrepancies could be explained away by the age of the children and the traumatic circumstances of the assaults.

" 'Besides,' the DA said to one of O'Sullivan's lawyers, 'there hasn't been a similar attack since your guy was arrested.'

"O'Sullivan went to trial six times and as I said the facts were identical, so much so that the police department's sex crimes unit characterized the attacks as 'pattern sodomies.' In every case the victim was accosted inside an elevator of a residential building by an assailant with prominent facial hair, sideburns, and a goatee, wearing a bright bandanna which partially covered his face as well as the facial hair. Each victim said the attacker was armed with a small silver plated handgun held against their head. The assailant spoke only once and then briefly. He was somehow able to bypass floors as he took each little girl to the top floor of the building, usually the sixth floor. He then took her roughly by the arm and dragged the terrified child to a metal staircase resembling a fire escape that led up to a room containing the machinery which operated the elevator system. He then forced the victim to kneel."

At this point in my story I decided to give Morty a glimpse inside the trial where I defended O'Sullivan. I wanted him to know what we were up against.

"The assistant district attorney carefully brought the tiny seven-year-old victim through her first contact with her assailant, making it quite clear that her identification was solid.

" 'As you waited for the elevator were there lights on in the lobby?'

" 'Yes.'

" 'Were they very bright?' The prosecutor knew it was an improper leading question but he also knew that the judge would not rule in my favor had I objected because of the child's age and the stress she was under. It didn't really matter because I had no intention of objecting, which I believed would have upset the child and had an adverse effect on the jury.

"The child answered, 'They were very bright.'

" 'Were you alone?'

" 'Yes,' she replied softly and then she added almost in a whisper, 'for just a few minutes.' Here the judge leaned over and said solicitously,

" 'Sweatheart, you will have to speak up so the jurors can hear you.' The little victim then pointed to Frank and blurted out in reply, 'Yes, until he came.'

"At this point tears streamed down her cheeks and she began to shake as she seemed to recall the ugliness of it all. I glanced in the the direction of the jury box and I could see the reactions of some of the jurors, from sadness to anger to disgust.

"After the assistant DA had established that the lighting conditions were bright aboard the elevator and repeatedly asked the child where she was looking as she was abducted and throughout the ordeal leading toward her testimony about the assault in the machinery room he had clearly demonstrated to the jury that she had had ample opportunity to identify her assailant." It was at this point as I recalled her testimony that I carefully watched Morty's reaction.

" 'What happened after you were forced to kneel down?' the prosecutor continued.'

"Now the child sobbed out of control as she described how her attacker zipped down his pants and . . ."

When I finshed describing the wantonness and brutality of the assault I looked at Morty and saw his face had blanched and that he was angry.

"How could you have defended that pig?"

"But Morty," I said, "the guy was innocent."

I completed the account of her testimony where she recalled that the assailant told her, "Count to fifty or else." Then to emphasize what he'd do if she did not, he cocked the gun and pushed it against her head. Then he disappeared out the door and quickly down the metal staircase.

"Frank went to trial six times represented in each case by an experienced and competent trial lawyer. He was convicted in each case on all counts, which included kidnapping, attempted assault, and sodomy. By the time I took him to trial the appellate division had reversed the two prior convictions and dismissed the charges citing the unreliability of eyewitness identification in general and in particular these two cases. In my trial, not only was the facial hair significantly different in color and in length, the attacker was described as having jet black sideburns and a fully developed jet black goatee. Frank's sideburns were blond like the rest of his hair and his arrest photograph showed a goatee with blond fuzz. There was also a serious problem with the height and weight description given to the police. The victim described her attacker as forty pounds heavier than Frank and at least six inches taller." None of that mattered any more than it mattered to Morty, and Frank O'Sullivan was once again convicted.

"By this time O'Sullivan had been fired from his job following his first conviction although he was appealing the ruling by the FBI. That administrative review by the bureau was rendered moot after his next conviction. Of course, his administrative appeal was put back on track after the second reversal which once again was halted upon his third conviction. Finally his marriage of ten years ended in divorce and he lost custody of his nine-year-old daughter. His wife, Rosemary, had stayed with him through the third trial but then said that she could no longer be sure of his innocence and that she was afraid for their daughter. At this point Frank, whose physical condition had deteriorated and who was fighting depression, said he that he was pretty much resigned to what had happened to him and that he fully understood Rosemary's decision.

"Several months later Frank's third conviction was reversed and the case dismissed but the DA refused to change his decision to continue the prosecution. Frank was tried and convicted three more times and in each case there was a reversal and dismissal based on what the appellate court concluded was a flawed eyewitness identification. But it was the language of the court's sixth consecutive reversal and dismissal of *People v. O'Sullivan* that sent a clear message to the district attorney. In what would be the appellate division's last unanimous decision in the O'Sullivan matter, the presiding justice of the court, Honorable R. Herbert Dayon, wrote with eloquent yet direct language, 'No piece of evidence has so disturbed the courts of this state as that of the testimony of an eyewitness without any other support. While this Court does not reject such testimony entirely, every prosecutor who wishes to do a fair job must carefully weigh this evidence with a full appreciation of its potential for a perverse and unjust result.' Dayon then added these words: 'How many times must this Court reverse based on the facts in the O'Sullivan case before the district attorney of Kings County more fully understands that his job is not just to convict but to do justice?' O'Sullivan would not stand trial a seventh time."

Morty, who had recovered from his emotional reaction as he

began to understand Frank's predicament, asked, "So what happened to him?"

"He was restored to duty with back pay," I replied, "but the last time I saw him a few years ago he was still in pretty bad shape and doing everything he could to restore his marriage. A few months later I called him at his office in St. Louis where he was reassigned and he told me he was still not having much luck convincing Rosemary to take him back."

We both realized that the O'Sullivan travesty had consumed most of our lunch, not leaving much time to discuss corruption, and at this point Morty, now in his late sixties, said, "By the way kid, you ain't ever gonna end police corruption. They've tried everything and nothin' works." I smiled and shrugged my shoulders.

Following a delicious meal of veal francese and a side of spaghetti drenched with garlic and oil, we skipped dessert and opted instead for some espresso and a touch of anisette. Suddenly Morty stood and said, "There's some guys at the bar who would like to meet you." "Like who?" I said warily. These were alright guys, he said, a few reporters from the courthouse, a prosecutor, and a defense lawyer. "You know most of them, and," he assured me, "it'll be off the record."

It was Friday afternoon, getaway day, when court calendars were adjourned, and as we entered the bar area, I recognized, at the far end of the room near the door, Bobby Kaminsky, a homicide prosecutor with twenty years in the New York County DA's office, talking to Carlos Rivera, a kick-ass defense lawyer for the last fifteen years. Rivera earlier in his career had ten years in the office of the New York County district attorney. He had just been nominated to the State Supreme Court and with the support of the Democratic organization was assured of a fourteen-year term after the November election. He and Kaminsky were celebrating.

Rivera and Kaminsky were very close, some said like brothers. Carlos Rivera was a solid five feet eight inches tall, with a barrel chest, carefully hidden by tailored Baroni suits. He favored broad-brimmed fedoras and dark gray tweed overcoats with velvet Chesterfield collars. His black Italian leather shoes were always spit-shined, a habit he'd kept from the Marine Corps. His speech was street tough, with salty language picked up and retained from his years of growing up in El Barrio—Spanish Harlem. His jet black hair glistened and was always combed straight back. His friendship with Bobby Kaminsky developed when, as a veteran homicide prosecutor, he was directed by a supervisor to break in Kaminsky. Bobby Kaminsky was six foot five, with a trim two-hundred-pound frame kept solid with a daily exercise regimen that began each morning at five. He had a full head of sandy-colored wavy hair, and as a forty-five-year-old bachelor, he was very much in demand. Kaminsky and Rivera always seemed to be together at Forlini's, either in the restaurant or at the bar. Neither drank much, preferring the give-and-take of the bar scene, mostly sipping Diet Coke or an occasional beer. Their respective statures reminded older patrons of the comic strip characters Mutt and Jeff.

Standing between them were three reporters: Sid Lyons of the *New York Daily News,* with an ever-present series of chain-smoked cigars; Jimmy Fess of *Newsday,* short, fat, and loud; and Barney Golden of the *New York Post* with his checkered sports coat. The three were heavy-duty drinkers. I recognized the reporters from the court scene, but I don't think I ever spoke with any one of them. I knew both Kaminsky and Rivera as superb trial lawyers. It was difficult to get a seat at one of their trials. When they competed, all the brotherly love was left outside the courtroom, and a furious struggle ensued until a jury announced its verdict.

Morty quickly introduced me, more by title than by name. Fess of *Newsday,* barely bothering to acknowledge me, spoke first and offered the following unsolicited observation: "If the state doesn't go broke, the only thing you can be sure of from your fuckin' job is a paycheck every two weeks, because there's no fuckin' way you'll ever do anything about cop corruption, or for that matter judge corruption! It's an institution!" When I asked Fess why he was so certain, Sid Lyons gruffly interrupted and said, "If you don't know why, what the hell makes you qualified to be our special state corruption prosecutor?" To underscore his sarcasm, Lyons slowly and carefully pronounced each syllable of my job title. Kaminsky jumped in and said, "Hey, give him a break, he hasn't even started." Now both Rivera and Golden of the *Post* chimed in, shouting over one another. "Bobby, tell the kid about Mulvey," Golden said. "Tell him," said Carlos Rivera, "how that fucking blue wall destroyed a good cop." Golden continued, "Ya see, every cop knows what happened to Mulvey, and while most of them are honest, hardworking Boy Scouts, because of Mulvey and what the police department did to other cops, no honest cop will ever help you end police corruption." "And," added Morty, "that's why you'll be just another flop in a job that should have been abolished years ago. But in the meantime, take Jimmy Fess's advice. Relax and enjoy your paycheck." I wasn't particularly surprised by the cynicism; it was nothing new. But I wanted to hear about this cop Mulvey.

What they told me that afternoon was shocking enough, but what happened to Mulvey's nephew years later was outrageous. The story of that young cop, Steven Robert Holt, and his uncle, Sergeant Robert Mulvey, is a profoundly tragic example of the culture that created the NYPD's Blue Wall of Silence and why it had to be destroyed in order to end the cyclical evil of police corruption in New York. This story of police corruption begins in an unusual way. It begins with murder.

# 1

Suffolk County, Long Island, New York,
December 20, 1990, 7:30 A.M.

"Oh my God, David." Alyson Keeler sobbed uncontrollably at her gruesome discovery. "Come here, quickly," she pleaded, her body trembling.

Alyson had soft blond hair with streaks of chestnut, worn slightly above her shoulders. Her large hazel eyes were deeply set above high cheekbones in an oval-shaped face. Her aquiline nose was neatly sculpted, and her lips were drawn up in what seemed to be a perpetual smile. She was very pretty, perhaps even beautiful, but this morning her lovely face was twisted by fear, contorted with revulsion at the sight of what lay on the ground only a few feet away from where she stood. She looked at the bodies lying there and then looked away, only to look back again. She repeated this sequence a few times until her fiancé, twenty-three-year-old David Rapp, joined her and held her closely, protectively. The bodies of two young men, who appeared to be in their early thirties, lay there on the snow-covered beach looking peaceful enough, staring skyward. A brief glance might have suggested that they were lost in contemplation of their majestic surroundings. But on close examination, each man had a bullet hole on the left side of his temple, haloed with a small pool of coagulated, frozen blood.

Alyson Keeler, twenty-one years old, was a sophomore at the Stony Brook campus of SUNY, or the State University of New York, located in Long Island's Suffolk County. She was enrolled in the school's premed honors program. David was in his third year of premed at the same school. They had driven earlier that morning to Robert Moses State Park, named for New York's notorious master builder. They arrived early enough to see daybreak. It was their favorite time of day at their favorite place.

Alyson's shocking discovery was two dead men dressed in denim shirts and trousers. They wore canvas jackets with cheap imitation black fur collars and sleeves. Their footwear was worn black work boots.

When she had somewhat recovered, Alyson used a nearby phone booth to summon police. As soon as Alyson's call to the Suffolk County 911 Police Emergency Operation Center was transmitted to a police car patrolling the perimeter of the park, every emergency unit with a police monitoring scanner would, with flashing red lights and blasting sirens, begin to roar toward Robert Moses State Park. Police cruisers from both the Suffolk County Police Department and the New York State Police, fire engines, emergency medical vans, and investigators from the Suffolk County district attorney's office would soon be joined by a full armada of news media.

Two murdered men found five days before Christmas in a crime-free suburban state park was a twenty-four-hour news story. Who these murdered men were would only increase the interest.

The first responding police officers notified their patrol sergeant. "We got two male Hispanics, apparently shot to death with one bullet each to the head. It looks like they were carried here from the main road after they were shot. We found pay stubs—probably their own—from a factory in Brooklyn on each of the bodies."

Ned Leon, the on-duty reporter for Long Island's cable television Channel 21, was the first reporter to hear the call over his police scanner, which was mounted on the dashboard of his mobile van, along with his unauthorized red police emergency light. Leon had been a police reporter for more than a dozen years, having spent much of his early days with the now-defunct *Long Island Press*. His heavy drinking and chain-smoking were habits he intentionally acquired trying to fit the image of a hard-bitten, leather-tough street crime reporter. These abuses were having predictable results on Ned Leon, who was afflicted with chronic coughing and bleeding ulcers and the sad and drawn look of an old man. Leon and, for that matter, all so-called police reporters loved the trappings or the instruments of police authority. Some carried phony police badges, and some even carried licensed guns. They flaunted these symbols, without having to deal with the awesome responsibilities and the dangers faced by real cops. Still, Ned was respected by the cops and the other police reporters because he had the uncanny investigative skills of a street detective. His ability to analyze raw data often led to the solution of a case before an arrest was made.

Two Hispanics killed execution style in 1990 meant one of only two things to Ned Leon: These two victims were taken out in a bad drug deal in Brooklyn, or the murders were racially motivated. A veteran reporter like Leon, whose workday went from idle speculation to the ugly reality of homicide, abused wives, and abandoned kids, could not conceive of any other reason. Since the factory where the two murdered brothers, Hiram and Ramon Rodriguez, were employed was in a notorious Brooklyn neighborhood where drug-related murder was commonplace, and since race relations in New York City, and even its eastern neighbor counties of Nassau and Suffolk, could not have been worse, Ned Leon's guesses were not merely cynical. But his conclusion wasn't even close.

"Jimmy," said Suffolk County Police Chief of Detectives Phil Pitelli, "my homicide detectives think that those two guys we found in Moses State Park yesterday morning were killed by a city cop."

"What proof do they have?" DA James Crowley demanded.

"Frankly," Pitelli responded slowly, "they don't have much other than a few facts and a cop's instincts. The ME places the time of death, based on the degree of rigor mortis, sometime between six and eight hours before the bodies were discovered. Since the victims were from Brooklyn, my guys figure that they were killed there and brought to Moses to be dumped." Pitelli waited for DA Crowley to respond. When he didn't, the chief continued.

"The doc retrieved two rounds, one from the head of each victim. Our ballistics lab identified the rounds as those used in a .38-caliber Police Special, which, as you know, is a revolver issued to the NYPD. And then there's this: A gas station attendant on the Northern State Parkway gave a fill-up to a guy in a van about two in the morning of the twentieth, the day the bodies were found. He said that the driver looked like a cop and that the two passengers in the van also looked like cops. Finally, the attendant said that when the driver took out his wallet to pay for the gas he had a gun butt protruding from his waistband."

"Well," Crowley observed, "now if we only had a confession."

"Now, Jimmy," Pitelli scolded, "just be patient. My guys are working with the NYPD's Internal Affairs. Who knows, if we get the right photo maybe we'll have your confession."

"Why not?" replied Crowley. "With thirty thousand city cops, maybe you'll get lucky and give me that confession before my term ends in '93."

# 2

Kenny Rattigan,
1990 and 1991

In 1989, W. Carlton Richardson won a stunning victory to become New York City's first African American mayor. The Brooklyn district attorney, Sherman "Buddy" Cooper, an old friend and ally of Richardson, recommended Kenneth J. Rattigan, his Rackets Bureau chief, as Richardson's first corporation counsel. The corporation counsel is the city's lawyer, whose staff represents all New York City agencies in claims brought against them. Traditionally, the corporation counsel is not only the mayor's chief lawyer but also his closest confidant. District Attorney Cooper thought Kenny Rattigan was a perfect choice. Rattigan's judgment was near flawless, and he was fiercely loyal.

As Rattigan was completing his first year, he was loving every minute of the job. Despite no experience on the civil side of the practice of law, Rattigan adjusted by recruiting first-rate lawyers with extensive experience in a number of specialties, including corporate, financial, and real estate law, as well as hard-fisted trial lawyers he deployed to the combat zone of negligence law. Rattigan particularly enjoyed being part of the mayor's inner circle with its direct access to Richardson, giving him a say in virtually all major policy decisions.

Following the appointment of the corporation counsel, the next critical appointment is the police commissioner. Since Kenny Rattigan was the only member of Richardson's cabinet to have experience in law enforcement, the mayor accepted his recommendation and appointed a little-known captain, Sean J. Nevins. It was a startling development that sent shock waves throughout the hierarchy of the police department. It would also set in motion a major offensive on one of the department's most enduring problems, police corruption. The appointment did much to establish Rattigan's influence with Mayor Richardson.

Mayor Richardson's power base was Brooklyn's Bedford-Stuyvesant section and South Jamaica in Queens County, both black enclaves, every bit as rich in African American tradition as Manhattan's world-famous Harlem. The rivalry among these communities was mostly friendly except when it came to politics. Richardson filled his inner circle with his political supporters, who were in the main African Americans, leaving Corporation Counsel Rattigan very much in the minority. But he looked forward to each new day and each new challenge, and he enjoyed fending off the good-natured comments from the other members of the mayor's kitchen cabinet, especially one deputy mayor who would wonder aloud, "Does our white guy have any colorful thoughts this morning?"

The daily meetings at Gracie Mansion began promptly at seven o'clock and quickly became free-for-alls—loud debates presided over by Richardson, a workaholic who seemed driven by the need to prove himself all over again every day. The exhilaration of each morning's often fierce debates was for Kenny a natural high, and it filled the vacuum created by the separation from his first love, the battleground of the trial court.

But Rattigan's time at the mayor's elbow soon ended. In November 1990, Sean Patrick, who had served as the Queens County district attorney for more than a dozen years, suddenly resigned. At Mayor Richardson's urging, New York State's governor and fellow Democrat David Laurel appointed Kenneth Rattigan the interim Queens County DA. The appointment would last until the next general election, in November 1991. The mayor convinced Rattigan to take a shot at elective office. He promised and delivered the support of the powerful African American community in South Jamaica, and in November Kenny Rattigan was easily elected to fill the remainder of Patrick's term.

"Kenny, it's Rose. The boss wants you." Rose Chauf was Brooklyn DA Cooper's longtime secretary and confidant. To Kenny Rattigan, despite the fact that he and District Attorney Cooper were colleagues, Cooper would always be the boss.

"Kenny, I have some terrible news." Cooper knew that Rattigan would be shocked, so he chose his words carefully and uttered them very slowly. "The Suffolk cops have been investigating the murder of two young Hispanics found shot to death in Robert Moses State Park."

"Yeah, Boss," Rattigan interrupted, "I remember the case."

"Well, they were tipped by telephone, anonymously," Cooper continued, "that if they searched a certain factory in Brooklyn they would find the body of Scott Ruben, a cop who disappeared some time ago. The caller added that the guy who murdered all three was a New York City police officer and that if they recovered his gun, they would have all the evidence that they needed."

"Who's the cop, Boss?" Rattigan asked anxiously.

Cooper replied, "The caller said that it was a Sergeant Steven Holt."

"Ah, that's just bullshit, Boss." Rattigan was angry.

"Wait a minute, Kenny. The medical examiner's office checked the dental records of the corpse found in the warehouse, and it was identified as the body of Scott Ruben. The word is that Steven was furious when Ruben somehow managed to avoid being arrested in that roundup of all those corrupt cops last year."

"Yeah, but that's quite a leap to conclude that he killed him."

"But Kenny, what if the tip is right about Steven's gun?"

"I still wouldn't believe it, Boss. Hey, I'm sorry, I gotta make a call." With that, Rattigan abruptly ended the conversation.

Rattigan's first call was to Robert Mulvey, retired and living with his family in upstate New York.

"Robert." Rattigan tried to sound casual. "How do I find your nephew?"

"He's still at the Seven-five in East New York over in Brooklyn. Is there a problem?"

"Nah," replied Rattigan, "a question came up about a case we worked on."

"Seven-five Precinct, PAA Sloan, how can I help you?

"May I please speak with Sergeant Holt? This is a personal call."

"May I tell him who is calling?" responded the police administrative assistant, a civilian working for the department.

"Sure, this is the Queens County district attorney, Ken Rattigan, but this call is unofficial."

Moments later, the PAA was back on the phone. "I'm sorry, Mr. District Attorney, but Sergeant Holt is in conference, and he can't be interrupted. I'll tell him you called."

# 3

East New York, Brooklyn, the 75th Precinct,
April 23, 1991

Inspector Thomas Newell and Sergeant Reggie Jobloviski, both of Internal Affairs, greeted Sergeant Steven Holt. Holt had met both men some months before when he was interviewed by them for a position in the Internal Affairs Bureau of the New York City Police Department. Shortly after the arrests in a major police corruption case in Brooklyn during 1990, Holt had responded to a departmental order issued by Police Commissioner Sean Nevins inviting officers of all ranks to apply for a transfer to a "new" Internal Affairs Bureau.

While both Newell and Jobloviski were impressed with Holt's intelligence, enthusiasm, and knowledge of corruption, particularly what he said about its causes and various strategies he thought should be used to contain it, they were not inclined to recommend him for transfer to the revamped corruption unit for two reasons. First, his age. He was, after all, the youngest sergeant in the police department. Second, his answers to some of their questions suggested that he needed more maturity. They were particularly concerned that he considered the elimination of police corruption not only a priority mission for the department but a personal passion.

Sergeant Jobloviski concluded in his report that Holt's application for a transfer to IAB should be put on hold for a year or two to allow him more patrol experience and time to gain the necessary maturity. "The applicant is very bright and will surely hit a fast promotional track, but at this stage of his career, his concerns about corruption allegations within the department cloud his objectivity and judgment," he wrote.

Today, though, Inspector Newell and Sergeant Jobloviski were not in the captain's office at the 75th Precinct to discuss Holt's transfer application. Steven was puzzled to see others in the room, particularly a few uniformed officers with shoulder patches identifying them as members of the Suffolk County Police Department.

Inspector Newell made the introductions. "Sergeant Holt, this is Assistant Chief Phil Pitelli, chief of detectives for Suffolk County. Detective Sergeant Brenda Murphy, who is in charge of the Homicide Division for the Suffolk County Police Department, and Assistant District Attorney Wallace Goss, chief of the Suffolk County district attorney's Homicide Bureau."

The scene would have been comical with all of these people jammed into the captain's modest-sized office except everyone's face was so solemn.

"These folks would like to ask you a few questions, Steven. Any problem with that?" Newell continued.

"None that I can think of, sir," Holt replied.

Chief Pitelli motioned to Sergeant Murphy and said, "Brenda, why don't you begin."

"Sergeant, how well did you know Police Officer Scott Ruben?"

Holt was immediately curious, because Sergeant Murphy referred to Ruben in the past tense.

"Not well at all. We both work here at the 75th Precinct, but he works a steady tour supervised by another sergeant."

"And who is that?" she asked.

"There are several. I don't recall their names."

"Did you know two brothers, Hiram and Ramon Rodriguez"—Holt thought, *She's using the past tense again*—"who were employed by Leib Electrical Supplies, located in the Bush Terminal in Brooklyn?"

Holt looked at each of the three people in civilian clothing who had been identified as officials from Suffolk County. He glanced toward each of the uniformed officers, also from Suffolk but not introduced. He then directed a question to Inspector Newell. "Has anything happened to these guys?"

"Yes," Sergeant Murphy replied, not waiting for Newell's response. "They are all dead. Ruben, too. They were murderd."

Holt shot out of his seat and, raising his voice, said, "I think maybe I should speak to my SBA delegate before we go much further." A police officer's union—in Steven's case, the Sergeants' Benevolent Association—would be the first line of defense in such a situation.

Inspector Newell stood and walked to where Holt was standing and said, "Sergeant Holt, that of course is your right, but I must ask you officially if you are willing to proceed with this interview."

"No, sir, I am not, at least not until I speak to my union representative and decide whether I should be advised by a lawyer. By the way, am I in custody?"

Chief Pitelli, assuming his best folksy manner, put his arm on Steven's shoulder and said softly, "Of course not, son, and if you want to wait until you consult a lawyer or a union rep, you can and you should."

Inspector Newell said, "Sergeant Holt, as a result of a preliminary inquiry, I am authorized by the police commissioner of the City of New York to suspend you for a minimum of thirty days, and I am directing you to immediately hand over any weapons you have in your possession and to surrender your shield. And finally, I order you to report to the office of the chief of detectives tomorrow morning at One Police Plaza at 0800 hours. Am I clear?"

Holt could feel the anger building. His cheeks were red hot, and he felt frustrated and humiliated. "Yes, sir," he finally blurted.

But the ordeal was just beginning for the young police officer, because it was Assistant District Attorney Wallace Goss's turn to speak. Clearing his throat for his moment, Goss clumsily removed from his inside coat pocket a piece of paper, orange in color and perhaps three-quarters the size of business stationery. He handed the paper to Holt, who did not offer to accept it until he noticed that Goss's hand was quivering.

Goss solemnly intoned, "Steven Robert Holt, the grand jury of Suffolk County hearby summons you to appear before it to give testimony in the matter entitled *The People of the State of New York Against John Doe.*" The name John Doe or Richard Roe is used in the identifying title of grand jury investigations when that body has not received sufficient evidence to name or charge a particular individual.

Holt took the paper, folded it up, and began to leave. He stopped, however, at the door and addressed Newell and Jobloviski. "What you two have done today is just disgraceful."

Newell tried to interrupt, but Holt cut him off. "No, Inspector, be decent enough to listen to me. I assure you that I will not be as disrespectful to you as you have been to me. I have put my life on the line for the people of this city. I fought the corruption that this department permitted to fester and grow unchecked for decades. And now, in the presence of strangers, you didn't grant me the common courtesy or fundamental rights you would give as a matter of routine to some street mutt who injured or killed a police officer."

The room had become eerily silent. Pitelli was genuinely embarrassed by what had occurred. Even Goss looked uneasy.

Holt finished, "What you have done today is a huge mistake. You should all be ashamed to call yourselves law enforcement professionals."

Suddenly Holt was gone, out the door, not waiting for any complaints or comments.

The following morning, Steven Holt reported to One Police Plaza. There Chief Pitelli was waiting, accompanied by two Suffolk County detectives and a lieutenant from the NYPD IAB. They approached Holt, and Pitelli said quietly but firmly, "Sergeant Holt, please turn around and place your hands behind your back."

Steven complied immediately, allowing Pitelli to rear-cuff him, but when the chief began to give him the Miranda warnings—"You have the right to remain silent . . . anything you say"—Holt interrupted.

"No, don't you dare treat me like a perp!" he shouted. "I am a sergeant with the New York City Police Department, and I damned well know my rights. Don't you disrespect me in front of the other cops."

Pitelli raised his voice and said, "Son, I have no choice. It's the law."

What wasn't either the law or a procedural requirement was to march Steven, handcuffed from the rear, through the hallway of the headquarters of the New York City Police Department, past cops and civilian employees, to an elevator and then to the garage for his ride in a gated police van to the Suffolk County jail. It was something Holt would never forget nor forgive, and years later he certainly would recall that it was April 24, 1991, his birthday. He was twenty-seven years old.

# 4

## Steven Holt, Brooklyn, 1964–1969

Steven Robert Holt was born on April 24, 1964. At his baptism into the Roman Catholic faith he was given the middle name Robert to honor his mother's brother, Robert Mulvey. Robert Mulvey, then twenty-one, was a brand-new member of the New York City Police Department, assigned to the 67th Police precinct in the Flatbush section of Brooklyn. Mulvey's strong young body was neatly packed into a six-foot frame that easily supported 180 pounds of carefully conditioned muscle. His sharp facial features, in particular his pointed chin, his broad, large nose, his jet black hair, and his dark searching eyes made him look like a descendant of Native Americans rather than one whose ancestral roots were in County Derry, Northern Ireland.

Police Officer Robert Mulvey, who wore shield number 1050, was so very proud to be a member of the department that he dressed for the baptism in his crisp blue uniform and specially shined his gleaming black shoes. He was particularly proud that that his sister Mary had asked him to be Steven's godfather. During the baptism ceremony, Steven's father, Harold, perpetually drunk and out of work, could not contain himself from mocking this serious young police officer. Harold became so loud and abusive that

Father Dwyer ordered him to leave the baptistry. Harold happily obliged and headed for the nearest gin mill.

As Steven grew up, he became more and more attached to his uncle. And Robert Mulvey soon became much more than an uncle, especially after he kicked Steven's father out of the family's apartment in 1968.

Typically Harold's episodes with alcohol made him increasingly violent. He began to direct his violence against Steven's mother, first with humiliating sarcasm and then with an occasional slap across her face. The physical assaults escalated, and he beat her so severely early one morning that she had to be rushed to the hospital, where she needed sutures to close a deep gash over her left eye. For Mary, the worst part of this ordeal was that it was inflicted on her in front of their son, Steven, who was at the time only four years old. Soon the frail little boy began to have terrifying nightmares about these beatings, and Mary decided that they would have to leave.

Not long after she reached this decision, her brother Robert dropped by unexpectedly. As he approached the front door, he heard Mary's screams and his nephew Steven's convulsive sobs. Mulvey burst through the door and found Mary lying on the floor of the kitchen with Harold's foot drawn back about to kick her in the head. Mulvey grabbed the drunk's raised foot and threw him backward into the kitchen stove. Harold hit his head and lost consciousness. Steven, his little heart beating so rapidly he thought it might explode, watched all this while cowering under the kitchen table. When Harold came to, he was on the sidewalk in front of the home he would no longer share with his family. Robert had piled all of his clothing and two suitcases neatly next to where he had thrown Harold. "If you ever go near my sister again, I will break every bone in your body." Mulvey said this as he was holding Harold's hair, pulling his head back so he was staring directly at him and so there could be no mistake about the seriousness of his threat. Harold never saw his wife or son again, although he did try to contact her and Steven a few years later while he was serving time in a federal prison for tax fraud.

Uncle Robert Mulvey was not only a surrogate father to Steven, he was his idol and best friend. During the summer of 1969, Mulvey taught the little boy how to play baseball. He took him to the movies and to Mets games at Shea Stadium. It was the Mets' magical summer, the year they won the World Series. When Robert's sister chided him that someone nearly twenty-seven years old should marry and settle down, Robert would say that between the job he loved so much and the time he spent with his "best buddy" Steven, he had little time for anything else. He managed to say this in front of the boy, and the five-year-old beamed.

Not long after, a tragedy struck the City of New York that would have lasting repercussions for Robert Mulvey, and for his little nephew Steven.

# 5

Flatbush Avenue and Avenue U, Brooklyn,
August 23, 1969, 2:25 P.M.

By early afternoon Brooklyn was experiencing one of its annual August dog days when the sun seems, in that turn of the calendar, to stand still. The temperature had reached 96 degrees by 1:30 P.M. and with humidity above 90 percent, Brooklyn was baking.

Overheated automobiles on both Flatbush Avenue and Avenue U, where the two major arteries intersect, were proof of the futility of attempting to use the relatively new automobile air-conditioning. The result left many of these vehicles, not much more than helpless metal hulks, clogging the streets.

No one paid much attention to the battered dark blue Ford sedan pulling over to the curb on Flatbush Avenue, a few feet west of the intersection. The unmarked but unmistakable detective squad car contained Detective Harry Lewis behind the wheel and his partner of more than a dozen years, Detective David Cordo, in the passenger seat. They had gone a short distance outside of their assigned area, so that Lewis could buy some cigars at his favorite tobacco store.

In 1969, cigars and wide-brimmed porkpie hats were the trademarks of a New York City detective, and Harry Lewis was every inch, and with every move, a New York City detective. A thin little Dapper Dan of a guy, with elevated lifts in his shoes, he was just a hair below five feet seven inches tall. His eyes betrayed more smiles than he'd allow his lips, but they communicated more cynicism than humor, the result of years interrogating suspects. His high forehead would draw attention to his receding hairline, but it was always concealed by the way he wore his porkpie hat, down but jaunty on the left side of his head. He thought this made him look like Humphrey Bogart. To complete the picture, Detective Lewis always wore loud striped and oversized sports jackets. The large jacket was used to conceal his cannon, as he called his huge Colt revolver. He could very well have just stepped out of Central Casting.

As Lewis walked slowly toward the store, Detective Cordo stepped outside the police cruiser to escape the heat trapped inside. Cordo was originally from Puerto Rico. He preferred neatly pressed dark suits, blue shirts, conservative ties, and highly polished shoes. His look was more FBI than NYPD, the polar opposite of his partner, Lewis. He smiled broadly and constantly with his gleaming white teeth, at nothing in particular. His high cheekbones and a perfectly sculpted nose and jet black wavy hair blessed him with the swarthy good looks of a Latin matinee idol complemented by a firm, lean body. He could have easily passed himself off as a recently retired professional athlete, perhaps a major league baseball player. As Cordo rested against a nearby telephone pole, he began to think how good the ice-cold beer would be at McNulty's, the favorite haunt of the cops and detectives of the 67th Police Precinct.

The sight of a tall, thin young woman, with bleached blond hair neatly shaped in pageboy style, walking slowly down Flatbush Avenue in his direction distracted Cordo. Her yellow tank top barely hid her supple breasts; her overall look was very inviting. She smiled sweetly, acknowledging his attention. She slowed, seemingly interested in stopping, at least for a moment. Detective Cordo started to speak when suddenly, from the cigar store, he heard the popping sounds of a handgun. He instantly drew his .38 and started racing toward the store. His adrenaline shot up and his heart was pounding against his chest, but his training took over as he quickly assessed his first tactical problem.

The store's entrance was guarded on the side nearest Cordo by a large green bench, which held an assortment of daily newspapers. The back of the bench was about four feet wide and nearly six feet high, completely blocking Cordo's view of the store's interior from that side. Cordo passed this partition cautiously. Detective Lewis's body was sprawled across the entranceway. Harry was on his back, motionless, with his empty hands outstretched against the wall. At the rear of the small store behind a six-foot-long counter, some fifteen feet from the entrance, Detective Cordo spotted an elderly man, arms raised in the air, with a terrified look on his face; he seemed to be motioning with his eyes to someone off to the side.

Cordo shouted, "Police, freeze!" and assumed the shooter's crouch. Two blurred forms suddenly appeared from each side of the counter, firing their guns repeatedly in response. *Pop, pop, pop, pop*. Detective Cordo took two bullets in the chest and two in the stomach. He was dead before he fell to the sidewalk.

Detective First Grade Harry Lewis, age fifty-one, was married and the father of five children, and Detective Second Grade David Cordo, forty-six, was the widowed father of two girls and two boys. They became the fourth and fifth members of the New York City Police Department murdered in the line of duty in 1969.

Steven Holt would always remember the morning of August 24, 1969. His mother had just finished preparing Steven's breakfast when they heard the two familiar knocks followed by the opening of the door to their apartment. Robert looked at Mary and Steven, then stopped abruptly at the doorway. Robert's ever-present smile was gone. His eyes were moist and red. It was clear that he'd been crying. He was clutching in his right hand a copy of the *New York Daily News*. As he unfolded the newspaper they saw the terrible headline: "Two Detectives Executed in Brooklyn."

Every uniformed cop in the 67th Precinct knew Lewis and Cordo. Mulvey especially looked up to these two charismatic detectives. One of his dreams was to one day get the gold shield of detective in the NYPD.

# 6

Church of the Holy Innocents, Brooklyn,
August 27, 1969

Perhaps the most cherished tradition of the New York City Police Department is the tribute it gives to those of its members who fall in the line of duty. It is called an inspector's funeral, probably because it was thought that the ceremony would be fitting for someone of that rank, although no one recalls a funeral for a police inspector who died in bed ever equaling the one given to police officers below that rank who are killed on the job. The tradition dates back many decades. With its pomp, pageantry, and ornamental trappings, the ceremony is not unlike a majestic church service.

As the time for the funeral Mass grows near and the street becomes filled with people, tension builds with mournful anticipation. No one who has attended such a funeral will ever forget it.

When Detectives Lewis and Cordo were murdered, tradition at the time gave to the commanding officer of the precinct the privilege of selecting the honor guard from among the police officers who worked under his command. That unit, usually a contingent of ten, took turns, two at a time, standing guard at attention on each side of the casket during the viewing hours chosen by the family. The honor guard also remained with the body during all public displays until the burial, vaulting, or cremation.

Captain Sean J. Nevins, the commanding officer of the 67th, chose Robert Mulvey as the first member of this elite unit. He did so for reasons other than Mulvey's flawless appearance and exceptional personnel evaluations. Mulvey's evaluations were indeed outstanding, and with his looks, his physique, and the way he cared for his uniform, he could well have been the ideal model for a police department recruitment poster. But Nevins chose him for his character and in order to send the message to the rest of the officers assigned to the 67th Precinct that in the eyes of their commanding officer, integrity counted above misguided loyalty.

Mulvey's appointment to the honor guard at the joint funeral of Detectives Lewis and Cordo would affect his nephew Steven in a way that was impossible to predict at the time. And it set in motion circumstances that would change Robert Mulvey's life forever.

The inspector's funeral and Mass was held at the Church of the Holy Innocents, in the Flatbush section of Brooklyn. The church is a huge Gothic structure built in the late nineteenth century, a third of a city block wide and a full block deep. It is constructed mostly of sand-colored blocks of stone of various sizes and shapes, with some dark-colored pieces creating a unique design. The [illegible] trance is located on East 17th Street and has three twelve-fo[illegible] arched doorways made from darkened oak. The lower t[illegible] of these doors, which lead to the church's vestibule, are inlaid with morocco leather imported especially for the church by one of its parishioners, an enormously wealthy investment banker. The upper portions of the doors, composed of stained glass, depict various scenes from the life of Christ. Each of the doors has huge brass rings, polished regularly so that they glisten in the sunlight.

In 1969, the Church of the Holy Innocents was the crown jewel of the Diocese of Brooklyn, which includes all Roman Catholic parishes in Kings and Queens counties. Holy Innocents Parish included worshippers such as the Trumps, who built thousands of affordable housing units in high-rise apartment houses in Brooklyn and in neighboring Queens County. The McAllisters, whose tugboats dominated the harbor, were also prominent members of the parish. Both families were extremely active in every aspect of church life, particularly fund-raising. Successful lawyers, bankers, and physicians poured contributions into the maintenance of this magnificent structure. No expense was considered too much by these important lay leaders. Of course, not all of the parishioners were wealthy. Most of the other church members were from comfortable middle-class families, including teachers, small business owners, firefighters, and police officers.

The Church of the Holy Innocents was chosen for the joint funeral for the two detectives mostly because Harry and Monica Lewis and their children were members of the parish and devout Catholics. The Cordos were not practicing Catholics and claimed no parish for their own. Muriel, David Cordo's wife, had died of cancer when she was only thirty and left behind four little children to be raised by their father. Her death left David angry and bitter. Although initially David followed Muriel's wishes and raised the children as Catholics, he and they soon fell away from all association with the Church. So when the oldest Cordo child, twenty-three-year-old Billy, a probationary New York City firefighter, was asked if he had a preference for his dad's funeral, he replied that his father and "Uncle Harry," as he called Detective Lewis, "should remain partners, even at the funeral."

The day of the funeral was another August scorcher. By nine o'clock, the temperature readings were nearing 80 degrees with 75 percent humidity. Sanitation workers scurried along East 17th between Cortelyou Road and Beverly Road, cleaning every inch of the asphalt roadway, the curbs, and even the sidewalks on either side of the street. The sun rose rapidly, quickly burning off the small veil of fog. The sweat poured through the sanitation workers' shirts, but no one complained. Their job, willingly and proudly done, was to make this city street spotless, a fitting place of honor for two heroes who would soon be delivered in their coffins to begin their funeral Mass.

Mary Holt and her son stood on top of the rectory's stoop to observe the funeral procession. Mary's face was ordinarily a sad one. Her hair was gray and rapidly turning white, and the skin below her left eye was permanently discolored, the scar left over from the last beating by the fists of her husband, Harold. During that vicious attack, the bones above and below her eye were shattered and she suffered a concussion. Her brother Robert would later recall that after that brutal assault Mary rarely ever smiled again. She always maintained her erect posture, holding her head up in a dignified way. Her clothing was mostly hand-me-downs from close friends or family members, but today she wore a tasteful dark blue linen suit with soft makeup including pink lipstick. Sheer stockings complemented her shapely legs, and with her dark blue pumps, she appeared taller than her five feet five inches. Her outfit was completed by an elegant white straw hat with a dark blue band around the crown, which she angled sharply and wore on the left side of her head. It was worn in a way to conceal her substantial hair loss, the result of the aggressive chemotherapy administered by her doctors to destroy the cancer cells surging through her body. Nevertheless, for one rare time, Mary Holt looked stunning.

Little Steven, with long, tousled blond hair, possessed a sweet and yet devilish smile. He had been smartly dressed by his mom in a starched white oxford shirt, a blue-and-green-striped tie, and navy blue shorts with matching knee socks. His black loafers that he'd shined earlier that morning sparkled in the sunlight.

By ten minutes before eleven, thousands of uniformed police officers from New York City were joined by hundreds more from cities throughout the country, including Boston, Chicago, and Washington, D.C. The massive contingent created a wall of blue filling both sides of East 17th, five deep, for its entire length. The mayor and the governor had arrived, together with other politicians and union officials. All the officials took places in front of those police officers who were lined up directly across from the church.

From about three blocks in the distance, the vast crowd began to hear the unmistakable strains of several bagpipes with no identifiable tune, just sad noises as the pipers rehearsed with their instruments. Suddenly there was an eerie silence. It lasted a full ten minutes. Many of the mourners had begun to look in the direction of the last sounds when all at once the slight beat of muffled drums was heard in the distance. The beating of the drums grew louder as the contingent of pipers and drummers came within view of the church. Soon the twelve drummers were just a few yards from the line of dignitaries, and the powerful beat of their drums and the click of their leather heels against the asphalt caused goose bumps to rise on more than a few of those in attendance. The drummers led fifty silent bagpipers, each carrying his instrument on his right side parallel to the ground.

This part of the ceremony meant that the heroes had arrived, led in historic tradition by a protective band of warriors with drumbeats marking the pace—the proud members of the Pipe and Drum Corps of the Emerald Society of the New York City Police Department. Dressed in dark blue jackets with bright-colored tartan kilts, each carried on his right hip an automatic pistol in a leather holster. Completing the uniform was a broad green, white, and orange sash, the colors of the Republic of Ireland, fastened at the top of the left shoulder and worn diagonally across the chest and down past the waist. Their black shoes were spit-shined for the occasion, and they wore dark blue knee socks with bright green trim. A long, sheathed knife with a huge black handle hung on the outside of the stocking on each man's right leg. The pipers marched solemnly, parading ever so slowly toward the Church of the Holy Innocents. Their leader, the drum major, Ryan O'Farrell, was in full command at six feet four inches, with flaming red hair laced with puffs of white. O'Farrell's high, ruddy cheekbones stood guard over his ample and sharpened nose, with its reddening tip. His broad, powerful-looking shoulders bulged from his tunic, as did his swollen belly, the result of years of beer drinking. He used his graveled smoker's voice effectively, shouting out commands. The regal way he wielded the six-foot-long silver baton slowly from side to side as he marched, almost with a prance in his step, completed the picture of decorous authority not tolerating any challenges.

Suddenly the drums grew louder when a robust roar of engines was heard—the sound of forty motorcycles as they made their way slowly toward the church. They came two abreast, each one ridden by a young policeman. The riders wore dark blue tunics with highly polished copper buttons—from which the slang word for police officer, "copper," or "cop," is derived—and soft uniform caps trimmed in black leather, different from the blocked and steam-pressed caps worn by other police officers. Each had a black leather strap worn diagonally left to right across his chest, attached to a belt of the same material. On the right side of each belt was a black leather holster carrying a .38-caliber police revolver. The motorcycle cops completed their uniforms with dark blue trousers, more like the jodhpurs worn by horseback riders. They also wore jet black, well-polished boots, coming to just below the knee. The NYPD cyclists were followed by at least twenty more motorcyclists from police departments in Suffolk and Nassau counties as well several cities in New Jersey and Connecticut. The final motorized contingent included twenty green-and-white police patrol cars, ten on each side of the street. The NYPD patrol cars were followed by another twenty patrol cars from police departments across the tristate area.

Now came the funeral cars bearing the bodies. They moved deliberately down East 17th Street, hulks of polished steel, one jet black, the other a deep dark gray, glistening in the late morning sun, first the one carrying the body of Detective Harry Lewis, followed by the hearse carrying Detective David Cordo. At the front and rear of each hearse, the members of the police honor guard, with their shoulders back and their heads erect, strode with military precision, in a determined silence broken only by the cadence of their heels beating on the pavement.

Steven, his little heart pounding, immediately spotted his Uncle Robert marching at the right front fender of the car carrying Detective Lewis. Little Steven Holt later would remember that Uncle Robert was everything he wanted to be. The honor guard carefully began removing the caskets of the two detectives, and at that exact moment a voice loudly commanded, "Detail, attention." The order was dutifully responded to by the thousands present. Once the caskets were removed and placed on the shoulders of the officers assigned to the honor guard, and the various members of the families lined up in sight of the caskets, the voice commanded, "Detail, hand salute." Immediately the uniformed thousands brought their hands to the brims of their uniform caps while the civilians brought their right hands across their chests.

As the bodies were carried toward the church entrance, a lone piper played the strains of "Amazing Grace." When the sound of the instrument stopped, the voice boomed, "Ready, two," and all the mourners brought their right hands to their sides. The families and as many of the officers as the church could accommodate, together with the politicians, filed in and took places in the pews for the solemn Mass of the Resurrection. For those who could not cram into the church, the entire ceremony, including a particularly moving homily by the senior Roman Catholic police chaplain, Monsignor Patrick Kellchan, was heard through large loudspeakers placed in various spots near the front of the church and down the complete length of East 17th Street.

When the service concluded, those police officers in the church poured out to join their comrades once again, setting up a blue wall of tribute. Soon they were joined by the mayor, the governor, and the other politicians and union officials to await the families and then the caskets of the two heroes. When the families exited the church, they stood off to the side. As the caskets left the church, the American flags covering them were carefully folded and offered with an attentive salute by two lieutenants to Monica Lewis and Billy Cordo.

As soon as the flags were presented, an NYPD detail of helicopters flying in a missing-man formation appeared from the eastern sky and passed over the funeral scene below. During the flyover, the piper played taps, followed by "America." The final scene began as the Pipe and Drum Corps led the cortege from the church for several blocks. The tune they played was "Going Home." The maudlin cry of the bagpipes, at first hitting high notes and then low notes, wailing the lyrics, "Going home, going home," was accompanied by the deliberate beat of muffled drums. As Robert Mulvey passed by Steven and his mother perched on the rectory's stoop, admiration and pride overtook the youngster, and he threw up a smart hand salute as tears ran down his cheeks.

Someone else at the funeral noticed Police Officer Mulvey. That someone, Captain James Patrick Connolly, would have a profound influence on Robert Mulvey's career, and his life.

# 7

Larry Green,
April 25, 1991

"Kenny," the voice of Robert Mulvey quivered, "they're going to railroad my nephew. We need help."

Mulvey explained to Queens County District Attorney Ken Rattigan that Steven Holt had been arrested for a triple murder and was being held without bail in the Suffolk County jail. Of course, news of the arrest of a New York police sergeant for a triple murder was headlining radio and television programming all morning, so Mulvey's call was no surprise to Rattigan. What was a revelation was that Steven had been given a subpoena by the chief of the Homicide Bureau of the district attorney's office allowing him the "opportunity" to appear before the county's grand jury investigating the deaths of Scott Ruben and Hiram and Ramon Rodriguez.

"Stay calm, Robert," Rattigan answered. "I know the Suffolk County district attorney, and there is not a fairer prosecutor in this state."

Mulvey paused, holding back a sob, and said, "But Kenny, what if the evidence makes it look like Steven is connected to all of this? I mean, they took his gun." He now sobbed out of control. "This is my sister's only child. Please, you gotta help us."

"Larry, do me a favor, take a look at this for me, will you?" Rattigan detailed for Larry Green as much as he knew, which wasn't a whole lot, and finished by saying, "This is very important to me."

His plea was answered, first with a grunt and then with Green's trademark growl, "Hey, Kenny, you're a fucking prosecutor, but you sound like a goddamned social worker."

Lawrence Lewis Green was fifty-eight years of age and still at the top of his game. He was almost bald and kept whatever hair was left at crew-cut length. He had a portly appearance maintained by a gourmet diet with generous amounts of special vintage French red wine consumed over long lunches. His perpetual scowl, like his acerbic and confrontational style, was part act and part gout, caused by his affection for his favorite red wines. When asked by his doctor, who was bold enough to suggest a change in his diet, whether he drank a lot, his answer was "As compared to whom, W. C. Fields?"

Throughout the years that Buddy Cooper served as the Brooklyn district attorney, Larry Green was always his first choice for an appointment as special DA in those cases where the district attorney was faced with a conflict of interest. For example, if one of Cooper's assistants was a crime victim, it would not be appropriate for him to remain as chief prosecutor. And for all those years, it was not uncommon to hear District Attorney Cooper's raspy voice bellow to his secretary, Rose Chauf, "Get me Green."

Larry Green was a natural in the courtroom and a Brooklyn legend. His trial skills, while marked by his unique brand of bellicosity, were rounded out by meticulous preparation of the facts and knowledge of the law. He refused to let anyone conduct any investigation unless he supervised each step. One prosecutor, who had dismissed him as a one-man band after what turned out to be a regrettable miscalculation of Green's ability, soon changed her mind. Following an acquittal in a case she thought was a slam dunk, she said, "He's no one-man band, he's more like the damn New York Philharmonic. He served me with thirty-seven fucking motions. I had to assign three people from my Appeals Bureau to work full-time just to stay even."

For the next several days, Green met with Sergeant Holt, Inspector Bernard Pressler, a longtime friend and mentor to Steven, and a number of Holt's friends and associates so he could get a full picture of just who this young man was and determine whether anything about him suggested that he was capable of murder. He also met with Suffolk County District Attorney Jim Crowley and Crowley's Homicide Bureau chief, Wally Goss.

Green had known Crowley for several years, and they had teamed up and lectured many times to meetings of the New York State District Attorneys Association and at law enforcement conferences held in various parts of the country by the National District Attorneys Association. Before Crowley's election as Suffolk County's district attorney, he had been Long Island's most celebrated criminal defense attorney, and since Green was the Brooklyn DA's top pinch-hitter as special district attorney, the two would take turns acting out the parts of prosecutor and defense attorney. Their styles contrasted dramatically: Crowley the blustering Irishman who tried to dominate the courtroom, and Green his cantankerous adversary, the quintessential Brooklyn Jew whose speech inflections suggested to most people the way the notorious mobster of Murder Incorporated, Meyer Lansky, must have sounded. Between these two characters, a dynamic was created that regularly filled lecture halls to standing-room-only capacity. Green and Crowley both enjoyed a drink or two . . . or three, so their professional respect for one another developed into a social relationship.

So Green's meeting with Crowley was friendly enough, with a half hour or so devoted to war stories, which had a different hero depending on who was the narrator. Crowley, large and gregarious, sat in front of his long mahogany desk, wearing a huge white Irish-knit sweater. His gray hair, streaked with black strands, was more like a mane that fell long over his ears and flowed over and covered most of his neck. His thick black eyebrows loomed over his deeply set dark eyes, which twinkled regularly in concert with a disarming smile.

When the good-natured ribbing had run its course and the meeting turned to the charges against Steven Holt, it did not look good, and Larry Green was very troubled.

Green's last interview before reporting his findings to Kenny Rattigan was with Robert Mulvey and his wife, Shannon, a retired special agent with the Federal Bureau of Investigation.

Green got right to the point with Mulvey. "So you had trouble in your career until someone at One PP saved your ass. Why did they do that?"

Shannon attempted to speak, trying to protect her husband, but Green raised his voice and continued, "How much of this did your nephew know, and when did he find out?" Then Green faced Shannon and shouted to her, "Listen, lady, get this straight. I don't like feds, and it doesn't matter to me in the least that you're retired, because you never lose your inflated sense that you're better than everyone else."

Now it was Shannon's turn to shout. "Dammit, don't you dare put me in one of your FBI mental cubicles, and don't you treat my husband like this. Robert Mulvey was and is a hero, and he was screwed by the NYPD. You know nothing of the circumstances that nearly destroyed both of us, so don't you be so fucking callous."

Mulvey stood and said slowly and firmly, in a way that was clearly intimidating, "You can ask anything you want about me, but stay away from my wife, you hear me?"

Green replied, "I hear you, and I'm sorry, Mrs. Mulvey, that was out of bounds." Green was very calm, and he spoke in a deliberately measured tone. It was the soft side of Green he usually tried to hide. He felt guilty about the way he was treating them, but he didn't offer more than that flat apology because he had to make it clear what they were up against.

However painful it was for both Robert and Shannon Mulvey, Robert told Green the entire story of his fall into the gutter and how Kenny Rattigan and Inspector Bernie Pressler saved him and finally how Police Commissioner Virgil Sampson permitted him to remain a police officer. He also told the lawyer, who was taking copious notes on a yellow legal pad, that he had told Steven none of the details but only that he had some difficulty and was then assigned to Internal Affairs.

Green looked up at this point and said, "And you spoke to him sometime in 1990, right?"

Mulvey looked puzzled and said, "Is it a problem that I didn't tell Steven what I just told you?"

Shannon asked, "Is someone suggesting that there's a motive?"

Green permitted himself a rare smile. "I thought you were an FBI agent, Mrs. Mulvey. You sound more like a major case squad detective."

"It's Shannon, Mr. Green, and I was a brick agent."

Special agents of the Federal Bureau of Investigation who were assigned to field or street investigations, in contrast to those who reviewed books and records to build fraud cases, were known as brick agents, and they were every bit as effective as any New York City detective. Larry Green certainly knew as much.

Green did not respond directly to this but simply said, "That's about it, and as you both probably know, a prosecutor in state court doesn't have to prove motive, but it sure helps them when they have one."

Because of their backgrounds in law enforcement he told the Mulveys a little more than he would usually be inclined to reveal. "Your nephew was furious that Police Officer Scott Ruben and his partner, Police Officer Gabe Perone, were crooked cops and were permitted to remain on the police force. You both know how quiet and reserved he is, but he has repeatedly displayed anger and frustration and has told anyone who will listen how wrong it was for them to have escaped and remained on the job. He feels outraged by the way you were treated by the department, transferring you to a unit that was held in contempt by most members of the service."

"Are you suggesting," Shannon asked, "that Steven felt that Robert's transfer was disrespectful and that, coupled with the department's lax attitude toward police corruption, led him to execute three people?"

Green paused to let everything he'd said sink in and then said, "Shannon, he has worshipped Robert all his life."

Shannon walked over to where Green was sitting and asked, very softly, "And do you think that kid could kill three people . . . out of love for his uncle?"

Green looked up, and Shannon thought she saw a flash of anger as he said, "A lawyer's nightmare is to be forced to defend an innocent person, but right now my biggest problem is that I don't know whether he's innocent."

"Kenny," said Green, "let's get a beer."

When they had finished their first drink, Green stared directly into Rattigan's eyes and said, "The only real hope is that asshole Wally Goss. Why Crowley would assign someone like him to try the case is beyond me. It's as if he's going into the tank, throwing the case. But that's not like Crowley."

"Well, Goss is the chief of the Homicide Bureau," Rattigan responded.

"Yeah, he's supposed to be a good investigative lawyer, but I can't find anyone who can remember the last time he's been on trial. Besides, during our meeting with Crowley, it was clear that he didn't know dick about trial strategy. He kept repeating that his case was a lock, as if that was supposed to scare me."

Rattigan observed, "Well, maybe Crowley thinks it's such a tight case that he doesn't need a heavy-duty trial lawyer, and he's rewarding Goss for making the case."

# 8

Suffolk County Jail,
May 28, 1991

Steven Holt was held in isolation for two reasons: one, he was a police officer, and two, given the brutal nature of the charges, and that he faced upon conviction three consecutive prison terms of twenty-five years to life, there was a serious concern that he was a suicide risk. He was guarded around the clock in three shifts, with two deputy sheriffs assigned to each shift. He was kept in a comfortably sized bedroom, with a double bed and a writing table with a small chair and tabletop lamp. During evening hours, the lamp remained lit. The door to the room was made of bulletproof glass, permitting the deputies to view Steven at all times. He was given access to any newspaper he chose, and he was permitted to read any of the books that were kept at the jail library. He was fed in the room three times a day, and when he needed to relieve himself, he was marched to a secure bathroom on the same floor that was available only to him.

"Hey, Sarge," one of the deputies shouted, after knocking on the translucent jail door, "you've got a visitor." Standing in the doorway was Sergeant Joseph Kurland. Though he was wearing civilian clothing, a blue windbreaker and khaki pants, Steven recognized the heavyset but powerfully built Kurland from the 75th

Precinct in East New York, where Steven had been assigned after graduating from the Police Academy. Kurland occasionally had the duty of the turnout sergeant, the supervisor who presided over roll call at the beginning of each shift. Since Steven had virtually no contact with Kurland during the few years he served at the Seven-five, he was curious about the visit.

Kurland spoke first. "I just wanted you to know, son, that the entire SBA is solidly behind you. Last night, I was at one of the beer rackets." Kurland watched Steven's reaction. There was none. He continued, "And I told the membership that I knew you at the Seven-five, ya know, not personally, or close, but I knew you was a great cop and a decent guy who could never have done what they're claiming. They told us that a ballistics test matched the bullets from your service gun to the bullets taken from those three dead guys. Do you have any idea how that happened?"

Steven finally spoke. "Sarge, I have no idea. All I know is that I never killed anyone."

Kurland followed up quickly. "But they say you knew Scott Ruben, and you didn't like him because he was a crooked cop—"

Steven interrupted, raising his voice. "Listen, Sarge, my lawyer said I was not to speak to anyone about this case, so let's end it here. Ruben was a crook, and worse than that, but I am not going to discuss it with you or anyone else. But the fact is that I had nothing to do with his murder. Is that clear?"

"Sure, son, and don't get angry with me. I'm here to help."

"I think you'd better go," Steven said firmly. As Kurland turned to leave, he stopped and, grabbing Steven by the shoulders with his powerful hands, said, "The membership is running a fund-raiser to help you pay for your lawyer. Larry Green is very good and very expensive, so we're gonna come up with as much as it takes so that you're not in a hole."

Now Steven smiled. "Thanks," he said. He waved as Kurland was leaving.

As Steven sat back down his thoughts were about Chief Connolly and how it might have been different for his Uncle Robert if he and Connolly had never met. He began to reflect on the ironic parallel path his life was taking, rapidly descending toward chaos very much the way Uncle Robert's life hit some rough times. Oh, to be sure, their paths toward descent were quite different. Robert, after all, nearly succumbed to job-related stress. Steven, on the other hand, was plainly and simply the victim of a diabolical frame-up. Yet Steven could see the dark connection between Robert Mulvey's hero worship of James Patrick Connolly and his own worship of an uncle who was his guardian angel for most of his life. He was the reason Steven was a cop. And becoming a cop was why Steven sat in this makeshift jail cell in Suffolk County facing life in state prison for three murders he did not commit.

# 9

Captain Connolly and the Christmas List,
September 1969

James Patrick Connolly at age thirty-seven was one of perhaps a half dozen bright young executives in the New York City Police Department who were known to be all job. "All job" was a description given to very few officers, particularly bosses, and it meant a total commitment to police work, together with fierce loyalty to the department.

At the time of his baptism into the Roman Catholic faith, Connolly was named for James Connolly and Patrick Henry Pearse, both martyred heroes of the Irish Revolution.

By 1969, James Connolly was one of those young captains in the New York City Police Department considered to be the future leaders of the department. In fact, some senior chiefs saw in Connolly a potential police commissioner. He had rugged good looks with a broad face and a high forehead. His broad, powerfully constructed jaw and his large, prominent nose were softened by wavy light brown hair and pale blue eyes. He was solidly built with 185 pounds on a frame slightly under six feet. His otherwise handsome face carried a jagged five-inch maroon-colored scar that started just under his left eye and traveled down his face, ending just above his lips. He had been attacked while he was attempting to arrest a knife-wielding maniac who was threatening one of his cops.

In lightning fashion, Connolly passed the promotional tests for sergeant, then lieutenant, and finally captain, the highest rank available for civil service testing. All higher ranks are attained solely by the appointment of the police commissioner upon the recommendation of a police promotional review board. The ranks of deputy inspector, inspector, deputy chief, and assistant chief are so political that one bitter senior captain observed that in order to be promoted you had to kiss ass and undergo a frontal lobotomy. This frequently passed-over captain added, "And don't make waves . . . ever!"

None of that, though, seemed to apply to the hard-charging James Connolly. He consistently took maverick positions during policy discussions with his bosses, but he never contradicted his superiors once they had made a decision. He carried out each command assignment with skill and exuberance. For example, when he was put in charge of the 60th Police Precinct in Brooklyn's Coney Island section, drug houses had virtually overwhelmed the neighborhood. Connolly, armed with search warrants and battering rams, led wave after wave of raids against these drug dens until every last dealer had fled. During one of the raids, a drug dealer armed with a shotgun blew off part of Connolly's right shoulder, but he was able to return fire, and the cops assigned to the Six-oh had one less drug dealer to bother with.

Connolly soon acquired the reputation of being a cop's cop. Anyone familiar with the politburo mentality at police headquarters at that time knew that it was not a recommended part of the formula for promotional advancement. But James Connolly was different. The bosses liked him, and while at times he would disagree with policy, it was always done respectfully. When he was overruled, it was always answered with a "Yes, sir," and Connolly made certain that the policy was carried out in meticulous detail. What the super-chiefs saw in young Captain Connolly was a superb police executive and a future leader.

Just past Labor Day in 1969, Police Officer Robert Mulvey was summoned to Captain Connolly's office at the site of the 1964 World's Fair in Queens County. The Special Operations Division, or SOD, of the New York City Police Department could mobilize to meet any contingency. New York City, the borough of Manhattan in particular, is a mecca for huge indoor and outdoor events drawing crowds at times into the tens of thousands. Special Ops will, depending on the size of a gathering, typically assign hundreds of foot patrol officers reinforced by a dozen "scooter cops" and mounted police officers. This kind of crowd control is fairly routine, but Special Ops is particularly effective in responding to spontaneous demonstrations that have the potential of escalating into a riot. In this division, Connolly had command override, the power to supersede command authority for any police unit. If, for instance, there was a concert in Prospect Park in Brooklyn and the fans became rowdy, the local police precinct commander could notify Special Ops and a directive would be sent by Connolly ordering all police commands in a predefined area near Prospect Park to respond and take up positions and implement crowd control. Every detail of this procedure is part of a preset plan regularly practiced by police units throughout New York City. Connolly's selection as the commanding officer of the SOD was a clear indication of how well his career was developing.

Mulvey knocked at the captain's door and was told to enter. "Sit down, son, and just relax."

Mulvey could not relax, so he sat at attention.

Connolly pretended not to notice. "Do you like the job, son?"

"Yes, sir," Mulvey replied, trying to avoid Connolly's searching eyes, which peered out from either side of his massive yet perfectly shaped nose, set in contrast with soft rounded cheeks, marred by the massive scar on the left side of his face. Connolly's deep tan was maintained by a daily run along the beach near his home at Breezy Point in Queens, a peninsula nestled between the Atlantic Ocean and Jamaica Bay. Connolly's imposing figure and his very direct way of speaking intimidated the young officer.

"How long have you been assigned to the Six-seven, Officer?"

"Ever since I graduated from the academy, sir."

"Do you know why you were picked for Detectives Lewis and Cordo's funeral honor guard?"

Mulvey reddened slightly as he softly said, "No, sir."

"Because your captain didn't want any fucking crooks guarding two heroes!" Connolly replied. Although he rarely used that kind of language, it seemed to him appropriate for the circumstances.

"Now, tell me about the Christmas list," he demanded.

Mulvey's face was now fully crimson, and he could not immediately reply.

Connolly rose abruptly from his seat and continued, "Listen to me good, Mulvey, there is a line drawn on the floor of this office and you better goddamned well see it. You can step over it and be with me, or you can stay there, take off your shield, spit on it, and throw yourself in with those fucking dirtbags on Snyder Avenue."

The fury of Captain Connolly's ultimatum so unnerved Mulvey that he was having difficulty speaking.

Connolly shouted again, "Tell me about the fucking Christmas list or get the fuck outta here."

Suddenly Mulvey recovered and stood. As he stepped back from Connolly, he tripped and all but fell into a nearby chair. He put his face in his hands, and as anger, guilt, and fear of the consequences nearly overwhelmed him, he froze with concern and uncertainty. Connolly put a reassuring hand on his shoulder and waited. After a few minutes, Mulvey began to talk of last year's Christmas season.

Before the NYPD began to replace police officers with civilians in certain clerical jobs, virtually all tasks were performed by uniformed police officers. It was neither efficient nor cost-effective, and it took police officers away from fighting crime. One of these positions was the job of station house administration. Each precinct had an officer who was known as the "124 man," taken from Section 124 of the Police Patrol Guide, the NYPD's detailed bible of protocol for just about everything. As the name suggested, the 124 man was the precinct's paper shuffler, who recorded everything involving the police personnel assigned to the station house. These tasks included the essential duty of recording each police officer's days off, sick leave, and vacation time. The information was vital to the decisions made by the precinct commander, who had to know available patrol strength to make appropriate deployments of his officers.

The importance of the 124 man was never taken for granted by anyone in the station house, and to the extent he had virtual control over the roster, he was respected if not feared by the officers assigned to the station house who might need his grant of a favor.

By the mid-1960s, a 124 man received a nominal tip from a police officer who wanted a day off, usually a ten-dollar bill. He also designated which police officers on patrol would be assigned the Christmas pickup list from local merchants who would be asked to give an annual contribution to the officers who regularly patrolled in the vicinity of their stores. It amounted to only a few dollars each year, but no store owner was ever known to refuse.

In some police precincts the 124 man was also the CO's bagman, who would regularly collect bribes from the more substantial store owners in the precinct for a variety of favors. The bagman would turn over most of the bribe money to the boss and would receive a 10 percent share. Of course, there is no honor among thieves, and many of the bagmen would pocket some of the money before turning over the rest of it. In the 1960s these 124 men, particularly those who operated as the precinct's bagman, became all-powerful, and their requests for tips became demands; they might get as much as a hundred dollars from a police officer, depending on the kind of favor allowed. A police officer who paid this tribute typically would recover that cost by taking tips from motorists stopped for violations, who in return for ten or twenty dollars would be let off with a warning.

Police corruption of this kind had become pervasive in New York City by 1968. Honest cops looked the other way. One anticorruption police chief described the crooked cops as falling into two very different categories: the grass eaters and the meat eaters. Grass eaters would take money only when it was plainly opportune—say, from the stopped motorist who with a toothy smile would offer a driver's license and an automobile registration folded around a twenty-dollar bill.

On the other hand, meat eaters would start every tour of duty with the resoluteness of a perpetrator, or a perp, singling out targets for prey. They would enter a bar tightly regulated by the SLA—the State Liquor Authority—go into the bathroom, and steal the soap required by the SLA and the city's health department to be available to customers. Then the officer would boldly approach the bartender and say, "Hey, pal, what kind of a pigpen do you run? You know the SLA rules about soap!" In 1968, most bartenders, familiar with the routine, would silently turn to the cash register, hit the No Sale key, and remove a ten- or twenty-dollar bill and pass it across the bar discreetly to this guardian of the public's hygiene, who swiftly left to be on his way to the next score. The practice was briefly interrupted with the arrival of soap dispensers, a momentary inconvenience for the meat eaters, until they found a way to remove the liquid soap from its container.

The 124 men of the late sixties were so organized they appeared to have their own membership association—a cadre of crooks from which precinct commanders could draw for replacements. Commanders of the various police precincts who were getting kickbacks from their 124 men would exchange these officers when the need arose, but without giving much information or direction to the reassigned officer. This practice led to sloppiness and the assignment of clerical police personnel who did not have the ability to identify those officers in the precinct who could be trusted.

So it was that Officer Hartwell, the 124 man of the 75th Precinct in the East New York section of Brooklyn, got himself in serious trouble and inadvertently caused an eruption and near chaos at the 67th Precinct in the Flatbush section of the borough, where he was temporarily assigned during the holiday season of 1968.

Meyer Hartwell was as unlikely looking a cop as you could imagine. Short, overweight, and mostly bald, Meyer had grown his black hair as long as he could from the left side of his head and then folded it over to cover the rest of his bald pate. The effect was an unintended burlesque look. Meyer had a perpetual crown of perspiration hanging on his forehead. His distinctive and certainly in no way attractive face brought attention to itself with a large, bushy black mustache flecked with gray and strange-looking pieces of debris that remained from a recent meal. His tiny dark and deep-set eyes were obscured by a long, thin nose discolored by popping blue and red veins. Protruding aimlessly from his nostrils were several strands of nose hair. Police Officer Hartwell appeared to have selected his uniform each day from the bottom of his closet. Frayed and always wrinkled, his uniform shirt with the lower two buttons missing hung over a belt forced out by his bulging stomach. His black shoes were almost gray with scuff marks. None of this mattered, though, because he had graduated third in his class from the Police Academy, and because of his grades his first commanding officer at a police precinct in the Bronx tapped him to be the 124 man. It was soon clear that Hartwell and his CO were a perfect match. They were both crooks. It was this first assignment that Meyer Hartwell used to hone his skills as a 124 man, providing for the needs of every officer at the precinct willing to meet his price. That experience, and even more his reputation, helped to land him a spot at the 75th Precinct, a particularly fertile place for a 124 man to make extra money.

Police Officer Meyer Hartwell's reputation in the Seven-five, as an aggressive meat eater quickly earned him the nickname of "Meyer the Buyer." Meyer had a price list, which included a fee for every favor offered to the police officers assigned to the Seven-five, from thirty dollars for an unscheduled day off to seventy-five dollars for a choice seat in a police patrol car on the midnight to 8:00 A.M. shift. This late tour was infamous as most conducive to police scores, because there were fewer sergeants around, so there was little or no supervision. It was known throughout the job as the theft shift, where two aggressive cops could make up to three hundred dollars a tour by raiding bars that failed to stop serving booze after 4:00 A.M. and pulling over drunk drivers who would be forced to pay the officers twenty, fifty, or a hundred dollars to avoid an arrest.

Some of the Yiddish-speaking merchants on Pitkin Avenue in East New York, whose businesses were patrolled by the police officers assigned to the 75th Precinct, when observing Officer Hartwell strolling down their street would exclaim, "Oy vey, here comes Meyer the Buyer!"

On one occasion, Mendick the kosher butcher said to Hartwell, "Meyer, why don't you go bother the goyim? I have no more gelt for you."

Hartwell smiled and replied, "That'll cost ya!"

Hartwell had a friend at the New York State agency that supervised the dietary laws required to be observed by kosher butchers in the preparation and sale of meat to observant Jews. His inspector friend would regularly drop by Mendick's market, look around, and, as he left, exclaim, "Meyer says you run a good store. You know, he's right!" Every six weeks or so Meyer would receive seventy-five to one hundred dollars from Mendick for his stamp of approval, which he would split with the kosher meat inspector.

Shortly before Christmas 1968, when Meyer learned that the 67th Precinct's 124 man was going on a short leave, he asked his uncle, a captain assigned to police headquarters, if he could arrange for a transfer.

So, early in the third week of December, Meyer Hartwell arrived at the Six-seven to begin his 8:00 A.M. to 4:00 P.M. shift as the temporary 124 man.

Meyer fingered his way distractedly through the paperwork on the desk until he found a sealed white business-sized police department envelope. It was addressed simply "Hartwell." Opening it quickly, Meyer found a note from the previous 124 man listing the names and locations of businesses for each assigned police patrol sector of the precinct.

Meyer marveled at the number of businesses listed in each sector. His eyes danced with delight as he read over the parenthesis by each business. The numbers varied between $50 and $250. The high figure of $250 was assigned to Bloomstein's department store at the corner of Flatbush Avenue and Snyder Avenue, only half a block from the station house. The hundreds of stores stretching side by side for miles down Flatbush Avenue would produce quite a bundle of money. Each list was headed by the name of the police officer assigned to the 8:00 A.M. to 4:00 P.M. patrol that day—except for Sector Charlie, which had no assigned officer.

A note attached to the list stated simply and directly, "Meyer, thanks for filling in for me, but don't get sticky fingers. Billy!"

As Meyer happily reviewed the Christmas list, which he expected would yield for him a generous share, the morning routine of the precinct was carried out. The turnout sergeant conducted the morning's roll call. Police Officer Robert Mulvey got excited before each tour. For this young and dedicated police officer, it was another adventure about to start, with no way of predicting how it would end. Also, roll call always reminded him of Sergeant Bernard Pressler, the tough, powerfully built instructor at the Police Academy whose military bearing and manner Mulvey so admired.

Standing at attention, his firmly proportioned five-ten frame erect, Pressler had once said something Mulvey never forgot: "What makes us so different from the people we are sworn to protect is the uncertainty. We never know whether we will be injured or killed before our tour ends." The words shocked Robert, but he always seemed to remember them just before he took any action. He began to regard those words as his safety net.

As the turnout sergeant concluded his roll call instructions, he said quite matter-of-factly, "Those officers on Flatbush Avenue patrol, see the 124 man." Each police officer so assigned stepped over to Hartwell's desk and received his typed Christmas list—everyone except the police officer assigned to Sector Charlie.

"Who's got Charlie?" Hartwell shouted.

"I'm sorry," replied Police Officer Robert Mulvey nervously. "I've got it. I was just assigned this morning."

"Okay, kid," said Hartwell, handing Mulvey the list. With a chuckle, he added, "Don't drop any singles."

Curious, Mulvey took the list. As he walked across the precinct floor, glancing at it, he became more and more perplexed. "Brockman's grocery store, 740 Flatbush Avenue (50); Mickey Brennan's Bar and Grill, 836 Flatbush Avenue (100); Sid's Stationery, 850 Flatbush Avenue (50) . . ."

As Mulvey got to the front door, suddenly the turnout sergeant ran up to him and, grabbing the piece of paper out of Mulvey's hand, shouted, "That's not yours, kid. It's a mistake."

"But what is it?" stammered the young police officer.

"It's nothin'," snarled the sergeant. "Now get out there on patrol, like you're suppose to!"

Still confused, Mulvey stumbled down the concrete front steps of the station house and began walking toward Flatbush Avenue.

He couldn't hear the turnout sergeant's screams as he slammed Meyer the Buyer against the wall of the precinct's locker room. "You fuckin' asshole, are you outta your head? Who the fuck told you to give that list to that fuckin' Boy Scout?"

Robert's mind raced as he walked back and forth patrolling Sector Charlie. Everything had happened so quickly. As he recalled looking at the typed sheets, recognizing the names of businesses located on the patrol route next to the parenthetically enclosed numbers, then thinking about the sergeant's bizarre behavior, all of it seemed surreal. He decided, with nothing more than instinct, that something was wrong, very wrong.

"Let me speak to the captain. It's Police Officer Mulvey."

It was 1315 hours, or 1:15 P.M. Mulvey was on meal break, although he couldn't eat.

"Boss, this is Mulvey, Officer Mulvey," he sputtered when the captain picked up.

"I know, you called me" was Captain Nevins's gruff but typical reply. "What do you want?"

"Boss, I've got to see you after my tour."

# 10

Lookout Point, Nassau County,
Late Summer 1992

For New York Police officers and firefighters, particularly retirees, Lookout Point was a kind of Shangri-la. It was home to people who enjoyed the summer tranquility of a bungalow colony and who at season's end would join other snowbirds in various settlements on both coasts of southern Florida. There they would remain until Memorial Day weekend would summon them back to what they lovingly called "Nassau-by-the-Sea." Yet some of the regulars who stayed behind in the off-season knew that Lookout Point was an incredibly peaceful oasis.

One of these was retired New York City First Deputy Police Commissioner Brendan Moore. While most of his neighbors headed toward warmer climates, Commissioner Moore and Peggy, his wife of forty years, enjoyed the turn of autumn by the seashore.

"Brendan." The voice was unmistakably Robert Mulvey's, although many years had passed since they last spoke. "I promise not to take more than an hour of your time."

"Sure," Brendan replied, "come on down."

"Thanks, and do you mind if I bring Shannon with me?"

"Of course not. Peggy and I would love to see both of you. Why not come in the afternoon and plan to have dinner with us and stay over? We've got plenty of room."

# 11

Suffolk County Jail,
January 1992

During the months that followed the Suffolk grand jury's finding, charging Steven with three counts of murder in the second degree, his physical condition steadily declined. His once firm and wiry body had lost considerable weight. In deference to the fact that he was still a police officer, and one holding the rank of sergeant, he was not required to wear the coveralls and T-shirt issued to other inmates. The collared sports shirts he favored seemed draped onto his body, and his khaki trousers were so loose at his waist that he had trouble finding a belt to hold them up. Steven's dark brown eyes were set back in shrunken sockets made more prominent by his bony cheeks. His light brown wavy hair was showing spots of gray, and his hairline was receding. The deputy sheriffs who watched him constantly were beginning to become alarmed because he would sit for hours in his desk chair with an expressionless stare. At times, when they tried to make conversation, Steven appeared to be listening politely, but they knew he understood little of what they were saying. The only time he came alive was during the daily visits from his fiancée, Lee Moran.

Lee was in her midtwenties and was also a New York City police officer with the rank of sergeant. She shared the anguish of

Steven's nightmare from the very beginning. She had long, soft, blond hair with a touch of red, frequently swept back in a ponytail. Her emerald green eyes set in an oval face were disarmingly gentle and yet quite sexy. Lee Moran literally turned heads each day as she glided up the steps of the county jail on her visits to Steven. Her body had near perfect proportions, with full rounded breasts enticingly concealed in a woolen sweater, or sometimes in a soft blouse or tailored jacket. Her narrow waist, her firm, attractive, and softly curved calves, and elegantly turned ankles completed the picture of a very attractive and photogenic young woman.

Since Steven's arrest and detention in the Suffolk County jail, where he was held without bail, awaiting trial, he had managed to keep his sanity through the comfort this lovely creature brought him each day. On leave from the police department without pay, Lee Moran was a constant source of reassurance and hope. Waiting for Lee was no different this morning, although the hour was approaching noon and Steven was becoming anxious. He was suddenly roused from his thoughts by a sharp tap on his translucent door.

"There's a certain sergeant here, Sergeant," Deputy Sheriff Foley announced with his usual broad smile. Of all of the deputies, Foley was Steven's favorite. When Foley had the duty he would regale the young officer with endless war stories and lots of unsolicited legal advice. "It's really too bad that my nephew Liam is a government attorney. There's the lad who could spring you from this hoosegow!" he once burst out.

"You okay?" Lee asked hopefully.

"With you here, it's always okay." Breaking into a laugh, he motioned toward the cell door. Deputy Sheriff Foley insisted on covering the glass door with a blanket to give Steven and Lee privacy. It didn't matter at all to Foley that this serious infraction could cost him a heavy sanction, or even the loss of his job. It didn't matter to Foley because he was convinced that Steven had been framed.

"Any word from Green about a trial date?" Lee asked.

"Unfortunately, if we don't get started within the next month or two, Larry is committed to a trial in federal court in Manhattan. It's scheduled to go the beginning of April. It's a racketeering case, and he expects that it will go for at least four months."

"I just don't know how you're able to get through this, Steven. What are you going to do if Green gets stuck in federal court? Are we sure he's the right lawyer for us?"

"It's bad enough to be innocent, but the one break I got, apart from you, was getting my lawyer. Usually when someone is jammed up for the first time and doesn't know anything about the system, finding a lawyer is a stab in the dark. That's the way I felt when they threw the handcuffs on me and put me in a holding cell. But thank God for Uncle Robert and his friend District Attorney Rattigan. Their recommendation was really all I needed. And now that I've watched Larry Green in action at the pretrial skirmishes with that asshole of an assistant DA Wally Goss, I know I have the best." Steven stood up, leaving Lee Moran sitting on his bed alone. He walked a few steps and then turned around. She could see the hint of tears in his eyes as he said, "You know that next to you, I loved nothing more than being a member of the service. It's something I've wanted to do since I was a kid. Be a cop and do good. And regardless of what they did to my uncle or do to me, I will never stop being a cop."

Steven returned to his bed, sat down beside Lee, and gently kissed her on the forehead.

Lee stared silently at Steven for a minute or two and then began to speak. "I don't think you ever told me why you decided to become a cop."

Steven smiled and sighed. "It's a long story, but we have plenty of time."

# 12

## Steven Holt's Road to the Job

Steven's mother had over several years been in remission from cancer, which had attacked different parts of her body, but finally in 1984 she lost her last fight to lung cancer diagnosed the year before. His father drank himself to death nearly ten years before that. So Uncle Robert was his only living relative to attend the ceremony at historic Madison Square Garden in Manhattan when he graduated from the Police Academy in 1985. Afterward, Robert took Steven to dinner at a venerable downtown Brooklyn restaurant, Gage and Tollners.

"Be safe, Steven," Robert began, "and most of all be true to the memory of your mother. Don't do anything that would not make her proud. And if you ever have the slightest concern about anything, just call me, at any time, day or night."

While there was never any doubt in Steven's mind that he would become a police officer, as he grew up he seemed to go out of his way to make that dream impossible. In the fifth grade at Our Lady of Angels elementary school in Brooklyn, he was expelled for being disrespectful.

Immediately after Steven's expulsion, Mary Holt used some savings she had accumulated from a few odd jobs and placed him in St. Peter Julian Eymard Preparatory, a private Catholic school in Manhattan, which was staffed by a religious order of brothers known for their strictness and propensity for corporal punishment. Mary thought that the brothers would be an effective substitute for the boy's father, who was rarely around and very rarely sober.

Steven's first few years at St. Peter's Prep were uneventful. His behavior was carefully controlled by strict discipline administered most often at the end of a stick. The brothers were otherwise friendly, and many were athletic young men who taught Steven and his classmates the fundamentals of basketball and baseball. Nevertheless, they would not tolerate any disruption in class or laziness in academics. They demanded that their students reach above-average levels in reading, mathematics, and grammar. These requirements were serious problems for Steven. While he didn't dare disrespect the brothers, because they hit much too hard, he had a quick temper with his fellow students, and he frequently used boxing techniques taught to him by his Uncle Robert to terrorize his classmates. He was very quick and extremely effective with his fists. On several occasions when an instructor had to leave the classroom to attend to something, Steven would use the time to settle a grudge against another student. Of course, when the brother returned to the classroom, Steven was severely beaten and denied his weekend pass. As his bullying and other erratic behavior increased, he was denied more and more weekends at home.

As these separations from his mother and Uncle Robert increased, Steven suffered from depression and began to withdraw from most school activities and contact with his classmates. He began to have recurring nightmares, vivid replays of the vicious beatings his father frequently gave to his mother. He would not or could not study, and soon he placed dead last in all his classes except gym. It was the only place that provided an outlet for Steven's aggression. His speed on the basketball court and his solid fielding as a first baseman were noticed by the school's athletic director, who coached both sports, but Steven's chance to join either of the school's teams was abruptly cut short when he was informed one day by the dean of academics that his grades disqualified him from all extracurricular sports. That evening while the seniors were having dinner in the school's cafeteria, Steven went to their dormitory and stole a draft card from a night-table drawer. His plan was simple. Early the next morning he would slip out of the school, find a recruiting office, and join the United States Army. He would become a paratrooper, and when he returned home after training, dressed in his freshly pressed uniform with gleaming paratroop boots and the silver jump wings worn proudly on his chest, everyone would look up to him the way they looked up to Uncle Robert. He would even go back and visit St. Peter's and see the envy on the faces of the brothers and those little creeps who made fun of him behind his back. He would never again have to put up with that "Mickey Mouse bullshit discipline from the brudders."

Steven's grand plan had a number of problems. When he forged the name of the eighteen-year-old senior whose card he stole, it was a botched job. He used a whitener to remove the inked signature and then clumsily wrote his name over it. In his panic over what seemed to him to be the crime of the century, when he noticed that the date of birth on the card didn't match his, he changed it in the same clumsy way. What the hapless forger didn't realize was that the alteration proclaimed his true age, sixteen! The Army recruiting sergeant took one look at the draft card, then at Steven, who immediately confessed and was in short order on the way back to face "the brudders."

Everyone in the family seemed to remember this incident as a turning point for Steven. The brothers treated the incident as a silly prank by a kid, but they also recognized the danger signs in this behavior, so one of the brothers was assigned virtually full-time to tutor Steven and bring him to an acceptable academic level. His classmates also looked a bit differently at him. "Geez," said one, "this guy's got some balls." Some of them even became his friends, really the first Steven ever had. While all of this did have a definite positive effect on Steven and allowed him to graduate closer to the middle of his class, his real change, a kind of an epiphany, didn't occur until several years later when he was accepted by the New York City Police Department to begin training at the Police Academy.

Steven threw himself into his studies. He drove himself to exhaustion during the physical training periods. He studied and analyzed every theory and application of police strategies and techniques, spending many hours after class in the academy's library. And he spent hours peppering his Uncle Robert with every question he could think of. At the conclusion of all this, Probationary Police Officer Steven Robert Holt had two achievements. He was given the Leadership Award by a majority vote of his class, and he graduated from the academy fourth in his class.

Holt's first assignment was to the 75th Police Precinct in the East New York section of Brooklyn.

"Of course," Steven continued, "what gave me the confidence and the desire to become a police officer was my Uncle Robert. He was and is my hero." Suddenly a pained expression overtook Steven's face.

Alarmed, Lee asked, "What is it?"

Steven was thinking again of his uncle and the infamous Christmas list. He began telling Lee the rest of his uncle's story.

# 13

## Captain Nevins and the Christmas List, December 1968

Captain Sean J. Nevins always seemed to be at attention, even when seated. His prematurely white hair was at crew-cut length; his jaw was perpetually clenched, and his mouth seemed always clamped around a very long, never lighted cigar. He had soft blue eyes, perpetually darting with activity. A recovering alcoholic and former chain-smoker, the captain rose early in the morning, giving himself enough time for ninety minutes of physical conditioning. When he spoke, his arms and hands moved in the animated fashion of a marionette manipulated by a master puppeteer. In those rare moments when he released his cigar, you could see his tight, thin-set lips, which appeared to form a constant scowl or sneer. They were just below a huge, flattened nose, the result of years of unsuccessful amateur boxing in his youth. He had a bulging chest made larger by the contrasting narrowness of his waist. At forty-four, he had been a police officer for nineteen years. His reputation among the police brass and among the union officials of the Patrolmen's Benevolent Association, or the PBA, was one of uncompromising inflexibility. They all hated Nevins. His troops, on the other hand, loved him, and that was all that mattered to him.

Once when a rare job action bordering on a strike threatened police patrols in the South Bronx, Nevins was assigned to turn the police officers out on patrol after roll call. He stood in front of the assembled cops and said, "There is no job action on my command," and as he said the words a kind of force field of electricity seemed to develop. "Does everyone understand that?" he bellowed.

One veteran police officer, a guy named Winter, raised his hand. "I'm the delegate in this precinct, and I want a chance to speak to the borough trustee."

Every police precinct has two union delegates, and every borough command has a PBA trustee, who sits as a member of the central board of trustees, the operating body for the twenty-thousand-member organization. Police Officer Winter was the fullback on the police department football team, called the Finest. At six-three and 240 solid pounds he seemed more than intimidating. Captain Nevins walked directly up to Winter, peered up at his face, and slapped it so hard that it made a pop like a firecracker. Winter screamed with pain.

"You get the fuck out on patrol or I'm going to kick the shit out of you in front of your constituents so they can all see what a piece of garbage you are. Now move," Nevins commanded, "all of you!"

The police officers moved quickly toward the door and on to their patrols.

Nevins shouted, "Hey, Winter, after you finish your tour you have that turd your trustee see me." He paused for effect, threw his head back, and howled, "That's if he has the balls to see me!"

The morning following Police Officer Mulvey's report to Nevins, there was a directive from the captain posted prominently throughout the 67th Precinct station house ordering all officers to meet in the assembly room fifteen minutes before turnout, with no exceptions.

"When I took over this scurvy house," Nevins began forcefully, "I warned you fucking people that if I caught you stealing I would personally put the handcuffs on you." Nevins's face was a frightful red hue as he spit out his anger and frustration. He had until this moment believed that the sheer force of his personality together with his unique command style developed as a Marine officer in Vietnam was enough to elicit total obedience to his orders. And for most of the police officers of the Six-seven Precinct, particularly the young ones, it was. They adored Nevins, who time after time would lead raids against the hijackers who preyed on the truckers who made deliveries to the commercial strip along Flatbush Avenue. He led them with all the lust of the military operations he conducted in Vietnam.

"Whoever started a goddamned Christmas list," he continued, just below a shout, "committed a goddamned crime. Cops don't take fuckin' gratuities, at least real cops don't. You got twenty-four hours to return whatever you took from those humps on Flatbush Avenue. Those of you who don't, I'm gonna fuckin' lock you up." Glaring at all the police officers standing at rigid attention in the muster room, he shouted, "You got that?"

"Yes, sir!" came the screamed response.

"Now get the fuck out of here!" ordered the captain.

The following afternoon, Nevins marched along Flatbush Avenue, a solitary figure of impressive stature. At each stop along the way, he received repeated denials from the store owners. Some replies were delivered so sheepishly it confirmed for Nevins that he was visiting a member of the now-defunct Christmas list.

To each store owner he gave a direct promise delivered with an unmistakable threat. "You give money to my people again and I will lock you up!" One of them was so frightened that he complained to a local Democratic district leader who forwarded his concern to Sherman Cooper, the Brooklyn district attorney. So it was that Sean Nevins and Kenny Rattigan, Cooper's Rackets Bureau chief, first met. Years later, they would recall the incident and laugh about how much both of them had changed.

Nevins, incidentally, was fined two weeks' pay for slapping Winter, the PBA delegate from the South Bronx, during the attempted "job action." It was the proverbial straw that broke the camel's back. In the years that followed, Nevins would never receive a promotion above his civil service rank of captain, a fact that didn't seem to bother him.

Nevins did one more thing. He assigned Officer Mulvey to be the full-time 124 man of the 67th Precinct. The corrupt payoffs to the 124 desk stopped, of course, and few police officers at the Six-seven would have anything to do with Mulvey. After all, he couldn't be trusted.

"But how did the Six-seven, or the rest of the job, for that matter, get so screwed up in the first place?" Lee asked.

"What my uncle always said was that it was a deadly combination of bosses who cared only about covering their asses and their careers after they left the department and a PBA leadership more interested in their political power and perks than in the well-being of their membership," Steven replied.

"Hey, Sergeants," interrupted Deputy Sheriff Foley, "do you have any idea what time it is?"

Both Lee and Steven blurted out an apology for talking away the afternoon, including a full hour past the authorized visiting time. Lee planted a quick kiss on Steven's lips and was out the door.

# 14

The Annual PBA Convention,
August 1990

The Concord Hotel and Resort was one of the few remaining jewels of the once great summer vacation resorts located in Sullivan County in upstate New York.

In the 1940s and '50s, the Borscht Belt hotels of the Catskill Mountains were the summer places to be, but by the late 1960s and '70s, interest in the Catskills had waned. Concord and just a few other resorts survived by offering especially attractive deals for organizations like the Patrolmen's Benevolent Association, which held annual conventions at the spacious resort.

The PBA's annual convention was the highlight of the union's year. The officers and the board of trustees of the PBA used the event as a way of saying thank-you to their delegates from the various units of the NYPD. In fact, all of the delegates and their spouses and children were treated to a week at the convention "on the arm"—police parlance for free.

By 1990, there were several hundred delegates from the more than seventy police precinct houses and other units of the police department. The delegates comprise the ruling assembly, whose particular power ordinarily is limited to the approval or rejection of the contract covering the wages and other benefits for the union's members. This negotiated settlement between the PBA's executive board and New York City's Office of Labor Relations is then proposed to the delegate assembly of the PBA for an up or down vote. The assembly historically approves these contracts with limited controversy. Nevertheless, this membership body remains a sleeping giant, and when aroused it can be the catalyst for throwing out the officers and the board of trustees. Hence the delegates of the assembly are treated very, very well by the union's hierarchy.

Although by 1990 more than a third of New York City's police officers were women, African Americans, Latinos, Asians, and other minorities, the seven members of the board of trustees were all white males, and the organization stubbornly maintained its official name as the Patrol*men's* Benevolent Association. Although from the beginning of the twentieth century the problems of police corruption apparently had a cyclical recurrence every two decades, no one could ever recall any initiatives proposed by the PBA to prevent this blight. Instead, the union's leadership either steadfastly denied the existence of corruption and condemned any investigation into police corruption as a witchhunt or simply ignored it.

The president of the PBA was the all but invincible Pasquale Russell Russo. By 1990, "Rusty" Russo had held the office for almost twenty years. His administration was popular with the rank and file and was regularly reelected. Russo gave the PBA much-needed stability, which forced the city fathers to bargain seriously with the union on relevant issues, in particular the all-important subject of wages.

President Russo presided over a membership of more than twenty thousand, giving him substantial political clout. No one ran for any elective office in New York City without seeking a PBA endorsement, and, since a growing majority of New York City's police officers then resided outside the city, no one ever contemplated a run for statewide elective office without courting the support of the

PBA. These endorsements were sought not so much for the votes they might produce as for the money they generated, as well as the status and recognition. An endorsement by the PBA carried with it the imprimatur of "pro law enforcement," hence tough on crime.

At fifty-four Rusty Russo maintained a trim and muscular frame with daily visits to the gym. He stood exactly six feet and never weighed more than 170 pounds. He had a small, thin face that was offset by a large, powerfully constructed square jaw. All of his hand-tailored Armani suits were dark, and his Oleg Cassini shirts were all blue. Of course, no outfit of his was complete without designer shoes and ties by Ferragamo. Rusty was very much in demand and accessible to the news media. His face had the manufactured tan of a sunlamp, part of a daily routine, and his blow-dried straight black hair was seeing its first signs of gray. His eyes were large, and their color appeared dark, almost black, because of his bushy black eyebrows. His eyes seemed to peer out from his face, emphasizing the man's intensity. He had high, puffy cheekbones and a pug nose. To some the image was that of a boxer who had taken too many head shots, but the fact is that Rusty always avoided physical contact. The total image Russo projected was success, a powerful leader of the largest police union in the United States.

Rusty Russo's speech pattern was distinctive. His predecessor was a tough street cop whose "deese, dose, and dems" and a nasty habit of repeatedly attacking public officials and the media became an embarrassment to his members. By contrast, Russo's flair for language gave him, at least to his membership, the sound of a college professor. He brought class to his position. Rusty chose his vocabulary for its sound, its length, and most of the time for its content. Slipping an occasional malapropism into his speech led Murray Kempton, one of New York City's top political columnists, to observe that "the ubiquitous Pasquale Russell Russo has never met a polysyllable or a metaphor he didn't like."

Shortly after the last plate of dessert was served, Pasquale Russell Russo mounted the rostrum of the Concord Hotel and Resort's grand hall.

"My brothers and sisters, elected officials and guests, welcome once again to the magnificence and splendor of the Concord."

The grand hall's luncheon arrangement featured a three-tiered dais filled with other PBA union officials, as well as representatives from other unions and an appropriate mix of police executives and elected officials. Attendance was a must for the police commissioner, the New York City mayor, the state's governor, several dozen members of Congress, and more than a few state and city legislators. Finally, as a show of unified support from the law enforcement community, the five elected district attorneys of New York City, representing Brooklyn (aka Kings County), Queens, Manhattan (aka New York County), Staten Island, and the Bronx, made the annual trip to the Concord, a mandatory entry on their appointment schedule.

"Regard this day and the remainder of your brief sojourn here as our way"—Russo majestically gestured toward the beaming trustees seated on either side of the lectern—"of expressing our profound gratitude to you for your unstinting and unselfish devotion to those magnificent modern warriors who daily stand between the criminals and the decent people of our city. And let us now give tribute to those heroes."

At these words, a roar of approval filled the hall and everyone jumped to his feet. The dais snapped to attention so abruptly that one candidate for mayor nearly lost his toupee. Russo would have his twenty-minute address interrupted eight more times by standing ovations.

Eventually he continued. "Because of an inextricable confluence of calamity, the loss of family virtues, today those verities have been inexplicably replaced by violence, a growing welfare-dominated society, and the all too meddlesome influence of the American Civil Liberties Union—and if you are a police officer, that means ACLU lose!"

This line caused a cascade of laughter, which filled the dining hall. Russo now raised his hand and brought instant silence. He looked sternly first at Mayor Richardson, then for dramatic effect at each of the city's five elected district attorneys. His voice began to rise as he continued.

"We are now seeing the ravages brought upon our society by the 'street mutts.'" The term was one of only a few diversions Rusty permitted himself from his affected patrician speech, as a way of saying, *I'm still one of you guys.* "That milieu has created such an utter lack of respect for law and order that in far too many police precincts of New York City, cops are cuffed and criminals walk!"

This last piece of rhetoric brought Rusty's desired level of snarls and shouts from every police officer in the hall.

"So tormented are our lonely guardians of public safety that the words of Sir William Schwenck Gilbert of the renowned team of operatic composers Gilbert and Sullivan sadly but clearly apply: 'A policeman's lot is not a happy one.' But, my friends, the era of criminal coddling is about to end. From this day forward this union of brothers and sisters will issue its manifesto—a message to all prosecutors of New York City: We have had enough! This morning, your board and I have unanimously agreed that your eminent counsel, William Moreland, Esquire, and his capable staff of lawyers will draw up a protocol for all of our members that will include the demand that no police officer in any criminal case will speak to a superior officer or to an assistant district attorney without benefit of counsel."

Everyone except the five district attorneys, the governor, the mayor, and his police commissioner was on his feet, cheering wildly.

Russo shouted over the din, "If those who would elevate their evil ways to the detriment of society are by law decreed to be protected by lawyers, then those who daily lay down their lives to preserve society shall also be protected by lawyers, our lawyers. It is what they deserve. It is what they shall have." At the end of his speech, Russo thrust both his hands straight up in a victory sign and for a brief moment looked very much like Richard Nixon, as the rafters of the old hall shook with the thunderous applause of the police officers and their families, who leaped to their feet.

As Rusty began to descend the stairs from the dais, suddenly one of the district attorneys, the longest-serving of the five, stepped in front of him. The district attorney of New York County, Justin Rothchild, was furious as he contemplated the chaos that would result if every police officer who made an arrest demanded the presence of a PBA attorney before speaking to an assistant district attorney. At seventy-one years of age, a former United States attorney, appointed by President Kennedy, with a national reputation, Rothchild wielded enormous power. At a trim six foot two and still ramrod straight, he was a man no one wanted as an enemy. Staring eye-level straight at Russo, and with his index finger jabbing the union leader's chest, Rothchild said quietly but in a firm voice, "Rusty, are you fucking crazy? How do you expect to get away with this?"

Russo glared back and said, "Watch me." Then he walked away, immediately mobbed by his adoring delegates.

Police Officers Scott Ruben and Gabe Perone talked excitedly at their table about Russo's proposal. Ruben was short and squat; some said he looked like a fire hydrant. He had a seventeen-inch neck and a broad, powerful chest, and his muscular arms, made prominent by his form-fitting short-sleeved shirt, were thick with black hair. Not much more than five feet six inches in height, he had short, stocky legs, which made him quite formidable on the department's soccer team. Ruben's oval face had a large, crooked nose between bulbous eyes. His bald pate, above tiny ears, was compensated by a large black walrus mustache. His physical appearance, together with a perpetual scowl, made him a very intimidating man. It was probably one of the reasons he was elected a delegate at the 75th Precinct. Ruben's friend Gabe Perone was his alternate, and both were members of a special new breed of crooks. These two, like other delegates and alternates in every police precinct, knew about the increase of corruption in the NYPD, but they chose to look the other way. Unfortunately, most other cops during that awful period also chose that course of conduct. Ruben's reaction to Rusty Russo's challenge was "What a terrific idea—an instant lawyer, even if it's that scumbag Moreland."

Perone, a gaunt little man with a long, sallow face with slits for eyes and a long pointed nose, was puffing hard on a cigarette. His nasal voice whined, "Scott, whaddaya think, can Rusty carry this thing off?"

Before Ruben could answer, Perone's beeper went off. He quickly read the number on the display and said, "It's Frankie." Ruben nodded as Perone left the table for the pay telephone.

"Frankie," Perone shouted into the phone, "tell that fuckin' weasel if we don't get that package by Friday morning, he won't ever see his kids again." He slammed the phone down and excitedly lit up a cigarette.

# 15

NYPD Safe House, Prospect Park, Brooklyn,
Early March 1974

Captain Nevins's decision in January 1969 to reassign Robert Mulvey as the 124 man at the 67th Precinct following the Christmas list revelation a month earlier was a sound one for the commanding officer. There would not be the slightest chance of corruption with Mulvey in charge of that sensitive position. For the young officer, though, the assignment was an immediate nightmare. Not a single cop would have anything to do with him. In every way he was shunned as the precinct's pariah. The Blue Wall of Silence not only protected corrupt cops, it blacklisted any officer who would violate the code. Observers outside the NYPD could not comprehend why honest police officers, who were a clear majority, fiercely supported this code. The reason for this will be more fully understood before our story ends.

At no time during the more than nine months Mulvey remained at the Six-seven as its outcast did he complain or ask for a transfer. He had recurring second thoughts and even some guilt as the betrayer of fellow officers. His ordeal ended with his meeting with Captain Connolly at SOD in September 1969. At the conclusion of their meeting that day, Connolly arranged to have Mulvey transferred to the Emergency Service Unit of the NYPD. It would be the highlight of Mulvey's career.

The ESU is an elite unit within the New York City Police Department. Members of ESU respond to every kind of emergency in their geographic zone of operation. They pluck babies from the arms of suicidal parents precariously perched on a building ledge and then, using whatever distraction they can create, they save the life of the despondent man or woman seconds before an attempt to jump to certain death. They race across the city to assist their sister or brother police officers confronting an EDP—emotionally disturbed person—armed with an axe. They regularly visit elementary and high schools, where they demonstrate rescue techniques and teach lessons in crime prevention. They are, according to one columnist from the *New York Post,* "firefighters with guns," a description they reject because it suggests heroic parity with their rivals. One of Mulvey's buddies, upon hearing of this comparison, said, "No, we're firefighters with brains." This was said over a beer at a local bar, the hangout of cops and firefighters, and said loud enough to invite the usual and expected four-letter-word responses.

Mulvey imagined he could do this assignment forever, or at least until he got too old for the physical demands of the job. Forty or forty-five, perhaps. By that time he'd be ready to pack it in anyway and look for civilian work.

"Mulvey," shouted his ESU commanding officer, a deputy inspector.

"Yes, sir!" replied Mulvey.

"Report to Inspector Connolly at the 13th Division, forthwith."

As Robert left his command, an unmarked but clearly recognizable police cruiser blocked his path as he turned to cross the street. Two gold shields were thrust at him and withdrawn so quickly that Robert could not identify the rank.

"Officer Mulvey," the older man said, "please get in the backseat. Inspector Connolly told us to give you a lift." Mulvey quickly got in the rear of the car, not really thinking that he had an option.

It had been more than four years since the meeting with Connolly at the Special Operations Division. While Mulvey saw Connolly at police rackets, as beer parties were called, they rarely spoke more than a greeting. Two of those rackets were to celebrate Connolly's promotions only a year apart, first to the rank of deputy inspector and then, six months ago, to full inspector.

Soon the car was in Prospect Park, Brooklyn's huge main recreational green space. The cruiser stopped at what appeared to be a bandshell with a stage. The rear of the stage contained a door leading to a dimly lighted staircase. At the bottom of the second landing of what looked like a subcellar was a rust-colored metal door. Mulvey, left alone as he descended, was told to knock and walk in. The room contained a desk and two straight wooden chairs. At each end of the desk stood a flag: the American flag at one end and the flag of the NYPD at the other. Suddenly a door to the rear of the desk opened and there stood Inspector James Patrick Connolly, commanding officer of the Thirteenth Division police plainclothes unit.

Connolly was dressed casually in fitted gray slacks, a white collared shirt, a blue cardigan sweater partially buttoned, white gym socks, and highly polished brown loafers. He could have been a professor of literature at nearby Brooklyn College. The pipe he clutched in his left hand completed the academic look. The inspector pointed to a chair for Robert to sit. As he sat down, his eyes wandered for a split second to a corkboard, three feet by two, partially blocked by Connolly's body as he seated himself behind the desk. The board appeared to have pictures of young men and two or three young women in uniform.

"How is the job, Robert?" Inspector Connolly inquired.

"I love it, sir, and I'm about to be made a sergeant."

Connolly interrupted, "In October, yes, and you're getting pretty serious with a very attractive young woman, a special agent of the FBI, Shannon Kelly. And oh, I see you just bought a share of a place on Fire Island for next summer."

Mulvey was puzzled and a bit flustered as he saw that Connolly was reading from the pages of a blue three-ring binder.

"And you still attend daily Mass, usually at St. Rita's in Corona, Queens." Then, with a smile, "Or any other place you can find, depending on the demands of the job. Some mornings you've led us on quite a chase."

"Excuse me, sir," he said, summoning up some courage with a simple question, "but why are you following me?"

"Because, Robert"—Connolly got very serious—"I need you."

Connolly's earnestness was unsettling to Mulvey. Connolly seemed worried—not the usual supremely confident police commander—and the setting for their meeting made all of it seem ominous.

"I need your help as I have never needed anyone else before!"

For the moment, Mulvey was stunned. Connolly was someone whom he admired and would gladly help, but how? And would he have to leave ESU? His career dream was to stay in the unit, and if he was lucky enough to catch the promotional examination cycle, he could be a captain before he reached his midthirties, just like Connolly. It was unreal. James Connolly, at once the most respected, most feared, and most dynamic young police boss in the department, needed Mulvey's help so much he seemed to be pleading for it.

"Robert," Connolly began in a soft, almost inaudible voice, "what I have to tell you must remain here. You must swear an oath to God."

Mulvey's heart began to race. Fear took hold of him at the solemnity of the situation.

"Even if you decide not to help, or should I say especially if you refuse, you must under pain of sin never reveal my words." Connolly allowed the young cop a minute to reflect on the seriousness of all this and then said, "Am I clear?"

"Yes, Inspector," came the muffled reply.

"Do I have your oath?"

"Yes, Inspector."

"Do you want me to continue?"

"Yes, sir."

"Besides that business a few years ago with the Christmas list at the 67th Precinct, have you ever heard of or actually seen any other cops taking money?"

Connolly, of course, suspected the answer would be no, because Mulvey's ESU assignment placed him among a group of police officers whose integrity had never been in question.

"No, sir. Although I have heard the normal rumors you pick up at beer rackets. Nothing other than that."

"Well, Robert, here at the 13th Plainclothes Division, we have much more than a rumor."

# 16

NYPD Safe House, Prospect Park, Brooklyn,
Early March 1974

Inspector Connolly began by giving Mulvey an overview of the work of plainclothes units like the 13th Division and a history of their corrupt activities.

The 13th Plainclothes Division was one of a dozen similar units created by the department to deal with prostitution and gambling. Plainclothes units soon became known as places where cops could make a few extra bucks off of the bookies they were charged with arresting, or from the prostitutes who worked the streets and were regarded as neighborhood eyesores. These women would approach an undercover plainclothesman, offer to turn a trick, and routinely be arrested, but that didn't necessarily mean that the officer would take the prostitute to the station house for processing on the way to criminal court. Often he had other plans for her.

Since it was the duty of these units to contain, if not eliminate, these two evils, or vices, the men and the few women assigned to this unit were soon branded with the ignoble nickname of "vice cops." It became almost immediately obvious to those cops assigned to these squads that the attempt to contain, let alone eliminate, these two immoral public activities was an exercise in futility.

If no society in all of human history had successfully eradicated prostitution, the so-called world's oldest profession, how could any New York City cop do better? So why not make some money from the pros, as they called them, by releasing them in return for free sex or a tip, or letting them ply their trade in a particular area in exchange for a percentage of the action?

As for bookmaking, since to the general public it was of little concern or interest, the vice cops received no outcry from citizens. Quite the contrary; the prevailing attitude was: Who is really hurt by Joe the Bookie? There was little evidence that wives and children anywhere were being deprived of food or clothing because of a husband's excessive bets with a bookie. There seemed to be far more evidence of deprivation for the wives and children of drunks. The difference was that the politicians made booze legal and kept gambling illegal. This reality soon led to a type of containment not envisioned by the Police Department or the penal laws of New York State—containment by the creation of the pad.

The "pad" was the euphemism invented by vice cops and bookies for payment to the cops. The bookie every once in a while would take a collar. (The word "collar" came from the turn of the twentieth century, when most men, even criminals, wore high starched collars. When a police officer made an arrest, he would typically grab the person by the collar.) The arresting officer permitted him to keep his book, or his work. The work was the detailed record of the bets made with the bookie; without it every bettor would claim that he or she was a winner. The work therefore was the bookmaker's lifeline. Since the arrest was made without the evidence of bookmaking, which is a felony, the only charge that could be brought was the misdemeanor of loitering for the purpose of bookmaking. Of course, neither the district attorney nor the judges were particularly excited about cases charging bookmakers with that low-level offense. So the vice cops and the bookies created an arrangement that worked to everyone's satisfaction.

The main reason why bookmakers paid off cops in the first place and never seriously complained when an increase in the pad was demanded was that their business was very, very lucrative. Bookies make money from their customer's losses, through the "vigorish," or the "vig," paid to them. The first bookmakers in New York City were Jewish, so they used the Yiddish word *vyigrysh*, a charge placed on bets. The vig is usually 10 percent of the face amount of the losing bet.

Bookmaking is a major criminal industry in the United States except in those few states, such as Nevada, where gambling is legal. By the 1970s in New York City, the annual gross take from bookmaking was eight billion dollars—and, no surprise, it was, as it is today, totally controlled by organized crime. The five organized crime families of New York franchise bookmaking locations and receive a weekly percentage of the bookmaker's profits. These franchises are controlled by fear. Every bookmaker knows that any violation, such as skimming or hiding profits, would be met swiftly with a severe beating or even death.

The next act of this charade would occur at the courthouse, where the assistant district attorney, busy with more serious crime, would say perfunctorily, "Whaddaya got, officer?"

"I got a KG for loitering." KG is cop and prosecution slang for "known gambler."

The prosecutor would then ask the bookie's lawyer, usually a local courthouse hustler retained by the bookie for a sum of twenty-five dollars for each case, "Counselor, how about a plea to an attempt and a fifty-dollar fine?"

Quickly they agreed to the deal, which was presented to a judge who also didn't regard the criminal charge to be particularly serious and who would pronounce a sentence with the usual warning not to repeat this egregious behavior. So the accommodation arrest benefited not just the partnership between the cop and the bookie but also the criminal justice system, a speedy and efficient revenue-producing disposition of minor matters that could clog up the system.

Some judges, such as Judge Murray Shoenstein, who was preparing to run for the office of Kings County district attorney, always sought to curry favor—with the cops and the PBA. Shoenstein, a comically fat man whose facial features were disappearing into his jowls, had curly strawberry hair that he dyed because he thought it made him look younger. When he tried to stand, it was always a great effort; his short arms gave him no balance to support himself on his stubby legs. Ordinarily, and for obvious reasons, Judge Shoenstein avoided standing once he ascended to the bench and took his seat, but he loved to castigate bookmakers from a threatening, standing position. He would preface pronouncing the sentence he imposed on the bookie with a special warning.

"You may not think your crime particularly vile, and I suppose that even to the more sophisticated, your activity is at worst socially unacceptable, but let me tell you, sir, and make it clear, when you become the subject of this police officer's investigation, requiring him to engage in activity that puts him at risk"—at this point Shoenstein would raise his voice, demanding the rapt attention of all present, mostly other vice cops and other bookies with the same kind of accommodation arrest—"when you by your criminal conduct, require a police officer to use his training, his cunning, his intellect"—now Shoenstein was shouting—"you are placing him in harm's way with a high risk of injury or even death." The last part of his oration was uttered solemnly with a deep voice: "I can never get used to appearing at a police officer's funeral. So if you come before me again, I shall sentence you to a maximum period of jail time. Do you understand?"

The bookie would look wisely shaken—and chastened. The vice cop would usually beam and, depending on how effective the judge's presentation sounded, the courtroom cops and bookies alike would erupt with cheers and applause. Whereupon Shoenstein would announce, with a broad, satisfied smile, "This court stands adjourned!"

Of course, most of the bookies that found themselves as defendants in Judge Shoenstein's courtroom had been treated to this same ranting many times over—and of course he never jailed a single one of them. In Part 3 of Brooklyn Criminal Court, where pleas of guilty or not guilty were entered, all was well that ended well. The judge made a speech; the assistant district attorney got a guilty plea; the bookie got to keep his freedom, but more important, he kept his book going. The hustling courtroom lawyer got his twenty-five bucks, and the vice cop reensured the monthly receipt of his payment from the pad.

When Inspector Connolly came to the 13th Division, he became determined to find out the extent of the corruption affecting the police officers he was about to command. It did not take long before he discovered conditions within the 13th that were so shocking he decided to recruit Mulvey for a highly confidential undercover assignment. Although Connolly knew that this young officer was intensely loyal to him, he suspected that Mulvey would find this level of corruption repulsive and probably refuse the assignment. Nonetheless, Connolly would try.

"Just settle back, son," Connolly said gently. "How I learned about the 13th is a pretty long, sorry story, and before I can ask for your help you have to know all of it." Mulvey didn't respond, but he did relax and listen attentively.

# 17

*People v. Holt,*
October 12, 1992

Too many lawyers who put themselves forward as trial attorneys or litigators regard the process of jury selection to be not much more than a delaying distraction from the main event, the trial. But to premier trial lawyers like Larry Green, the voir dire—French for "to speak the truth"—is the essential prelude to the case. Indeed, Green was fond of calling the process of finding the right jurors the very *sine qua non* of any case. The Latin phrase means "absolutely indispensable."

"It is during jury selection," Green lectured his trial advocacy class at Fordham Law School, "that prospective jurors take the measure of the lawyers. If they like you, you have established a beachhead. If they don't like you, then you might as well be speaking Swahili! How," he would ask crankily, "can you possibly pick a jury if you don't know anything about them? And you will learn about them only by asking questions that elicit complete, comprehensive answers. Only then can you assess a juror for intelligence, knowledge of current events, and the ability to keep an open mind."

Now, that did not necessarily imply Green was looking for an impartial jury. His mission, as he saw it, was to pick the brightest people he could find, those he could persuade to embrace his theory of the case.

For Larry Green, just as it was for the great pro football coach Vince Lombardi, winning wasn't everything, it was the only thing, so he had little patience and much contempt for lawyers who regarded jury selection as incidental to the trial. Such a lawyer, fortunately for Steven Holt, was Suffolk County Assistant District Attorney Wallace Goss.

Goss gave a perfunctory thank-you to the panel of citizens waiting to be chosen for jury service, followed by a series of questions that invited a one-word answer, often grunted inaudibly. "Can you be fair?" "Will you accept the law from the judge?" "Will you demand more of the prosecutor than proof beyond a reasonable doubt?" These were answered always "yes," "yes," and "no." In some cases, the judge would admonish Goss not to ask that last question because matters of law were strictly for the judge, but no matter how many times Goss was warned, he didn't get it. He remained clueless.

Larry Green's approach to jury selection had two basic goals: find out something about a prospective juror by getting him or her to talk as much as was necessary for an appropriate assessment, and develop questions to aid his strategy to win the case. Of course, his approach turned on the weight and the quality of the evidence. One technique to achieve the first goal was to ask questions that probed a juror's previous experience with a trial.

"Mr. Sullivan, you indicated before that you had previously served on a jury?"

"Yes, sir."

"Did you and the other jurors deliberate?"

"We did."

"If you did reach a verdict, without telling us what that verdict was, can you tell me the facts of the case?"

The way the potential juror framed the answer—whether it was articulate, concise, and clear; whether it showed a good recollection of the case—said a lot about the person. Even an attitude toward the system could be elicited by these responses. When Mr. Sullivan, the prospective juror, replied to Green's question about prior service, he recalled, "It was about this robber." That description of the defendant, though brief, meant to Larry Green that Mr. Sullivan had a predisposition in favor of the prosecution. Of course, Green would add that his conclusion was at best a good guess, based on experience.

Green's second goal had very much to do with his analysis of the case, and in Steven Holt's, Green found little optimism for an outcome favorable to the young sergeant. Holt's gun had been surrendered to the Suffolk County detectives and showed a clean set of his fingerprints and palm prints. The ballistics test appeared to be conclusive; the test bullets from Steven's weapon matched the bullets recovered from the bodies of the three dead victims. Moreover, Steven had some hell of a motive for killing Police Officer Scott Ruben. He hated him, and it was not just because Ruben was a crook. There was something more, something Holt was not ready to reveal.

"Criminal defense lawyers in New York State have a powerful ace in the hole, assuming," Green lectured his Fordham trial advocacy class, "they understand how to use it. It only takes one juror to screw up a prosecutor's case and create a hung jury. In some states a verdict can be reached upon the agreement of four-fifths of the jurors, but New York requires a unanimous verdict. And," he added, with a rare smile, really a smirk, "sometimes you get lucky, when an argument meant to convince just one juror gets adopted by all twelve." Here he quoted, very roughly, the writer-critic H. L Mencken, who said, "When a person is arrested and charged with a crime, a presumption of guilt immediately attaches to the case, but should that person be convicted after trial, the public can be easily convinced that the person was railroaded by the authorities!" Green decided that he would employ a strategy to frustrate if not defeat the prosecution of Steven Holt, based on the cynically held belief of many that often defendants are charged with a crime as a result of fabricated evidence.

Green began his voir dire "Ladies and gentlemen, perhaps the greatest observation one can make of the jury system is that truth is found by the collaborative effort of sincere and honorable citizens with disparate experiences. So let me begin with this question: Is there any example in your lifetime experience of someone unjustly accused of a crime, and do you recall the facts of that case?"

A young African American stockbroker, perhaps in his early thirties, dressed in a blue blazer with a white polo shirt, open at the neck, leaned forward and said, "Lynchings in the South were all too common, even in the 1960s, and were frequently based on trumped-up evidence."

Although Larry spent some time discussing this blight on American history with Norton Marshal, the young prospective juror from Wall Street, he knew very well that Goss would use one of his peremptory challenges to send the sincere young man back to the stock exchange. In a criminal case, the lawyers have two types of challenges to remove a prospective juror. One is for cause, where it is clear that the juror should not be seated because of bias, and the other is a peremptory challenge, which does not require explanation but may not be used prejudicially—for reasons of race or religion, for example.

Several of the other prospective jurors had varying opinions about Green's inquiry. After each lawyer finished a round of questioning, the panelists were seated or rejected. Not very long into the process, Green caught a huge break. Esther Steinberg raised her hand.

"Yes, madam." Green nodded to her. "Do you have a question or perhaps an observation?"

"I do," she replied. With a broad smile she said quietly yet firmly, "*J'accuse.*"

"What?" exclaimed Goss.

"Oh, be patient," counseled Green. "I'm certain Mrs. Steinberg will explain."

For the next few minutes, Esther Steinberg, a matronly seventy-year-old who was impeccably dressed and stylishly made up, spoke of what is known as the Dreyfus case.

Captain Alfred Dreyfus, a Jewish artillery officer in the French army, was falsely charged with treason and then convicted at a court-martial in 1894. He was sentenced to prison on the infamous Devil's Island off the coast of South America. In 1896, the French military had indisputable evidence that Dreyfus was not guilty, but instead of freeing him, they withheld the information, and he remained imprisoned until 1899. In 1898, the great French novelist Emile Zola penned a four-thousand-word essay in the form of an open letter to the president of the French Republic; he entitled the piece *J'accuse*—"I Accuse." Zola made a strong and compelling case that condemned the injustice suffered by Captain Dreyfus at the hands of the French military court. Zola's words ignited a firestorm of outrage from officials within the French government. The essay also led to a vile wave of anti-Semitism that swept across France. Zola was tried and convicted of criminal libel and was sentenced to serve a year in prison. He fled to England, where he remained for more than a year. By then, Dreyfus's conviction had been reversed. The captain was retried and once again convicted. Nonetheless, the French government immediately pardoned him, and he was reinstated by the army. Thereafter he was promoted and awarded the Legion of Honor. In 1906, France's highest court formally found the captain innocent. The libel charge against Zola had been dismissed years earlier, but his support for Captain Dreyfus left him financially ruined. Twelve years after this monumental injustice began, Captain Alfred Dreyfus was honored with a dress parade military ceremony.

Green was determined not to lose Mrs. Steinberg, but he made sure that it didn't appear obvious to Goss.

"Mrs. Steinberg," he began gently, "may I ask you if are you Jewish?"

She reddened slightly and replied, "Yes, I am, but—"

Green quickly interrupted. "May I assume that your religious affiliation and your knowledge about the Dreyfus case would not interfere with your ability to listen to the evidence in this case, take the judge's charge on the law, deliberate with your fellow jurors, and render a fair verdict?"

"That is correct," she quickly answered.

Green continued, "Is there any reason why you cited the Dreyfus case when I asked you about examples of injustice? And by the way, do you think that the circumstances that led to the injustices in the Dreyfus case are the norm for the criminal justice system—say, for this country?"

"I regard the Dreyfus case to be a particularly egregious example of injustice," she replied, "but I also think that, given all of the safeguards contained in our criminal justice system, an abuse like the Dreyfus case would be rare in this country."

Her answer completely satisfied Assistant District Attorney Goss, and he accepted Mrs. Steinberg as a juror. Green was ecstatic!

# 18

## Chief Louis Guido, 1973–1974

By 1973, police corruption had reached epidemic proportions, yet the leadership at One PP was unable or unwilling to mount any strategy to contain it. It would take a new mayoral administration and an innovative commissioner to turn the tide, but given the political demographics of a city controlled by Democrats and an extremely popular mayor, that was unlikely to happen. Then along came Winthrope Hargrove. No one could think of a more unlikely candidate.

For the political machine bosses of the Democratic Party, Hargrove was the ideal candidate of the Republican Party as its quadrennial sacrifice. Winthrope Hargrove seemed to be just a goofy WASP with a prep school education, topped off with a Harvard undergrad degree and a law school diploma from Yale. In a city whose Republican registration was dwarfed by the Democrats by a margin of six to one, Hargrove did not loom as much of a threat, and his slogan, "Win with Winnie," was laughable if not ludicrous. It didn't seem to matter that the Democratic leadership's once reform-minded incumbent, Phil Kersey, had become a vacuous, self-pitying shadow of the man once so much admired by New Yorkers as "Mayor Eternal"—his words. Or that Kersey's repeated and ill-advised attempts at higher office—first a disastrous run for the United States Senate, followed several years later by a half-hearted attempt at a run for governor—had worn thin his appeal with the voters and left his reputation shattered. Nor did it seem much of a problem that of the five Democratic bosses controlling each of the city's boroughs, two were serving time in federal prison and another had himself committed to a psychiatric hospital suffering severe depression. Nearly a century of repeated election victories at every level in New York City had left the Democratic Party as detached from reality as the city's mayor, who insisted on running for an unprecedented fourth term.

A confluence of circumstances fueled by Kersey's contempt for just about everyone made the unthinkable the inevitable.

The Associated Press wire story flashed around the country. "Phillip Kersey, once the enormously popular mayor of New York City's middle class, courted by three candidates for the Democratic nomination for president to be their vice presidential running mate in 1968, only minutes ago became part of the bitter history of lost elections, and with him the Democratic Party's machine has been unmasked as a paper tiger. 'Winnie' Hargrove, repeatedly vilified by the worst negative campaign in New York City's history, has overwhelmed Mayor Kersey 57 percent to 41 percent."

The first priority of any mayor is public safety, so his appointment of a police commissioner is closely watched by the press. The way Hargrove met the man he chose was purely coincidental. The place was a United Auto Workers lodge in the Brighton section of Richmond County, in the borough of Staten Island, on a summer weekend of that particularly nasty campaign for mayor. Louis Guido was a one-star chief serving as the deputy to the borough commander. Guido's career, which had peaked when he led the prestigious Public Morals Administrative Division, rapidly descended after he ordered the arrest of "Bippo" Readon, a major sports bookie who happened to be the brother of a New York City councilman who chaired the powerful Finance Committee.

Hargrove was introduced by the UAW lodge steward and took the stage to say a few words. Suddenly a drunken Democratic Party worker appeared out of the crowd and began screaming, "You fuckin' Republican phony," and threw a filled quart bottle of beer at the candidate. Hargrove quickly batted the bottle away, deflecting it from his head. Guido, who had wandered into the lodge a few minutes before to check on Hargrove's security, leaped to the stage and, smashing the drunk to the ground, knocked him unconscious. In seconds, Chief Guido had the man's arms cuffed behind his back and handed him over to an astonished young sergeant to complete the arrest procedure. When the crowd recovered, they sent up a loud cheer for Guido as he bounded onto the stage and asked the smiling candidate, "Are you okay, sir?"

The police department acceded immediately to Hargrove's request that Chief Guido head up his security unit.

Chief Louis Guido's appointment as the new commissioner bypassed eleven senior chiefs, all of whom promptly resigned. Guido in turn chose another one-star chief, Keith "Cookie" Nolan, to be his chief of department. Nolan became the only police executive to wear four stars and was the day-to-day chief executive officer of a department with thirty-six thousand officers of all ranks and twelve thousand civilians.

Some years before his current assignment, Chief Nolan had been banished by the then-serving chief of department to an obscure part of the bureaucracy hidden in the bowels of One Police Plaza. His transgression, which he could not recall, was apparently some slight that his immediate predecessor imagined him guilty of during one of the chief's endless administrative conferences. His best guess was that during one such conference with a redundant agenda about the personal hygiene habits expected of senior officers, an exasperated Nolan uttered a slight groan. The next morning he was banished from the executive floor to the basement of the building and put in charge of the motor pool.

While the traditional interaction between the police commissioner and the top uniformed commander was policy setter to policy executioner, Guido's and Nolan's history with each other would make things quite different. They had been friends since their days as police officers in the South Bronx, after they both graduated near the top of their class at the academy. This new administration would be a true partnership. In public, Nolan would refer respectfully to Guido as "Boss"—the traditional term for a superior officer in the department—and Guido would call Nolan "Chief." In private, all formality was dropped, and they set about reforming the department they loved so very much. They were determined to eradicate systemic corruption, particularly in the plainclothes division, and so it was that they decided to call upon Inspector James Patrick Connolly to begin that reform. Connolly agreed after one request was granted: assign Sergeant Bernie Pressler to help him.

# 19

## Bernie Pressler from Brownsville

Ever since their first assignment from the Police Academy to the 75th Precinct in Brooklyn's East New York, James Connolly and Bernie Pressler had been each other's shadow. They were very different in many ways. Connolly, an Irish Catholic, was all spit and polish while in uniform and a meticulous dresser when he wore civilian clothing. Pressler was Jewish. He was opinionated and super street-smart. His clothes always looked as if he had worn them to bed. He was also an extraordinarily effective investigator who hated corrupt cops.

Bernard Aser Pressler was a Brownsville Jew, and if you were one, or knew what the Brownsville section of Brooklyn was like in the 1920s through the end of the '50s, those words had instant meaning. Brownsville was a lower-income village made up typically of wood-frame, one- and two-family, fully detached or semidetached homes and a large number of brownstone row houses, popularly known as railroad flats. This enclave was wholly populated by Jewish emigrants from Eastern Europe. These Polish, Russian, and Romanian settlers produced large families fiercely committed to a tradition that included a deep faith in God and a clear understanding that education was the ultimate liberator from their economic ghetto here in their adopted land. But just as other groups, similarly situated, drifted into crime as a more effective way out of poverty, some in Brownsville chose that path and were enormously successful. These hoodlums created Murder Incorporated, the Jewish mob that controlled all the rackets in Brooklyn until the emigration and the ascendancy of the Sicilian Mafia.

Brownsville Jews also dominated college basketball at Long Island University and City College of New York, which was the last college basketball team to win both the NCAA and the NIT in the same year. They even played for some of the Catholic schools: The St. John's University basketball team of the late twenties was called "the Wonder Five," and in 1929 four of the five starting players were Jewish. Brownsville also produced some of the most successful bookmakers in New York City, and some say they were behind the biggest college basketball point-shaving scandal in history.

Fighting under pseudonyms such as Battlin' Buddy McGirt and Looie the Assassin Mangano, Jews from Brownsville became highly rated professional boxers. They were the trailblazers for Jews years later who could fight under their own names. Champions like Max Baer and Gus Lesnevich would in their time pack all the major fighting arenas in New York City with a huge following of fight fans.

Brownsville also produced a haberdasher who was a man so devoted to turning kids from that neighborhood away from a life of crime to medicine, teaching, social work, and the law that he soon became a living legend. This man, Abraham Stark, was so successful that he was elected borough president of Brooklyn. For anyone today over the age of fifty, Abe Stark is remembered best for his haberdashery sign in right center field at historic Ebbets Field, then the home of the Brooklyn Dodgers. The clothing sign read, "Abe Stark—1514 Pitkin Avenue," and invited the ballplayers to "Hit Sign, Win Suit!"

While Brownsville produced its share of criminals, many more of its residents became educators, judges, great trial attorneys, physicians, and cops like Bernie Pressler. Bernie Pressler, who had a keen intellect with high-school grades good enough to get him into any of the colleges of New York City, came from a family of seven children. It was a family, like so many others in Brownsville, that was dirt poor and simply could not afford sending a child to college. The combined incomes of all the kids and the parents were essential for survival.

At five feet ten inches and weighing 180 pounds, Bernie had developed a daily regimen of weight training and jogging at a gym not far from his home. He became so accomplished on the speed bag that the gym's boxing coach tried to convince him to take up the sport professionally. That career option lasted as long as it took for Momma Pressler to issue a firm order. "No!" So Bernie took the examination to become a New York City police officer and finished fourth out of the thousands of youngsters who applied. He was soon sworn in and was on the way to the academy.

Bernie wore his jet black hair with a sharp part directly down the middle, the favored style of bartenders in the 1940s. His wide face contained bead-sized dark eyes, prominent high cheekbones, and a huge flattened nose, a trophy from his boxing days. His short, muscular neck seemed to disappear between his head and shoulders. His lips were thin and perpetually turned down like a Ringling Brothers clown's, and it seemed to require an immense effort for him to smile.

Bernie Pressler was on the job when the Irish Mafia still ruled the NYPD; the stereotype for Jews was that they were either doctors, lawyers, teachers, or highly successful businessmen, and that they never took tough jobs like cop or firefighter. The police department he joined was parochial and distant from most new immigrants, particularly European Jews, and so at times Jewish citizens and the few Jewish police officers would fall victim to anti-Semitism. Whenever Pressler was confronted, he acted swiftly. Soon after his assignment to the 75th Precinct, in one of Brooklyn's toughest neighborhoods, Bernie overheard a big-mouthed bigot refer to him as "that Jew scumbag." He invited the officer to come to the locker room, alone, where he left him in a pile of bruises and blood.

# 20

*People v. Holt,*
October 19, 1992

On June 4, 1991, Steven Holt had been indicted by a Suffolk County grand jury. He was charged with three counts of murder in the second degree in connection with the murders of Scott Ruben, Ramon Rodriguez, and Ramon's brother, Hiram. A combination of extensive and complicated pretrial motions and Larry Green's commitment to other trials had delayed the start of Steven's trial for over a year. Now, as the court convened, he finally felt some relief.

Judge Michael J. McGowan was speaking to the jurors.

"Furthermore, if you conclude beyond a reasonable doubt that Sergeant Steven Robert Holt intentionally caused the death of Ramon Rodriguez and his brother, Hiram Rodriguez, and that he caused the death of Police Officer Scott Ruben, then you must find him guilty of the crime of murder in the second degree as charged in the first, second, and third counts of this indictment." Here the judge paused for a moment, and then he continued, "And, of course, if you don't so find, beyond a reasonable doubt, then you must acquit Sergeant Holt."

Judge McGowan was merely going through his ritual of giving the jury preliminary instructions, but Steven Holt, after months of anxiety, was beginning to show signs of paranoia and at this point cringed, believing that the judge had emphasized the standard for a criminal conviction and understated the grounds for acquittal. McGowan, on the other hand, thought he was actually benefiting the defendant through clarity and repetition. He would repeat these instructions in greater detail during his final charge, or definition and explanation of the law, to the jury, after they had heard all of the evidence and before submitting the case to them for their deliberation. Finally, McGowan added, "Verdict, ladies and gentlemen of the jury, comes from the Latin word *veredictum,* which means truth saying or telling the truth. And that, after all, is what you must try to achieve."

Judge McGowan's voice was firm and strong. It resonated clearly through the huge courtroom, acoustically almost perfect, chosen by him because he anticipated correctly that a large crowd of spectators and reporters would attend the trial of a New York City police officer charged with a triple homicide.

The walls of the courtroom were of rich, dark reddish-brown mahogany. Its floors were inlaid with expensive oak, maintained at a high polish with daily care at the conclusion of the court session. Completing the majestic image of this palace of justice was the judge's bench. The front wall of the bench was a foot thick and measured seven feet high and twelve feet wide. It was made mostly of black-and-white marble with a tastefully designed ebony base, three feet by four feet, that featured a sculpture of Justice carefully chiseled into the glistening stone. The judge's lofty perch created a formidable barrier between him and everyone else in his courtroom. High above and behind the judge's oversized green leather upholstered chair, an ancient command from the Book of Deuteronomy was written in large gold script on the mahogany wall: "Justice, justice, thou shalt pursue." All of this created a most appropriate venue for the tall, trim, austere-looking Michael J. McGowan, chief administrative judge of all the courts in Suffolk County. At nearly six feet six inches tall, with snow-white hair and a deep bass voice, he commanded the complete attention of the jurors. They sat comfortably in their jury box nearby, in large chairs made from the same mahogany as the courtroom walls and luxuriously padded with the same dark green leather as Judge McGowan's chair. McGowan, of course, had full control over the lawyers and the courtroom spectators, because he simply would not have it any other way. When he spoke, the sound of his voice was the only thing heard in the courtroom.

At the beginning of the judge's introductory charge, delivered just prior to the prosecutor's opening statement to the jury, Steven was having difficulty reading him. McGowan's reputation was that of a no-nonsense, tough, pro-cop jurist who had little patience with defense attorneys. Most police officers thought he was great. Steven was watching very carefully to see how the judge felt about this case, his case. Since Holt had no guidelines or experience in such matters, it was really an exercise in futility.

"Now, a doubt can't be flimsy. It must be reasonable and not used as an excuse to avoid an unpleasant task," McGowan continued. Steven thought for sure that things were not going in his favor. As McGowan's words pounded against his ears like so many sledgehammer blows, he could feel the hot flashes erupting on his pale cheeks.

*How . . . how?* Steven thought as the fear those words caused surged throughout his body. *How the fuck did I get here?*

It was a question he frequently asked himself and rhetorically put to Lee Moran and his uncle. He had no answer. He certainly had no reason to kill two factory workers from Brooklyn he'd never met, and while he knew Police Officer Scott Ruben and didn't have much use for him, he had no motive to kill him—or anyone else, for that matter. And he didn't have a clue about how his police service weapon was used to kill all three.

It was at these times of reflection, either during moments of distraction at the trial or alone in his cell, that he would compare his plight to the circumstances that led to the poor treatment given his uncle. What united them, aside from their love for each other and the job, was their hatred for every vestige of police corruption, and while their service was separated by nearly twenty years, each was given the opportunity by bosses fed up with police corruption to eliminate it. What Steven couldn't know was that while the factors that almost crushed Mulvey and the forces that were threatening to put him in prison for the rest of his life grew out of their anticorruption efforts, the destructive paths taken by each of them were very different.

# 21

Connolly, Pressler, and the Plan,
January–February 1974

Inspector Connolly and Sergeant Pressler agreed that their initial strategy should be to set up a surveillance of a few selected locations within the operational area of the 13th Division. Pressler borrowed a van from Internal Affairs that was made to look like a utility vehicle operated by the Brooklyn Union Gas Company.

They began their observations early the following morning. At approximately 10:30, not more than an hour after they set up, they noticed some unusual activity at a liquor store and a grocery store located on the opposite sides of Nostrand Avenue about a hundred feet from the intersection of Nostrand and a major artery called Eastern Parkway. Through the smoked windows of the undercover van, they watched a steady stream of people enter the stores and leave empty-handed. Over the next two and a half hours, thirty-six people entered the grocery store, and forty-seven entered the liquor store; most of them left a short time later without a package.

While the conduct of these "customers" might appear suspicious, the law requires that a police officer have probable cause to believe that a crime is being committed before taking any action against a suspect. Connolly and Pressler decided to get some advice from Deputy Chief Virgil Sampson, commanding officer of the elite Public Morals Administrative Division.

While PMAD's main mission was to work with prosecutors to put major bookmakers out of business and into prison, occasionally it would catch some crooked cops and thieving lawyers who were in partnership with the major bookies. PMAD operated at an undisclosed location and kept its personnel strength a closely held secret. It had an unblemished reputation for integrity as well as effectiveness. Unlike Internal Affairs, which at the time was regarded as a joke by most cops, PMAD was the real deal. If PMAD detectives caught you, you'd stay caught!

Virgil Sampson stood about six feet four inches tall, with skin the color of brilliantly polished ebony. He was one of the few African Americans at that time who had reached the rank of chief in the New York City Police Department. His trim, firm body was held perpetually erect, disciplined by regular exercise and by Chief Sampson's will. His large, muscular hands, which appeared to be out of proportion to the rest of his body, were strengthened by a routine of chopping wood several days a week in the backyard of his home in a neat residential neighborhood in Brooklyn known as Crown Heights. The chief had a habit of staring through people, which intimidated most and belied the fact that he had a great sense of humor. From the first day in the Police Academy, through every promotional examination, Virgil Sampson was known as a student. While he was never at the top of the class in school or on a promotional exam, he strictly followed the advice of his late father: "Virgil, just make sure that you're competitive." Indeed, that was what all the long hours of study produced for this dedicated young man. Virgil was always in the game, always competitive.

Chief Sampson was very familiar with the area of Crown Heights where Connolly and Pressler made their observations. He had grown up in the vicinity, not far from his present home. He also knew quite a lot about the two stores Connolly and Pressler had under observation.

"The liquor store," he said, "has been in the Creighton family since they moved here from Georgia in the late 1940s. Luis Arroyo bought the grocery store from the Steward family, who started their business in late 1951 shortly after they moved to Brooklyn from the Cayman Islands. Both stores are known to handle a little sports betting action and some numbers on the side." Numbers is essentially a ghetto gambling game and the winning numbers are selected from the last three digits of the mutual handle, or the gross amount of money bet for the day at the local horseracing track. So for example if the total amount of money bet at Aqueduct racetrack in New York City in one day is $3,542,923, the winning number for the day would be the last three digits, or 923. The payoff for the right guess can run into the hundreds and sometimes into the thousands of dollars.

Pressler asked, "Chief, don't you think that so many people over a few hours indicates more than a little action?" Chief Sampson, with many more years of experience in the surveillance business than the sergeant, resisted the temptation to put Bernie down. Instead he put a question to both officers. "Well, what do think we've got?"

Connolly replied, "My guess is that either the CO of the Seven-one doesn't regard the two businesses as anything more than a nuisance, or that some cops from either the precinct or from the 13th Division are being paid off."

Mulvey cleared his throat, and although he was intimidated he got up the courage to ask, "Why was it so obvious to you, Chief, that some police officers were on the take?"

Connolly smiled, still trying without much success to relax his protégé. "The short answer is, son, that corruption in the plainclothes division has been an open secret in this department forever. The thing is, no one has been able to prove it, but that's what the commissioner wants us to try to do."

Mulvey froze when the Inspector said "us." He shifted uncomfortably in his chair. Connolly continued his story.

When Connolly had finished his analysis, Chief Sampson looked a bit puzzled, but for only a minute. Then he said, "Fine, let's see if we can find out." He pushed the intercom button and said to his aide, "Billie, get me Lieutenant Moore. If he's in the building, send him in. If not, reach him and tell him I want him forthwith."

Not ten minutes later, there was a sharp knock on Chief Sampson's door which was answered, "Lou"—Lieutenant—"if that's you, come on in."

Lieutenant Brendan Moore quickly stepped into the room. Moore's face could have been on a travel poster for Aer Lingus. His hair, which he kept short, was jet black. He had deep blue eyes, and his cheeks had two prominent dimples. He wore a bubbly smile, and you could sense the enthusiasm as he entered the room. His gray tweed jacket and his freshly pressed chinos, accompanied by black loafers with tasseled straps, was the wardrobe he chose because he thought it made him look older. Although he was in his late forties, he was always concerned that his youthful appearance would be mistaken for inexperience. This street uniform made him look like the investigative analyst he had worked so hard to become—at least he thought so. There was no one in the department quite like him.

After the introductions, Chief Sampson gave Lieutenant Moore the details and asked, "Brendan, do we have any informants we can send to either or both of those locations to see what's going on?"

"Sure, Boss," the lieutenant replied. "I've got a guy working off a Bronx case who lives on Eastern Parkway, a few blocks from those stores." By "working off a case," the lieutenant meant that a confidential informant, or CI, had a pending criminal case in one of the five counties in New York City, and if the CI provided evidence or useful intelligence for Lieutenant Moore, Moore would agree to ask the district attorney in that county to offer a guilty plea to a lesser charge, reduce a jail sentence, or even dismiss the case. If confidential information is the currency for law enforcement undercover in drug and gambling operations, Lieutenant Brendan A. Moore was the national bank for CIs. This twenty-six-year police veteran, with two decades of experience in undercover operations, was quite simply the most highly respected police officer in the clandestine art known as surreptitious investigation. The demand for Moore's expertise from federal and local investigative agencies had become so time-consuming that Police Commissioner Guido's predecessors had to severely limit the lieutenant's activities outside the police department.

Several days later and with the assistance of Lieutenant Moore's CI, the answer was crystal clear: Both Crown Heights locations had become major sports betting operations. Moreover, those businesses were part of a network of illegal betting franchises wholly controlled by the Gambino crime family.

Moore's information did not just startle Chief Sampson, it made him furious. How could something like this happen, under his nose, in his neighborhood?

Certainly Sampson was well aware that organized crime controls and, indeed, regulates illegal gambling, not just in New York City but across the country. He was, after all, the premier expert in this area of criminal activity. Until this very moment, though, he had believed the conventional wisdom that organized crime bosses generally ignored local, small-time bookmakers, particularly those whose business largely dealt with the numbers racket.

Neither the chief nor anyone else in the illegal gambling wing of law enforcement knew of a meeting of Gambino capos held eighteen months before, when the family made a decision to get out of the narcotics business because it created too much risk, and to expand control over every aspect of illegal gambling, particularly sports betting, wherever it operated. In a remarkably short time, the revenue stream from this source would amply fill the vacuum created when the mob got out of drug trafficking.

Both the liquor store and the grocery store followed roughly the same routine. Bobby Arroyo, Luis's son, and Lance Creighton, the son of Bernice Creighton, the Creighton matriarch and owner of the liquor store, would deliver the betting slips to what appeared to be an abandoned warehouse on Staten Island located near the ferry slip. Part of the warehouse was used as a highly sophisticated wire room—acting as the nerve center of the Gambino sports betting operation in New York City.

A wire room is the depository for all the betting action, the place where all the betting slips are centrally recorded to determine who is entitled to be paid after winning a bet. It also operates to lay off bets with another bookmaking operation somewhere else in the country if the action is too much to handle. For example, if the Giants were a heavy favorite against the Cowboys, the wire room in Staten Island would lay off part of the action. So that if there was an upset and Dallas won, the Gambino wire room wouldn't be wiped out.

This particular wire room in Staten Island was heavily guarded, secured by surveillance equipment and a central alarm system connected to a security company controlled by the family. Since the annual gross at the room was six hundred million dollars, it was closely watched twenty-four hours a day.

On a bright, frigid February afternoon, Connolly and Pressler decided to put their plan into action. The design of the plan was really quite simple: Grab the Arroyo kid with all the betting slips, charging him with maximum felonies that could guarantee him serious prison time, summon his father to the arrest scene, and use the leverage to get the old man to identify the crooked cops. If they got lucky they could be well on the way to dismantling corruption in the 13th. Not bad for a new police commissioner who only took office a month before, in January 1974. Of course, it was not going to be that easy.

As Bobby Arroyo's late-model blue Mercedes neared the entrance ramp on the Brooklyn side of the Verrazano Bridge, an unmarked car cut in front of it, forcing him to the curb. Connolly and Pressler lept from their car with their guns drawn.

"Show me your hands and freeze," commanded Sergeant Pressler, which upon later reflection he thought sounded a bit too melodramatic. Not so for poor Bobby Arroyo, who wet his pants, immediately before leaving his car with his hands over his head.

Arroyo's five-foot-four, 120-pound muscular body shook violently with fear, and his small pockmarked face with its perpetually sad look had turned ashen. He cried convulsively.

"Well, looka here, Inspector," said Pressler, showing Connolly two full shopping bags of betting slips.

"Officer," pleaded Arroyo, "can I call my dad?"

"Who the fuck do you think you're messin' with?" roared Luis Arroyo, his face scarlet with rage. As soon as he received the urgent call from his son, Arroyo raced to the secluded tree-lined service road under the Verrazano bridge on the Brooklyn side. Bobby had been allowed a minute to speak to his father alone. In appearance Luis Arroyo was an older version of his son; Bobby tried to match his father in dress and mannerisms, so much so that his friends and family called him Luisito, or little Luis.

"How much more money do I have to pay you motherfuckers?" Luis shouted, but he was stopped before completing the sentence by the pain from Pressler's fist crashing against his jaw, sending him hard to the pavement.

Pointing to Connolly, Pressler snarled, "This is a New York City police inspector, you little mutt. Don't you dare use that language with him."

Stunned, Luis Arroyo, with a voice and look showing disgust, said softly, "How much money do I have to pay to how many cops to avoid this bullshit?"

The command center of the police department's Public Morals Administrative Division was located in a closed bus depot in Staten Island. It happened to be no more than two blocks away from the Gambino wire room.

As Luis Arroyo laid out how the operation worked to Connolly, Pressler, Chief Sampson, and Detective Paul Garcia at PMAD headquarters, Connolly could feel the early signs of nausea. He was about to assume command of a police unit that, if you did the math quickly as he did, was substantially corrupt.

On the last day of each month, at a different location, Luis would meet with two police officers assigned to the 13th and give them one hundred one-hundred-dollar bills, or ten thousand dollars.

As soon as Mulvey did the math and realized that crooked cops were receiving annually one hundred and twenty thousand dollars in dirty money, he jumped up and exclaimed, "Please, Inspector, I've heard enough. Whatever you have in mind for me is not something I want to be involved with." Connolly stood and tried to interrupt the young cop, but he persisted. "If you're looking to catch crooked cops, I'm not your guy. They would see through me in a minute—"

"Robert," Connolly went on, "just listen to the rest of this and then to what I have in mind for you. If you still don't think you can help me, that will be the end of it. Fair enough?" Mulvey hesitated, and Connolly continued, "Please sit back down and let me finish."

Mulvey nodded warily and sat back down.

When Inspector Connolly reviewed the personnel roster for the 13th Division, he found that there were currently twenty-four police officers, three sergeants, a lieutenant, a captain, and an unfilled spot for an inspector, which Connolly would assume. In all there were twenty-nine officers. Connolly wondered how many cops were splitting the annual payoff of one hundred and twenty thousand dollars—from Arroyo alone.

Luis Arroyo explained that the money was given in return for all the usual benefits, including accommodation arrests for the misdemeanor of loitering for the purpose of gambling, and, of course, the gambling slips were returned to Arroyo's workers, commonly called runners. Arroyo explained that after the Gambinos took control of his operation and granted him the right to continue bookmaking, his business increased as they steered new customers to his store. The payoff demanded by the cops also increased, from six thousand to ten thousand a month. That this coincided with the Gambinos' decision to assert total control over all gambling operations in their territory was an even greater concern to Chief Sampson. Corrupt cops taking money from local bookmakers was evil enough, but the adjusted amount in the payoffs indicated a direct connection between crooked cops and the mob.

Arroyo explained that the passing of the money was accomplished in a brief meeting where no words were exchanged. Three days before the last day of every month, one of his runners would be told randomly by one of the cops, "*Muchacho, Feliz Navidad.*" That "Merry Christmas" meant that Arroyo was to telephone a special number to get the location for the monthly payment. Changing these locations was thought by the crooked cops to ensure against detection.

Luis Arroyo agreed to cooperate with the police investigation in return for the release of his son Bobby, although the betting slips seized from Bobby Arroyo's shopping bags were not returned. The only assurance that Luis Arroyo got was that an effort would be made to keep him from becoming a witness against the crooks if a case developed.

# 22

*People v. Holt,*
October 19, 1992

As Larry Green rose from his seat at the defense table to begin his opening statement, he smiled briefly at Steven and then walked toward the jury box. He sensed the futility of his case, but there was nothing in his demeanor that would disclose it. Out of the corner of his right eye he caught a glimpse of some of his law students from Fordham seated in the row reserved for lawyers. He turned to look at them, and with a wink he continued approaching the jury until he was about a foot away from the forewoman, a sixty-something retired banker, neatly attired in a charcoal gray business suit. From the start of the voir dire, Green had been impressed with Ms. Drew's answers to both his and Judge McGowan's questions.

At this point, Green thought about his law school lecture on the dynamics of an opening statement and how a defense lawyer should deal with a weak case: "One thing you never do is to waive your opening, unless," he would add cynically, "you're prepared to give your client a jailbreak plan. And that's particularly true if the prosecutor has made an effective opening." That certainly wasn't the case with Goss's opening, which was sterile, boring, and distracting. Nonetheless, as Green would caution in class, "even a lousy opening requires a response, but it has to be tailored according to the facts of the case, its strengths and weaknesses, together with any available pragmatic factors."

And so he began.

"May it please the Court, Justice McGowan, Mr. Goss, Madam Forelady, and ladies and gentlemen of the jury." Green's voice was soft and soothing. "The prosecution has brought to this courtroom a case which asks you to convict a much decorated police officer, a man whose record as a corruption fighter earned him the personal and heartfelt gratitude of the mayor of the city of New York and that of the city's police commissioner, and who was awarded the highest medal the New York City police department has to offer. And, Madam Forelady, given the clear direction you and your colleagues will receive from this learned justice, Judge McGowan, about the burden of proof required of the prosecutor, and Sergeant Holt's right to be presumed innocent, and added to that the paucity of the evidence promised thus far in these proceedings by young Mr. Goss in his address to you, I must tell you that these charges"—Green's voice was now rising steadily—"are among the most outrageous I have confronted in my four decades as a lawyer. Let me add that while for most of my career I have defended people charged with various crimes, I have often acted as a special prosecutor by the appointment of the state's chief administrative judge in a number of counties throughout New York State. And I say to you"—now Larry Green had reached his desired level of staged indignation—"that never before in any county of this state where I have had the honor of appearing, either as a defense attorney or as the prosecutor, have I encountered a case so reckless that it relies wholly on evidence, which will soon be offered to you, that is both gossamer thin and irrevocably flawed."

Suddenly Green whirled around to look at the gallery and those members of his trial advocacy class. He smiled knowingly at his young charges because he understood they would be surprised. After all, for most of the semester at Fordham he'd taught them that rhetoric and argument have no place in an opening statement. "An opening statement is," he would say, "a promise to prove. Save your arguments for summation." He would tell them later today that he taught this division of presentations purposefully throughout his course until the end so as not to confuse them, and that during the last class session, when he would treat them to a few beers or some wine at a local bar, he'd explain that an experienced trial lawyer could, where appropriate, blend in with the promise to prove compelling arguments designed to capture the jury's attention early in the trial. Defending Steven Holt against multiple murder charges demanded, Green would tell them, "that I take the prosecutor's case apart piece by piece and shake it from its baseless foundation!"

Green returned his gaze to the jurors. "What is it that young Mr. Goss has promised you, once you have cleared away his fog of obfuscation? He has Sergeant Holt's gun"—now he shouted in mock surprise—"and lo and behold, the weapon has both the sergeant's fingerprints and palm prints." Pausing for effect, slowly shrugging his shoulders, and with palms upturned, he threw back his head and cried, "Mr. Goss would have you believe that these conclusions are from forensic technicians who are the successors of the great Sherlock Holmes."

Green walked directly toward Ms. Drew and, leaning over to about a foot away from the forewoman, said in a soft and quiet tone, "Let me be clear, the gun that Sergeant Holt turned over to the Suffolk County detectives is his gun, and it is covered with his fingerprints and palm prints."

"Objection," shouted Assistant District Attorney Goss, "I can't hear what Mr. Green is saying."

"Overruled," Justice McGowan shot back. "Sit down and pay attention!"

"Then," Green continued, "added to this underwhelming offering, Mr. Goss assures you that the bullets from Sergeant Holt's gun and the bullets recovered from the body of each of the victims in this case are a match." Green paced up and down before the jury box, searching the eyes of each juror. He stopped suddenly and then said matter-of-factly, "I assure you that after this so-called forensic proof disintegrates before your very eyes, and is swept away by the cold wind of truth, your course will be clear."

Green turned and appeared to be returning to his seat at counsel's table, but he stopped just before reaching his chair. "Madam Forelady, and ladies and gentlemen of the jury, when you have heard all of this"—his face was now an angry mask, although he kept his voice calm—"you will ask how this flimsy case has taken away this young police officer's liberty for nearly sixteen months, and placed him under the looming fear of a state prison sentence for the rest of his life. You will wonder, sadly—"

Goss exploded from his seat, shouting, "Objection, objection, Your Honor. Counsel knows very well that sentencing and pretrial release conditions are not part of the jury's responsibility."

Green, wearing a Cheshire Cat smile, remained standing, awaiting the court's ruling.

Judge McGowan rose slowly and, assisted by his high bench, seemed to grow to an awesome size. "You had better understand one thing very clearly, young Mr. Goss. Don't you ever again lecture anyone in my courtroom about the law of this state." McGowan ripped off his reading glasses angrily and peered down at the youthful prosecutor, who looked terrified. "The law is my domain!" The judge waited to allow his admonition to achieve its full effect. "Moreover," he continued, "for whatever period of time that Mr. Green has remaining in his opening address to this jury, you are to stay in your seat and you are not to utter so much as a sound. Am I clear?"

At first Goss, stunned, didn't reply. McGowan, whose voice until now had been measured and level, raised it and asked, "Do you understand me?"

The young assistant DA rose, unsteady on shaking legs, and spoke softly, "Yes, Your Honor."

Judge McGowan took his seat and, turning to the jury, said. "Now, members of the jury, Mr. Green very well knows, and I suspect even young Mr. Goss knows, that punishment is my obligation, not yours, and so you must not consider it, any more than you can consider the manner in which Sergeant Holt is being detained. Neither issue may be considered by you in arriving at your verdict."

Judge McGowan then addressed Larry Green. "Now, Mr. Green, please try to resist the urge to demonstrate your vast experience as a trial attorney by engaging in this kind of tactic."

Green rose immediately and, with a polite bow, said, "Of course, Your Honor. I will respect your wishes. And now, if I may, I am about done."

McGowan nodded, and Green continued. "When you think about this case, with all of its ramifications to the victims, whose lives were snuffed out, to their families, and their indescribable suffering, and how this young sergeant has been punished, you will wonder about the meaning of those words which sit high over Judge McGowan's bench; the true meaning of the ancient command of Deuteronomy, 'Justice, justice, thou shalt pursue.' But no matter how you conclude those words apply to the prosecutor in this case, I am entirely confident that you will heed their profound direction, and that you will follow the learned charge on the law by Judge McGowan to reach a just verdict. And when you do, I know that you will find Steven Robert Holt not guilty. Thank you."

As Green walked to his seat, he knew that his opening statement was good theater but lacking in substance, because there was none. He also knew that it was the only thing he had to offer. He would put his hopes on Ms. Drew or Mrs. Steinberg or just one of the others to hang the jury!

# 23

The Plan,
February, 1974

"You want to take a break, Robert?"

"No, sir, Inspector, I'd like to hear more," Mulvey replied.

"Good," said Connolly, "because now it becomes fascinating."

The Friday following Arroyo's agreement to cooperate, he was informed by one of his runners that some cops had called with their familiar greeting, "*Feliz Navidad*," followed by the instruction that the meeting would be at the main public library in Brooklyn, located in Grand Army Plaza. That plaza, designed as a replica of the Arc de Triomphe in Paris, was built as a monument to the soldiers who fought for the North in the Civil War.

The instructions directed that the meeting take place at the last table in the law research section and that Arroyo bring a Nike box in a brown paper bag. This last instruction seemed to Inspector Connolly and the others to be right from the plot of a cheap spy movie. Luis explained that whatever was used to transport the ten thousand dollars would be exchanged for an empty duplicate container brought to the meeting by the cops.

Chief Sampson, Inspector Connolly, and Sergeant Pressler agreed that it was time to meet with representatives of the Brooklyn district attorney.

The evidence developed so far in the investigation was brought to ADA Kenneth J. Rattigan, chief of the Rackets Bureau in the Brooklyn DA's office, by the district attorney's new detective squad commander, Captain Sean J. Nevins. Chief Sampson told Nevins some of the facts and asked him to set up a meeting with Rattigan.

By tradition, each of the five district attorneys was assigned a squad of New York City detectives who worked from the DA's office. Since these detectives typically investigated organized crime and allegations of police corruption, they were supervised by each DA's rackets chief. Throughout the years these squads and their commanders were often recommended by the political bosses in each county, but shortly after his appointment as police commissioner, Guido decided to appoint squad commanders of unquestioned integrity, replacing some of the hacks who owed their assignment to Democratic political bosses. The commissioner wanted these commanders to be jointly chosen by him and the district attorney to cement the relationship between the city's five prosecutors and the NYPD so that there could be a coordinated strategy to eliminate police corruption. It was an inspired idea, which did not take long to yield positive results.

Kenny Rattigan was not only the chief of Brooklyn's Rackets Bureau. He was Brooklyn DA Buddy Cooper's confidant. When Commissioner Guido suggested his idea of a partnership of appointment between the DAs and him, he did it over a drink with Rattigan. Kenny thought it was a great innovation.

Guido then asked, "Any ideas who your boss would want?"

"Absolutely," Rattigan responded. "We'd want Nevins."

Guido, in his comic Brooklynese—most people didn't know whether it was feigned or real—replied, "Hey, Kenny, are you fuckin' nuts? Nevins is a straight guy, but he's a fuckin' loose cannon."

So Chief Sampson, Connolly, Pressler, and Squad Commander Nevins filled the musty, tiny corner room occupied by Brooklyn

Rackets Chief Kenneth Rattigan. At thirty-five, with a thin, pallid face and soft brown hair, Rattigan was an even six feet with a body so underweight that his business suit appeared two sizes too big and his white dress shirt and striped tie hung so loosely that people would focus on his huge Adam's apple. Rattigan looked so young that he was often mistaken for one of the baby-faced detectives assigned to the DA's squad. His annoying chain-smoking filled his little office with a constant cloud and a stench that gagged most nonsmokers. His attitude in dealing with investigators who brought cases to his bureau was "No bullshit!" Kenny had a knack of evaluating cases and making a decision to move quickly or shut them down. From what he'd been told so far about this new case, Rattigan was salivating.

The plan of action they discussed demanded surprise. They concluded that the most effective way to get a true picture of the extent of corruption in the 13th Division was to get one of the two 13th Division pickup cops who met Luis Arroyo at the Grand Army Plaza library to flip. But what could the police department offer a cop who decided to turn against his co-conspirators?

Chief Sampson, who raised the question, answered it himself. "Get the DA to agree not to ask the judge for a prison sentence?"

Rattigan thought for a moment and then replied, "That's worth shit, Virgil. All these humps really care about is their pension. They know damn well that judges don't send them to jail, so there's no reason to come with us."

Rattigan now paused for effect and counterproposed something he knew very well ran against the grain of every procedure held so dearly by the police department. Before this meeting, he had cleared it with District Attorney Cooper, whose parting words were "Well, Kenny, we will soon find out if the cops are serious."

Rattigan leaned forward and said, "What if we don't prosecute one of these corrupt cops who agrees to cooperate and you keep him on the job?"

Chief Sampson shot up to a standing position as if struck by lightning but in a measured reply said, "Kenny, this department flushes its garbage. It's no go!"

"Okay, Chief, then we got nothing else to talk about."

Connolly jumped from his chair, shouting, "But Kenny, what about all those crooked scumbags at the 13th Division?"

The confident young prosecutor stood up to play his trump card and, smiling as he stepped over some of the participants crowded in the tiny room, answered, "Hey, guys, go see your friends at the FBI. They do corruption, too!" Looking directly at Chief Sampson, he continued, "The district attorney and I are frankly fed up with this bullshit. You and the rest of your department are in fucking denial. You have the chance of a lifetime to dismantle, destroy, and send to prison an entire vipers' nest of corrupt cops, and instead you want to just pick off one or two. Oh, I am fully familiar with your policy. After the arrest of these two crooks who were dealing with Arroyo, you'll announce to the press that in order to avoid the appearance of impropriety the police commissioner will reassign all of the members of the 13th Division. And you will do this with the full knowledge that the majority of those cops are crooks and that it will not take very long for them to regroup and to steal again. You know damned well, Chief, that this policy is the major reason your department can never be taken seriously when it comes to rooting out corruption. So go play with the feds, because they don't have any problem playing your game. But just remember this, Chief, District Attorney Cooper and I know what you are doing. You are trying to cover up the most extensive corruption scandal in the recent history of your department, so don't think we are going to sit back and say nothing." He closed the door behind him and left for another meeting.

"Kenny," said an obviously concerned District Attorney Cooper, "I hope you know what you're doing, letting a case like this get away."

"Buddy, aren't you fed up with these one-case-at-a-time corruption prosecutions? Every time we lock up a corrupt cop, the union and the department say it's an isolated case, a bad apple in a barrel of good apples. You piss off honest cops and their familes, who feel embarrassed that their neighbors will look at them differently. Soon they and all their relatives and friends start to believe the PBA's bullshit, which is embraced by an anachronistic department which has never found a way to clean out its sewer. We have a chance that nobody may ever have again. We've got to show everyone that what we've got here is a fucking outrage; that the cops in one police unit are collecting a share of thousands of dollars. That's something that all the working stiffs in this city including you and me can understand and will not tolerate. And, Boss, if the department doesn't understand that, fuck 'em!"

At 2:30 the following morning, they were all back in Rattigan's cubbyhole of an office. On one side of the desk, sitting next to the rackets chief, were Inspector Connolly, Sergeant Pressler, Detective Garcia, and a scowling Chief Virgil Sampson. On the other side, jammed against the wall, sat Police Officer William Bosco. Bosco didn't really fit the image of a cop, certainly not at this moment. He was a short young man with not much left of his hair. His balding pate ran with nervous sweat. He was wearing a faded green jogging suit that seemed sizes too big for him as he slumped over to one side. His face was chalk white. His fingers were in constant motion, either tapping the sides of the straight-backed wooden chair he sat in or brushing away the perspiration flushing down his narrow face. His body occasionally twitched with fear and then heaved deep sighs as his eyes darted from face to face of the accusers who did not seem to take their eyes off him. Sitting inches away, glaring with his omnipresent unlighted cigar, was Captain Sean Nevins.

Many hours earlier, Bosco and his partner, Officer Benny Perez, met with Luis Arroyo at the library. Bosco placed an empty Nike box in a brown paper bag next to the similar package under the table in the legal reference section. Then, smiling, Detective Perez picked up Arroyo's package and said, "*Muchas gracias, muchacho,*" and both police officers quickly left and headed for their car.

A thorough background analysis of both officers included the facts that Bosco was twenty-eight years old, that he had two children, ages four and two, that his wife, Marie, was three months pregnant, and that they had recently purchased and moved into a one-family house in a suburb in Nassau County. All those personal and financial obligations made Bosco a prime target. By contrast, Perez was a twenty-six-year-old bachelor with a relatively carefree lifestyle who spent his off-hours driving a used MG, usually with a different girlfriend each week.

They decided to flip Bosco.

At about 12:45 Saturday morning, Bosco's four-year-old Ford station wagon had just crossed over the New York City line into the town of Valley Stream, in Nassau County. Bosco swerved sharply to the right, leaving the Southern State Parkway, onto the cement shoulder, halting at the grass. The reason for his sudden move was two unmarked black vans—one that rammed the rear of his station wagon without warning, and one that pulled next to him and turned a hard right into his vehicle, forcing it from the road.

It seemed to Bosco that more than a dozen people leaped from the two vans with guns drawn, screaming, "Freeze, police!"

Bosco shouted, "I'm a cop," while trying to show his police shield and identification.

"You're shit, dirtbag," came the reply from someone who added, "And show me your fucking hands before I blow your balls off."

Connolly stepped out of the shadows and asked the shaken young officer, "What were you trying to get out of your pocket, son? You nearly got yourself shot."

Bosco answered quickly, "I'm a New York City police officer, sir. I was just trying to identify myself."

"Well, son, I'm Inspector Connolly of the NYPD, and we've been looking for a guy driving a station wagon who robbed a convenience store in Maspeth, Queens, a few hours ago."

"Sir, that couldn't have been me. I'm assigned to the 13th Plainclothes Division in East New York, Brooklyn, and I didn't end my tour until midnight. My partner and at least two bosses can vouch for that."

"Put the guns away," ordered Connolly, to Bosco's instant relief.

After Bosco showed his ID, Connolly said, "I'm sorry for the hassle, son, but the creep who held up the store fired three shots over the head of the owner's twelve-year-old daughter, and it would help us if you could come meet the guy so he can see that it wasn't you. You won't mind, now will you?"

"I got no problem, sir, but my wife is pregnant and she expects me home."

"No problem. Sergeant Pressler here will take you to a pay phone on the way to our office," answered Connolly. "We'll have you home in two hours flat."

None of this was anything more than a ruse to take Bosco off his guard for the shock that would follow.

Once they arrived at the Brooklyn district attorney's offices, Nevins suddenly reached into Bosco's waistband and ripped his .38-caliber police special from its holster. He said matter-of-factly, "You're now an ex-cop, you piece of shit!"

Before Bosco could react, Rattigan spoke. "Mr. Bosco." He emphasized the word "Mister" to underscore Bosco's sudden change of status. "I'm Ken Rattigan, and I'm an assistant district attorney and chief of the Rackets Bureau."

It helped that Kenny had been involved in a number of high-profile police corruption cases, which were widely reported by the media. His name was known well enough by the police officers who worked in Brooklyn. He had a reputation for demanding prison sentences for cops convicted of bribery.

"Now, Mr. Bosco, I want you to sit back and close your eyes and imagine for the next half hour or so that you're sitting in the felony part of the State Supreme Court here in Brooklyn, listening to me outline my case against you, which will send you to state prison for about seven years. Do you understand?"

Bosco, who was now drenched in sweat, couldn't answer. Instead he nodded slightly.

Rattigan continued, "Mr. Foreman, and ladies and gentlemen of the jury, last year, inside Brooklyn's main public library at Grand

Army Plaza, at the legal research reference section, this defendant, William Bosco, then a New York City police officer, received the sum of ten thousand dollars from a major bookmaker, an associate of the Gambino organized crime family. The money was passed to this defendant in a Nike sneaker box, which was carried in a brown paper bag. The purpose of this extortionate bribe was to pay for police protection which was provided by this defendant and other corrupt police officers assigned to the 13th Plainclothes Division, a unit of the New York Police Department located here in Kings County, in the Crown Heights section of our borough." Rattigan paused for a moment and then said, "As a result of this corrupt activity, a Kings County grand jury has returned an indictment charging this defendant with numerous felony crimes."

As the rackets chief continued laying out a powerful recitation of the evidence, particularly the testimony of witnesses, each section of the facts he promised to prove at trial came as a hammer blow to William Bosco. His hands trembled and he began to feel faint. Interrupting Rattigan, he asked for a glass of water.

Rattigan returned his request with a stern glare and said firmly, "No, you'll wait until I'm finished!" Rattigan was too experienced a trial lawyer to tolerate a loss of momentum. He would make Bosco keenly aware of the consequences of violating his oath and selling his sacred trust.

As he concluded, Kenneth Rattigan rose dramatically, turned away from Bosco for a moment, paused, and then abruptly faced the distraught young cop and said, "I'm entirely confident, Mr. Foreman and members of the jury, that after you have heard all of this evidence and you have been given the judge's explanation of the law, and after your careful deliberation of the facts and the law of this case, you will return to this courtroom and you will deliver your verdict. When you publish your verdict in this courtroom, you will say clearly and eloquently that William Bosco has brought shame on himself, his wife, and his children and that he has dishonored the police department of the City of New York, because your verdict will be to find him guilty of every count of this indictment."

When Rattigan had finished, he went to the watercooler just

outside his office and returned with a cold glass of water, which he offered to Bosco and which was accepted in his shaking hands. Rattigan then sat down and allowed the silence to focus the young cop's attention.

After a few minutes, the rackets chief spoke. "You know, you don't have to go to prison, and you don't even have to give up your job or your pension." At this, Bosco seemed to recover from the shock, and he leaned forward and listened very carefully to Rattigan.

"What you did was disgraceful. You spit on your badge and you brought shame on other police officers, and for what?" Rattigan asked. Now standing, the veins in his neck bulging, he shouted, "A few hundred dollars a month of dirty money!" Bringing his face not more than an inch from Bosco's, he continued, "Have you any dignity left? Do you want to drag yourself out of the gutter?"

Kenneth Rattigan had made his final pitch, one he had used several times before, although he thought this was one of his better ones.

After a pause that completely stilled the tiny room, Bosco said simply, "I've got to talk to my wife, but you gotta tell me what you want me to do."

Rattigan did not respond immediately. Instead, to keep Bosco off balance, which was critical to the turning the shaken young cop, he looked up at the ceiling as if deep in thought.

In order to build a prosecutable case, the tried and true maxim is "To catch a thief, you must turn a thief." To turn the thief, everything had to be planned and in place.

So when Rattigan and the others chose Bosco rather than Perez to flip, part of the plan was to dispatch a female detective who was known as PMAD's diplomat. She and her partner were ordered by Chief Sampson to convince Mrs. Bosco that it was in her husband's interest to accompany them to the office of the Brooklyn district attorney. She was told only that William had been arrested for bribery and that she could help him.

"Your wife is in the next room," Rattigan said finally.

Bosco seemed momentarily stunned by the news, but before he could react, Rattigan laid out the deal.

"First you're going to tell us who else is being paid off in the 13th Division, and then you're going to wear a wire and help me send every crooked scumbag to jail." Rattigan's anger unnerved Bosco as the prosecutor carefully laid out each demand. "If you do this, my boss won't prosecute you, and the police commissioner will let you stay on the job until he figures out a way to get you retired. If you don't, then I'm still going to send a scumbag to prison—you! Now go speak to your wife."

Wearing a wire was necessary because even if Bosco agreed to testify against the other thieves, under the law of New York State he was a co-conspirator. His testimony had to be corroborated, meaning that independent evidence had to be produced to support it.

It did not take Marie Bosco very long. When she emerged from the room she said simply but very firmly, "Mr. Rattigan, William will do what you want, and if he does not, he will never again see me or our children."

According to Bosco, twenty-nine members of the 13th Division, over 70 percent, were on the pad. Twenty-nine police officers, including a lieutenant and two sergeants, were receiving monthly payments from the two gambling operations in Crown Heights, Brooklyn.

Mulvey was out of his chair again. "Inspector," he shouted, "Good Lord, twenty-nine crooks!"

"Hold it right there, Robert," Connolly hastily replied. "Just wait a few more minutes. I'm certain that when you hear the extent of this corruption, the depth of their evil acts and how they disgraced the reputation of every police officer who was ever privileged to carry the badge of the NYPD, including heroes like Detectives Lewis and Cordo, you will agree that you have no choice but to join me in a historic mission." Connolly thought he was being a bit too theatrical, but from the look on Mulvey's face he knew he'd been persuasive. He watched with disguised satisfaction as Robert once again took his seat.

"And Robert, once you have heard my plan you will understand that when we bring down these vipers, the effect of it will be an avalanche of publicity, which will change the culture in this department that permitted corruption to flourish. We have an opportunity that no one has ever had before, the chance to free this department from institutionalized thievery and to put in place a mechanism which will prevent forevermore a return to the cyclical corruption that has reappeared approximately every twenty years throughout the history of the NYPD."

Connolly certainly believed what he said, although he knew that seemingly nothing, not even something so dramatic as the arrest, conviction, and imprisonment of so many corrupt cops, could reverse decades of entrenched police corruption. Connolly, of course, couldn't know that his plan would nearly destroy this young sergeant. And he certainly couldn't know that the person who would be given the honor of eliminating the culture of police corruption in the NYPD would not be Mulvey but rather his nephew, Steven Holt.

As Bosco related each detail, the account was both astonishing and shocking. The payments were prorated according to the rank of each officer—for example, a monthly share for each plainclothes cop, a share and a half for each sergeant, and a double share for the lieutenant. In all there were twenty-nine corrupt cops. So the grocery store monthly payment of $12,000 and the liquor store monthly bribe of $7,000 was a combined annual pot of almost $230,000. The pad yielded about $600 a month for each of the twenty-six corrupt police officers, plus $900 for each sergeant, or $1,800 for the two of them, and a double share, or $1,200, for the lieutenant. The monthly total was astounding: a bit less than $19,000. In order to make the shares manageable, they rounded off the money and designated a treasurer to retain the excess, which was divided and distributed on a prorated basis to each cop at the end of each quarter of the year.

They rotated treasurers monthly to protect themselves against temptations that might be too much for any one cop. This arrangement was a result of a problem that developed when one of them who had been the permanent treasurer claimed that his automobile, which had a bag of cash in the trunk containing about $6,000, blew up in a gasoline explosion. The Corporation, which was the name they gave themselves, did not believe their treasurer for a minute, but without any proof, they could only create a procedure to guard against any further calamity. The former permanent treasurer was excluded from the rotation. Of course, their suspicions were confirmed when they learned much later that the wife of their former money handler had treated herself to a new kitchen.

The Corporation met regularly, usually the last Friday night of each month, to discuss a variety of ways to expand their financial interests.

Similar groups were formed in other plainclothes units around the city, and in time an organizational structure was put in place. An officer wishing to join had to tender corruption credentials that would be checked out during a period of two months. No share would be distributed to the applicant until this process was complete. This procedure was concocted to protect the group against infiltration by Internal Affairs officers or, worse, by the hated and feared cops from the elite group assigned to PMAD.

When department transfers were inevitably made, something over which these thieving groups had no control, a two-months' share would be distributed from the treasury to the departing crook, usually at his or her farewell beer racket. This way a crooked cop lost nothing.

When Inspector Connolly had finished recounting this shocking story of the extent of this pervasive corruption in just one police unit, he let a period of silence settle in. He watched Mulvey carefully until the young police officer dropped his head to his chest and stared at the floor beneath his chair. Mulvey, uncertain of what Connolly wanted, began to sweat as panic overtook him.

"Robert." Connolly finally broke the tension. "This assignment is the turning point of my career. It will either make or break me, and that's why I need your help so much. I also understand that what I am about to propose to you may well be too much to ask, so if you refuse, it will not diminish in the least my respect or affection for you."

Connolly explained that Bosco had agreed to do whatever was necessary to collect incriminating conversations against every crooked cop in the division, but the inspector did not trust, as he put it, "this corrupt little weasel for an instant."

He had a plan to guarantee a successful prosecution. First, he would have Bosco wear a wire for a period of six months, gathering evidence against as many of the crooks as he could. Next he would, with Kenny Rattigan's help, get a court-ordered listening device planted at each meeting place chosen by the Corporation. Recorded conversations from four monthly meetings, together with all the other conversations gathered by Bosco, should ensure that future meetings of the Corporation would be in Attica State Prison.

Just to be sure, Connolly's trump card would be Robert Mulvey. Robert would spend six months at an assignment chosen by PMAD, getting his corruption credentials, and he would then be transferred to the 13th Division. Following his two months of initiation, during which his corruption credentials would be cleared, he would take his place at the table at a regular meeting of the Corporation. Just two meetings recorded in Mulvey's presence would finish off the Corporation. The plan would lock Bosco in because if he reneged, Rattigan could send him to prison until he was a very old man. If any of the defense lawyers tried to discredit Bosco, they would have to face the undercover officer Robert Mulvey, whose unblemished record would make it very unlikely that the corrupt police officers would be found not guilty. If the cops' lawyers forced Mulvey to testify, and if any of these crooks were convicted, Rattigan would demand and probably get maximum state prison sentences.

Mulvey stood, and Connolly watched him guardedly for a very long period of silence. Finally Mulvey said, "Boss, you have been an inspiration to me, someone I admire and respect. I have serious doubts about this, but I'll do whatever you say."

"Thank you, son," Connolly replied. "In just a minute I'm going to introduce you to the man who'll be your direct contact throughout the operation." Connolly pushed a buzzer near his telephone, and a moment later Pressler entered the room. Mulvey stood up immediately, coming to attention.

Pressler smiled and said gruffly, "You don't need to stand up for me, young man. I'm just a sergeant." Now it was Mulvey's turn to smile, and at the same time to be relieved because he recognized Pressler as the academy instructor he so much admired. He thought to himself that if Pressler was going to be his contact it would turn out alright.

"You take this number." Pressler handed him a folded piece of paper. "If I don't pick up right away, I'll be automatically paged, and I'll be back to you almost immediately."

Mulvey looked at the number and then said, "Thank you, sir."

Connolly put his hand out and shook Mulvey's and said, "Sergeant Pressler will be in touch with you shortly. Now you can return to your command." Pressler shook Mulvey's hand, and the youngster quickly left the room.

"Well, what do you think, Bernie?"

"He's perfect, Boss."

Things often don't work out as well as they are planned, but neither Connolly nor Pressler could have predicted that at this point. The plan seemed like a sure winner.

# 24

*People v. Holt,*
October 21, 1992

Goss's prosecution proceeded much as expected. David Rapp, now twenty-five years old, and his former fiancée, Alyson Keeler, who had just turned twenty-four, testified about their gruesome discovery of the bodies of Hiram and Ramon Rodriguez on the snow-covered beach of Robert Moses State Park. Goss led each through every detail, emphasizing in particular the large holes rimmed by dried blood observed by them on the left temple of each victim. It was a predictable attempt by a prosecutor to highlight the violence.

At this point an incident occurred that began to reveal Goss's strategy and produced the first serious round of combat. As David Rapp described the wounds, a piercing scream erupted from the second row on the jury side of Judge McGowan's courtroom. Rosa Rodriguez, the mother of the two victims, who had flown from Puerto Rico to be present at the trial, began to wail convulsively. The best efforts of the female court officers could not console her, and Judge McGowan ordered a brief recess.

The jury left the courtroom. Larry Green waited for their departure, then stood and said, "Your Honor, may we meet in your chambers?"

McGowan, motioning to Assistant District Attorney Goss, replied, "Of course, Mr. Green. Come along, Mr. Goss."

The parties had barely entered Judge McGowan's inner office before he exploded, "Just what are you trying to pull in my courtroom, young man?"

Goss's face turned ashen. "I deeply resent that, Judge. What are you implying?"

"You know damned well what you are doing. By the way, who paid Mrs. Rodriguez's airfare from Puerto Rico, and who is financing her expenses while she's here?" McGowan demanded.

"We paid for her airfare and we are paying her expenses, Your Honor, and what's wrong with that?"

"Nothing," McGowan shouted, "except that it means that you have control of her in this county and you should control her emotions so that this jury is not unduly influenced. If you cannot, then don't bring her to this court again. Is that clear? Because if it isn't and there is another outburst, I'm going to hold you in contempt and you can try this case by day and spend your evenings in the county jail until this case has concluded. Is that clear?"

All Goss could say, in a voice barely heard, was "Yes, Your Honor."

David Rapp concluded his direct testimony without incident and without the presence of Mrs. Rodriguez. When Goss was finished, he turned and said to Larry Green, "You may examine."

Green rose and, looking first at the jury and then to the judge, announced what trial lawyers agree is perhaps the most difficult thing for a lawyer to say. "Your Honor, I have no questions of this young man." It was the same tactic Green used after Alyson Keeler finished her testimony. No purpose could be served by keeping Rapp or Keeler on the stand other than to confirm the accuracy of their horrifying discovery.

After the two youngsters had concluded, Judge McGowan noted that it was now past four o'clock. "Time," he said, "to give the jury a well-earned respite."

The jurors began leaving the room.

Now Judge McGowan asked, "Mr. Goss, what are your plans for tomorrow?"

"I plan to have the coroner, some police witnesses, and a ballistics expert, and that should be all," Goss replied.

Green, instinctively smelling a rat, asked, "May I inquire whether the prosecutor has plans to call anyone not currently on the witness list he has supplied?"

Goss, whose unpleasant exchanges with Green had reached a level of animosity where he would respond only to the judge, answered, "I have no plans at this time to expand the witness list, Your Honor."

McGowan glowered. "Very well, young Mr. Goss, but I warn you, don't play games in my courtroom."

"But, Your Honor—" Before Goss could say another word, Judge McGowan had left the bench.

Green turned to Goss and said, "Hey, have you ever tried a case before this judge? As a matter of fact, when was the last time you tried a felony case?"

Goss had no intention of giving him an answer, but it did not matter, because Green did not plan to stay to hear one.

# 25

Washington Heights, Manhattan, the 34th Precinct,
1974

Connolly had decided before speaking with Mulvey that if he agreed to help he would be placed in a police precinct known for its corruption.

His assignment to the 34th Precinct in Washington Heights, in the northern part of the borough of Manhattan, was done easily enough. No one paid much attention to ordinary transfers, and the fact that Police Officer Mulvey was leaving the prestigious Emergency Service Unit for a patrol assignment could be explained away as nothing more than his position high up on the sergeant's list, and his obvious interest in getting some time in the field before his promotion.

Mulvey replaced another police officer, who was transferred to the 60th Precinct in Coney Island, Brooklyn, a place notorious for the high incidence of driving-while-intoxicated arrests and so a place where considerable money could be collected by a two-officer team cruising in a patrol car. The reassigned police officer, like Mulvey, had been placed in Washington Heights as part of Lieutenant Moore's network of anticorruption moles, held in reserve for the right assignment.

Mulvey's assignment immediately gave him the opportunity to make some cash protecting a local Dominican entrepreneur who ran a cockfight for the neighborhood. The cockfight he would protect in exchange for a monthly payment would later secure his passport to the 13th Division.

Washington Heights for years had been the landing point for émigrés from the Dominican Republic. They brought their tradition of Christianity, family values, and hard work with them, along with the poverty caused by displacement and few employment opportunities. For the majority of the Dominicans, their dream, like most other immigrants', was to get work, any kind of work, put in long hours supporting themselves and any family that came with them from the Dominican Republic, and send money regularly back home to those members of the family unable to join them. Their language presented the usual barrier until they could learn some English to get along. During their off-hours, particularly on weekends, they looked for some diversion, and cockfighting was their favorite. It was their spectator sport of choice, and when it was combined with their favorite *cerveza fría*, it made for a pleasurable evening out with friends. However, there was one significant problem, and that was that cockfighting was against the law in New York State.

The combatants, gamecocks, were bred for physical strength, for speed, and for their killer instinct. Usually their feathers were of various bright colors. They had long spurs on their legs, and their breeders trimmed down these spurs and attached sharpened artificial spurs made of steel or brass over them. These weapons were used to tear at the flesh of the opponent until death ended the pain and misery caused by the violence.

The fight took place in an enclosed pit. Before the fight began, the handlers held the birds close to each other and permitted them to peck at each other with their beaks until they were angry enough to fight. Spectators who surrounded the pit bet money with the bookmaker, who was the proprietor of what was often a factory-sized floor of an abandoned warehouse.

To ensure against any interruption by the local police, an appropriate bribe was agreed to by the police officer assigned to the sector where the arena was located. The payoff ranged from a flat fee of $250 to, for the more creative cops, a percentage of the house receipts, which could yield up to $700 or $800 on a good night. While the $250 was not a particularly good score, it did provide the credentials that would be used to gain other corrupt opportunities for assignments such as antihijacking squads, where dishonest police officers were paid to look the other way when a truckload of liquor was seized, or as a springboard to a choice assignment in the plainclothes divisions.

The cockfight pit was run by D'Ario Santiago and Petie Perez, who had become Santiago's main man. Perez was the front man who, among other things, handled the payoff arrangements with the cops assigned to the 34th Precinct. Petie was also working off a drug sale, which could have sent him to state prison for a term up to life, so he was cooperating fully with Lieutenant Moore. Among the dozen or so crooks with badges who were part of the approximately 175 police officers assigned to the precinct, none would question why Mulvey was allowed to catch the cockfight. In their business, you didn't ask questions if you wanted to survive. So Mulvey was quietly assigned to the sector covering the cockfight, and Petie Perez arranged the appropriate payment for him. While Perez worked out the details of the payment, Santiago, who trusted no one, designated himself to make the actual payment of the bribe. He liked, as he would say openly, the feeling of owning a cop.

Mulvey detested taking the dirty money. Although it was limited to one fifteen-minute period several times a month and it was a charade, he loathed the thought of meeting D'Ario Santiago, who always reeked of cheap wine and garlic and would toss a filthy brown paper bag at Mulvey with a big smile and a "Here, *amigo*."

It did not matter to Mulvey that immediately after the transfer of the money he would go to the lot in the rear of the warehouse, where one of Lieutenant Moore's officers would count the money in front of him and have him sign a receipt. It did not help Robert Mulvey to know that the corrupt money would be vouchered for the day when that slob Santiago and his creeps would have their operation raided and shut down and that they would be locked up for many, many years. What filled Mulvey's recurring and restless thoughts while he tried to sleep the night before each money transfer was that this piece of shit thought he was just another crooked cop who could be bought for a few hundred bucks.

He got out of bed, found the piece of paper he got from Pressler, and dialed the number. After several unanswered rings he hung up and waited for the promised return call. When it hadn't come fifteen minutes later, he repeated the call. When that went unreturned, he found a bottle of vodka under the sink in the kitchen, poured a long drink, and sat on his bed wondering what was going on. He drained the glass and tried to fall asleep.

The monthly meeting of the Corporation was set for the basement of Officer Sharon Mickens's brownstone located in an upscale part of Bedford-Stuyvesant. Sharon's years on the pad enabled her to socialize with this moneyed class that included physicians, stockbrokers, lawyers, and entrepreneurs. Officer Mickens deflected questions about her apparent wealth with a story of a huge inheritance from an uncle in Panama.

For six months, Detective Bosco tape-recorded dozens of conversations involving corrupt payoffs to the police officers assigned to the 13th Division. These bribes were paid to the cops by the bookmakers they protected. The payments were always made to a pair of cops, partners working a particular investigative shift. By prearrangement, Bosco was carefully moved to fill in when one of the regular partners had a day off, was ill, or was on vacation. Soon, without attracting any particular notice, Bosco became the division's "relief partner." The subtlety with which this was accomplished was lost on the crooks, who were more interested in their payments than concerned about being detected. It was, of course, a fatal mistake. The plan that moved Bosco from cop to cop was enormously successful. Over the six-month period not only did he capture on tape virtually every corrupt cop assigned to the division, recording each one receiving a payoff from a bookie, but he recorded six monthly meetings of the

Corporation. All this evidence provided sufficient probable cause for Rackets Chief Kenneth Rattigan to seek a court order for eavesdropping devices to be installed at Mulvey's debut at a future meeting of the Corporation. The next meeting's location, the basement of Police Officer Mickens's brownstone, was turned into a sound stage, with listening microphones backed up by recording equipment everywhere. Seven different listening devices had been planted by a special unit of Lieutenant Moore's undercover squad. Not a syllable would be lost, not a whisper unheard.

Mulvey rose before dawn the morning of his first meeting as a full-fledged member of the Corporation. He had patiently waited out his two-month period at the 13th Division before his acceptance was granted. Some of the Corporation members had quietly checked out his credentials with their buddies at the 34th Precinct in Washington Heights. Richie Goodwin, one of the plainclothes cops at the 13th Division, made it clear to Mulvey that not only was he satisfied to have him as a colleague but he was very impressed with reports about how he handled his "cockfighting protection racket," as Goodwin called it. Still, as Mulvey dragged himself from bed that morning dreading his first formal sit-down with the crooked cops he despised, he had a knot in his stomach.

Richie Goodwin had a nose like Cyrano de Bergerac's and large, grossly deformed ears, and a scrawny body barely five feet eight inches tall. He was known by everyone as "the Weasel." His hair was thick with pomade and combed into a comical pompadour. If that wasn't enough, his body gave off a stench that could fill a room. Goodwin had not always been a slob. Prior to his assignment to the 13th Division he had worked for eighteen months in the Narcotics Bureau as an undercover cop. He played up his part as a mostly stoned junkie as if it were a movie role. He grew a beard, lost thirty pounds, and got used to sleeping in the street on some cardboard he kept hidden during the day. Without benefit of any regular bathing, his acquired filth became part of his act. He even occasionally peed in his pants so the smell of dried urine filled the air around him.

He was also a thief. His operation was really quite simple. He teamed up with his partner, Police Officer Billy McGinn. Goodwin would buy some drugs from a local drug dealer. Afterward he'd radio McGinn, who together with his team would swoop down on the dealer and arrest him. They would confiscate all the dealer's drugs and money. They kept all the money and most of the drugs, which were divided equally at the end of their tour among Goodwin, McGinn, and two other members of the team. For example, if they seized fifty bags of heroin or crack, they'd voucher ten as evidence and divide up the forty. Thereafter they would resell the drugs to some of the street junkies they worked with regularly for cash and information about other drug dealers they'd set up for a score on another day. When the defendant was taken to court, McGinn or one of the other two police officers would tell the assistant district attorney that they realized they had made a lousy search, that they got too anxious and really didn't have probable cause. The case would then be dismissed. On other occasions they would tell the prosecutor that the defendant was a cooperator or was a stoned-out junkie who needed drug treatment. They employed a variety of schemes resulting in the defendant being cut loose. All of this had the effect of producing a happy junkie who would never tell anyone that he or she was ripped off. To avoid creating a pattern that could be discovered, they were always careful never to use the same assistant prosecutor more than once. During his eighteen months as a narc, Richie Goodwin pulled in thousands of dollars, which gave him sufficient credentials to earn him membership in the 13th Division's Corporation.

The Weasel probably would have remained longer in the Narcotics Bureau except for an incident that began as an affair of the heart and ended in the arrest of a team of narcotics detectives operating very much like Goodwin's crew. Unfortunately for the NYPD, Goodwin's corruption cell was not unique in the Narcotics Bureau. There were small, very controlled nests of corruption in every part of the Narcotics Bureau in every county of New York City. The demise of one of these began in the bar at Forlini's, the fabled gathering place of the power brokers of the criminal justice system in Manhattan. Twenty-six-year old Blossom Zim, an associate attorney for the Legal Aid Society, was on her first date with Aaron Stevens, a thirty-year-old assistant in the office of the New York County DA. They were having a few break-the-ice drinks before adjourning to Forlini's dining room, and they were talking shop.

"You know, Aaron," Blossom began, "your office is too much a bunch of hardasses when it comes to dealing with junkies. Lucky for us that some of the narcs have the guts to admit making a mistake."

"Like what?" Stevens responded cautiously.

"Well, just in the last few months," Zim explained, "there's a team of narcs operating around Times Square who have admitted to me twice that they were involved in bad searches and told me that they jumped the gun without having probable cause."

"What did you do with that information?" Stevens inquired. "And what do these cops look like?"

After describing the team of narcs in some detail, Blossom continued, "Well, of course, I told one of the assistant DAs what happened, and after it was confirmed by the cops the case was dismissed. But why do you ask about the police officers?"

"Because those guys told me the very same thing last month. So I wonder why they would have made three tainted searches in just a few months. It sounds fishy to me."

"Now, that's the problem with prosecutors," Blossom huffed. "You are just too goddamned suspicious."

"Or maybe you guys are too naïve," Stevens quickly rejoined. "But what the hell," he added, "let's have some dinner." He said this not wishing to blow the first date, but he would surely look into these coincidences the next day.

It did not take much effort to uncover the scheme that Narcotics Detective Brian O'Hurley and his two buddies had cooked up, and once Internal Affairs got the cooperation of a dozen or so junkies it was over for at least that collection of crooks. Less than six months later each police officer pled guilty and received several years in the upstate prison system. Of course, long before that Richie Goodwin used his contacts and was on the way to the 13th Division to steal again. But there was no real need for haste, because Internal Affairs concluded its investigation with O'Hurley and his friends, refusing to believe that there was a pattern of corruption.

"Hey, Mulvey, whaddaya think?" the Weasel asked in his whiny nasal voice, leaning close to Mulvey. "D'ya have any way of getting a buddy of mine that cockfight deal?"

Mulvey held his breath, fearing serious danger to his health if he inhaled his environment. "No, Richie," he quickly responded as he began to walk away. Then he said vaguely, "They already have lined someone up."

"Okay, I understand," replied the Weasel. "I just thought I could pick up some quick bucks as a finder's fee!" Somehow Mulvey was not shocked, but he quickly became depressed as the Weasel shouted after him, "I'll see you tomorrow night at the meetin'. I'll sit next to you and sorta let you know what's goin' on."

That wasn't what was troubling Mulvey this morning, though. It had more to do with the apprehension he felt having to sit among a bunch of crooks who thought that he was just like them. He knew how dirty he'd feel, the same way he felt when D'Ario Santiago would throw him the dirty brown bag filled with money after a cockfight in Washington Heights. He decided to call Shannon Kelly. She'd know what to do. She always did.

"Robert," Shannon said, trying to wake up, "do you know it's not even six o'clock?"

"I know, sweetheart, and I'm sorry," he replied timidly, "but I need your advice. I just can't sleep."

"Alright," she said sympathetically. "I'll put on some coffee. Come on over, you big baby!" Shannon was the youngest of six children and the only girl, but as she reached young adulthood and trained to be a special agent with the Federal Bureau of Investigation, she soon became the commanding presence in her home, particularly after her mother died. Her father and all the boys constantly sought out Shannon for advice, sometimes for the simplest problem. Handling Robert Mulvey as she did so well came with years of training and experience.

He sat on her overstuffed brown leather sofa. At first he just studied his shoes, and after a few minutes he crossed his long legs and folded his arms. Then he held his right elbow in his left hand and cupped his right hand under his chin. He said nothing for nearly ten minutes.

Finally Shannon broke the silence. "Hey, friend, what do you say you drink that coffee I just put in front of you and let's you and I talk about this problem." She waited for that to sink in. "Otherwise," she added defiantly, "I'm going back to bed. It is after all Saturday." Now Shannon stood as if to threaten, and Mulvey began to speak.

"I can't go through with this. I don't want to sit in that room for five minutes with that group of lowlifes and let them think that I'm a piece of shit like them."

"Sure, honey," she replied. Then, carefully selecting her words, she proceeded. "It's your call, completely your decision, but you ought to think about a few things before you make up your mind. Like how you have already invested eight months of your life to infiltrate these dirtbags and that you just have two meetings to attend. And that you've already been through the roughest part: dealing with lice like that Santiago. And that you are so very close to breaking the back of one of the most shameful corruption conspiracies in the history of the NYPD." He listened very attentively, as he always did when she gave advice. "Besides, "she continued, "didn't you promise Inspector Connolly that you'd see this thing through?"

"But he's got Bosco, and that crooked bum's gonna walk away from all of this with his badge and his pension because he has everyone on tape."

"Sure," she rebutted quickly, "and any defense lawyer worth his salt will destroy Bosco and show him up to the jury for the rat he is. No, Robert, you are Connolly's ace in the hole. You can't take that chance and allow these crooks to be acquitted." Shannon paused for a moment and then used her strongest argument. "What does it matter what those worthless bastards think of you? You know who you are, and I certainly know who you are, and soon every cop in your department and every citizen of this city will know who you are. You put your life on the line in Washington Heights for half a year. Robert, you are a hero, and what's more you have been chosen, given an opportunity that is so rare in life. There is a reason why you go to Mass every day. It has led to a calling that you cannot ignore."

A full ten minutes passed before he finally responded. "Alright," Robert said quietly, and then got up to leave. "But can I come back here later tonight after the meeting?"

Shannon winked and threw him a devilish smile. "Sure, but don't forget the champagne. I've got a feeling we will have lots to celebrate about!"

The meeting in Police Officer Sharon Mickens's basement started typically late for a police affair. The beer immediately flowed, and Sharon had chosen a special bottle of Sancerre, which she planned to share with the only other female police officer on the Corporation, Tina Trumboli. Sharon and Tina reminded most people who met them for the first time of Stevie Wonder's near-legendary ballad "Ebony and Ivory." Both young women were in their late twenties and had magnificently proportioned figures, with beautiful, almost angelic faces, high cheekbones, lovely almond-shaped eyes, and small but sculptured noses. Their sensuous mouths were drawn up into a perpetual grin, and when they smiled their teeth were gleaming white. They looked very much alike. Even their skin color wasn't all that different. Sharon's was a light milky brown, and Tina had perfectly blended olive-colored skin derived from her Mediterranean roots. Needless to say, they were the object of numerous failed attempts at conquests by their brother police officers. They shared the dream of the perfect score, a husband with unlimited wealth, but in the meantime they shared another passion: They would make as much money as they could by protecting the bookmakers operating within the confines of the 13th Division.

Tonight's meeting of the Corporation would have its full board present, all twenty-two members. Mulvey marveled at them, so many cops with a collective dedication to greed. He glanced quickly at each, one by one, trying to determine if there was anything about them that would suggest that they were out of the ordinary. But there was nothing. Only twenty white males and two females, one black and one white, whose dress, looks, or mannerisms gave no clue about them. It was only when they spoke, as they did frequently, about their obsession with money that the enormity of their conspiracy was so startling—particularly to Robert Mulvey, whose belief in the honor of the badge was as deep as was his faith in God.

They sat around around a huge oak table, comfortably lounging in burgundy-colored upholsted leather chairs. Long ago Sharon Mickens decided that if her basement was to be the Corporation's monthly meeting room, its décor and appointments should appropriately reflect the style of a corporate boardroom. Accordingly she assessed an amount of money from the pad before its distribution to the cops, enough to buy a proper conference table, the matching chairs, the floor-to-ceiling thick velvet drapes, and the massive wet bar and full kitchen. Across the room at the opposite end from the kitchen was a comfortable seating area with two large corduroy-covered couches and four large matching club chairs facing a forty-inch television screen. It had what Sharon thought must be the look of an executive lounge. While the consumption of alcohol in all forms was encouraged, smoking was strictly prohibited.

The reason for the full house this evening was that there was a particularly significant agenda. The Corporation would formally consider Robert Mulvey for membership, which was perhaps the real reason he was so apprehensive. They were also going to discuss whether the time had come to demand that the pad payments by the bookies be increased, something that had not occurred in nearly eighteen months. Finally, Sharon had suggested she had her own item, which she refused to disclose in advance. She did say that it was so important that it required the attention of all twenty-two members.

The Corporation's meeting was chaired by Police Officer Tom Huss, an eighteen-year-veteran of the job. Although he was outranked by Lieutenant Franks and Sergeants Bowers and White, he had been elected chair because he held an MBA from John Jay College of Criminal Justice. A consensus had been reached long ago by the membership that they needed a good numbers person as chairman. Besides, Huss had all the attributes of a leader.

Huss, an imposing, trim, and athletic six-footer, was, despite his age—he was nearing forty—the mainstay wide receiver for the Finest, the NYPD's football team. He was also the team's captain. With sun-bleached, curly blond hair and deepset blue eyes, he had the perpetual tan of a Southern California surfer. He had a preference for casual clothes—jeans and polo shirts—which made him look considerably younger than his age. When he walked into a room, the way he carried himself exuded charisma, and whenever he directed a Corporation meeting to come to order, there was immediate silence. From the moment he stepped into Sharon's basement with his long, determined strides, wearing his custom-made boots of alligator leather, no one would question who was in charge.

Robert was fortunate enough to squeeze into a seat between Sergeant White and Officer Tina Trumboli, leaving a somewhat miffed Weasel Goodwin on the opposite side of the conference table looking particularly glum.

The first item, the proposed increase in the pad, was introduced by Sergeant Bowers. His case was built on the recent across-the-board police raise negotiated by the city with the police unions. "It's an outrage," he fumed. "We got fuckin' sold out. Nothin' in the first year with 2 percent in year two and 3 percent in the last year for a total of a measly 5 percent over the three years. If we don't increase the pad, that kind of raise won't even cover the cost of living."

A bemused Mulvey watched a spirited debate ensue that considered the pros and cons of increasing the percentage of a shakedown. It continued for more than an hour before Chairman Huss raised his hand and said calmly, "I think it's time for a vote, but just remember this fact. It wasn't that long ago that we had twenty-nine members on the pad splitting nearly nineteen grand a month. Today, because of transfers and retirements, we're down to just twenty-two unless we add Mulvey. The bottom line is our net take, which I remind you is tax free. It's a hell of a lot more than it was before, and none of the bookies are complaining. Why risk making one of these bums an enemy? Right now if they get banged by PMAD there's no incentive for them to cooperate against us. But if we get too hungry, who knows what they will do?"

It was the winning argument, and a vote wasn't needed.

Next Sharon's hand shot up. Huss eyed her sharply and asked, "You want to speak about this some more?"

"No, Tommy," she purred, leaning forward from across the table, revealing a tantalizing cleavage from her tight dark brown cashmere sweater. "But since we're talking about the pad, I'd like to go to my item before we consider Mulvey. It relates to both the pad and the need to discuss new members."

At this point, Tina Trumboli put her left hand over Mulvey's right, which she found resting on his knee, squeezed it, and whispered in his ear, "Just watch this, sweetie." Mulvey stirred uncomfortably and quickly put his hand on the table. He thought that Tina was taking too much time removing hers from his knee. She finally took her hand away but then placed it on the table near Robert's, which was quivering slightly. She giggled softly and whispered, "Don't worry, babe, I'm not trying to seduce you." She then added, "At least not for now." Mulvey could feel his cheeks redden and kept looking straight ahead without even thinking of answering Tina.

"Very well, Sharon, lay it out."

"Well, for openers," she began forcefully, "look around this room and what do you see?" The question was rhetorical, and she answered herself immediately. "Everyone here is a white male except for me and Tina, and I'm the only black cop. There is something wrong about this."

Mulvey watched in utter disbelief for another hour during a heated discussion, which at times came very close to acrimony. At its start, most of the boys, as they referred to themselves, thought Sharon's complaints were not made seriously, so there were heckles and catcalls. Those stopped abruptly when Sharon stood up and shouted, "No, dammit, you listen to me. There are three other black cops in the 13th who are just as anxious to make a few bucks on the side. Why can't these guys get in? And please don't tell me it's their skin color that keeps them out. Even if you think it, you better not say it."

This she uttered with a level of defiance that made Huss uneasy. He jumped in. "No, Sharon, this discussion will not be about color but about economics. It's about, Why should we shrink our take?"

"Okay," she shot back, "then why are we thinking about Mulvey, because he's white?"

"Not at all, Sharon. Mulvey has credentials." At this Robert cringed as he thought, *There, it's said; I'm a crook just like them.* Then all he could think of was how incredible this all would sound when it was played at the trial of these criminals.

Finally Huss ended the discussion by agreeing to an interview process that included Mickens, Trumboli, and the two sergeants. Huss would act as the chairman. The panel was given the task of checking out each of the three black male officers currently assigned to the 13th Division to determine if they were ever involved in corrupt acts that would qualify them for membership in the Corporation. In an offer that pleased Sharon, Huss said he would go out to other parts of the police department to see if there were other corrupt black cops they could trust. He committed to adding a total of three African American police officers to their membership.

Later, at Shannon Kelly's apartment, Mulvey's stories about his first Corporation meeting became more and more hysterical, particularly with each glass of champagne.

"One thing is for sure, honey," Shannon beamed, "whatever else the jury thinks about Ms. Mickens, after they hear these tapes, they sure won't compare her to Rosa Parks!"

The headline in the *New York Post* screamed, 22 CROOKED COPS NABBED. Even the conspicuously reserved *New York Times* devoted the full right-hand side of its front page, above the fold—generally where particularly important stories are placed—to the headline POLICE LIEUTENANT, 2 SERGEANTS, 19 POLICE OFFICERS

ARRESTED IN MASSIVE CORRUPTION SCANDAL; MOB TIES ALLEGED. The accompanying story about the indictment not only detailed the almost unbelievable allegation that more than 70 percent of one police unit was corrupt, it included unnamed sources who said that similar levels of corruption existed elsewhere in the police department.

At one of the many press conferences held in the days that followed these unsettling revelations, the mayor, the police commissioner, and Brooklyn District Attorney Cooper faced the media in the mayor's ceremonial blue room. The three officials were joined by an impeccably dressed, distinguished-looking man who appeared to be in his late sixties.

Judge George M. Scarpo, senior associate judge of New York State's highest court, the Court of Appeals, had agreed to resign from the court and undertake, as the mayor promised, "the most comprehensive review of police corruption in the history of this department." Judge Scarpo would head up an investigative panel appointed by the mayor to end police corruption forever.

"Judge Scarpo and other panelists, whom I shall appoint, will be supported by all necessary staff and other resources in order to institutionalize anticorruption efforts within the police department," said the mayor.

At the rear of the huge room, Captain Sean J. Nevins, with his ever-present unlighted cigar bouncing from one side of his mouth to the other, turned to Sergeant Bernie Pressler and said simply, "It's all bullshit, Bernie. This ain't ever gonna end until cops act like cops."

Overhearing this, the local police reporter from *New York Newsday* asked, "What's that supposed to mean?"

Nevins replied over his shoulder as he and Pressler left the room, "Was I talkin' to you, dickhead?"

"Well, what *does* that mean, Sean?" asked Pressler earnestly.

"It means, Bernie, just what it says." And the captain dismissed any further conversation about the subject.

The fact was that Nevins was correct. No commission, no new initiatives, no commitment of resources could address the recurring reality of police corruption. For those who studied the issue it seemed that in a workforce of twenty-five or thirty thousand people, just as in the general population, there would be some percentage of lawbreakers; there would always be some rotten apples. The difficulty in accepting this as fact was that these violators were police officers, sworn to protect the public and dedicated to upholding the law. Worse than that, police corruption had become by the mid-1970s so pervasive as to threaten the very purpose for which young men and women became police officers in the first place. After all, they had become police officers to do good, and it was a pity that Nevins's cynicism about how any attempted reform would be doomed to failure had history to support it.

Soon after the mayor introduced his corruption commissioner and issued his executive order declaring the end to institutional corruption in the department, he summoned Police Officer Robert Mulvey to join him at the podium. The mayor then nodded to the police commissioner, who took a place next to the mayor. Mulvey moved to the side and stood next to his family.

The mayor now spoke. "This department has been served nobly by the undercover efforts of Sergeant Robert Mulvey, whose dedication to the people of this city that he and the women and men of the New York City Police Department so proudly protect is exemplary. We are deeply indebted to him. In recognition of his unstinting courage in undertaking a profoundly dangerous mission, the commissioner will make a presentation." The police commissioner opened a blue felt box and lifted out a gold medal shaped in the form of a cross attached to a dark blue ribbon.

"Sergeant Mulvey," the commissioner commanded, "approach." The young officer snapped to attention and walked smartly in the commissioner's direction. As he passed the mayor, he paused and saluted. The mayor awkwardly raised his hand, attempting to return the salute. When Mulvey reached the commissioner, he stood directly in front him and came to attention. He brought his right hand smartly to the brim of his uniform cap. He waited until the commissioner returned his salute and then brought his hand to his side. Next Mulvey removed his cap and bent his head slightly as the commissioner spoke.

"Sergeant Robert Mulvey, I now present to you, on behalf of a proud department and a grateful city, our second highest honor, the Combat Cross." After placing the medal around the young sergeant's neck, the commissioner raised his hand in a salute, which was quickly returned by the somewhat embarrassed young officer.

The Commissioner continued, "The citation which accompanies this medal recounts the eight long months of undercover work carried on by this heroic police officer who daily risked his life knowing that his cover would be broken and that he might be seriously injured or killed. His actions led to the breakup of what was the most pervasive example of police corruption in the history of our department and will stand out for all time as a clear warning to those who would think to defile their badges. Sergeant Robert Mulvey now joins the ranks of those special few who have contributed to the well-being of this city and made their sister and brother police officers proud to wear the uniform of the NYPD."

As Mulvey, in his immaculately pressed uniform with a chest full of ribbons, smiled for the horde of cameras, his girlfriend, FBI Special Agent Shannon Kelly, and his little nephew Steven stood next to him beaming with pride. Only a few feet away, Mary couldn't take her eyes off her brother. At one point he returned her smile, sadly knowing that she would soon die from the cancer attacking her body. All eyes were on Robert Mulvey, but none at this triumphant ceremony could have suspected what was in store for him.

# 26

*People v. Holt,*
October 26, 1992

Assistant District Attorney Wally Goss was thorough and methodical to the point of mind-numbing boredom. Goss's preliminary witness list included chemists from the forensic unit of the NYPD who droned on endlessly about the condition of the bodies of the Rodriguez brothers and Police Officer Ruben when they were discovered. The testimony of the experts included evidence of the trajectory of the bullet to the head of each Rodriguez brother and gunpowder residue found at the temple of each victim to establish that the gun had been fired at very close range. This highlighted the fact that the murders had been done execution style. The testimony about the decomposed body of Officer Ruben brought outcries of sobbing and gagging. After it was stipulated by Green that the murder weapon was owned by Holt and that it contained his fingerprints and palm prints, it remained only for the ballistics expert to testify that each of the bullets came from Steven's weapon.

Finally, there was the question of motive. While motive is not necessary to support a conviction for murder in New York State, there was evidence that Steven was angry at the way his uncle was treated by the department following his heroic role as an undercover cop in the 13th Division scandal. He was particularly infuriated that

Ruben, a notoriously corrupt cop, was allowed to remain a police officer while Robert Mulvey was set adrift from that very same department and permitted to descend into drug abuse, despair, and disgrace.

When Steven wasn't trying to listen carefully, he found himself repeatedly distracted by thoughts of his uncle and the department. It somehow made him forget for a time how shabbily he was being treated by that very same organization.

# 27

Lookout Point, Nassau County,
Late Summer 1992

Peggy Moore answered the door. She greeted Robert and Shannon each with a kiss and then ushered them into the Moores' comfortable and tastefully decorated study. Brendan Moore had made a fire a few minutes before the Mulveys arrived. To the right of the ornate fireplace of marble and cobblestone were floor-to-ceiling windows. They took up the rest of that side of the study, providing a breathtaking water view. Presently Brendan Moore entered and hugged both of his old friends.

Peggy brought in a tray of coffee, and the four settled around the center of the room facing the water.

"Brendan, we don't know where to turn," Robert Mulvey began. "Since Steven's arrest, we've had an opportunity to review the evidence. Quite frankly, it looks overwhelming."

Shannon added, "They've got forensic evidence and motive." Although Shannon appeared to interrupt her husband, they had agreed before the meeting with Brendan Moore that she would lead the plea for help, because Robert was too emotional about all that was happening to his nephew. Despite Shannon's strongest arguments, Robert believed that he was at least partially responsible for Steven's indictment, but his more serious concern, which he did not dare mention to Shannon, was a nightmare that haunted his sleep: that somehow the charges against Steven were true.

After laying out the case against Steven, Shannon paused to assess Moore's reaction. There was none. He had learned after two decades of investigative experience that no benefit is gained by showing a reaction, unless it is a planned reaction. Shannon continued, "The prosecution is prepared to offer witnesses who will establish that no one had a better motive than Steven, and—"

Now it was Brendan Moore's turn to interrupt. "Look, Larry Green is probably the best criminal lawyer in New York today. By the time he gets finished with the DA's forensic experts, they will be performing magic tricks for the circus. I've seen this guy in action."

Shannon's response was almost distraught. She was growing desperate that she was not convincing Brendan how much he was needed. "But Brendan, Larry thinks that Goss, the assistant district attorney, has a witness he hasn't told us about." Shannon saw that Moore was beginning to understand her anguish. "Steven believes that the Blue Wall of Silence exists not just among honest police officers who protect the crooked ones out of some misguided fraternal obligation, but that this damned wall, as he calls it, has been permitted to exist for the benefit of brass at One PP to cover their backsides against any media exposure, until they can move on to some cushy job as security director for some department store chain." As Shannon concluded, she could feel she was losing it, but she managed to say, "And Brendan, you know very well that for too many years, that's the way it's been. Steven is obsessed by his firm conviction that this policy nearly ruined Robert and probably destroyed or nearly destroyed many other decent young men and women who signed on to serve the public in this city and instead were corrupted by that fucking wall."

Moore blanched at Shannon's profanity, and she immediately apologized through a torrent of tears. Moore waited until Shannon seemed to regain her composure, responding to Robert's hugs and gentle kisses as he tenderly wiped her cheeks dry. Then he said, "Shannon, Green will tear that theory to shreds!"

Now Robert spoke. "Brendan, we are at our wits' end. Larry, as usual, poured himself into the law books looking for anything that might be used to dismiss the indictment. He found no way out. And as you know, the reason he works alone is, there is simply nobody his equal when it comes to legal research or creative strategies to end a prosecution pretrial. He used a team of his best investigators to conduct a complete canvass throughout the Bush Terminal complex, where Ruben's body was found. Nothing. No one has been found who can tell us anything about Ruben's murder. We told Larry about your network of informers, and he said that we have to find someone soon who might have been at the terminal that evening, or someone who might have seen something, anything."

Moore protested, "You both know just how quickly sources dry up. Informers get busted and go to jail, they overdose on drugs and die, or they become someone else's stoolie. That can happen in just a few months. I'm out of the job for almost a year. You know I'd like to help, but I'm out of this stuff and I don't want to get back in. Look at the life Peggy and I have now. I'm very sorry."

Robert and Shannon got up to say good-bye and to thank Brendan for listening, until Peggy Moore, who had been listening carefully to every word, took Brendan by the hand and said, "Sweetheart, won't you at least try?"

# 28

From Lookout Point to Suffolk County Jail,
Late Summer 1992

During the long automobile ride from Lookout Point to their home in upstate New York, Shannon and Robert at first barely spoke. While Shannon drove, Robert settled back and pretended to sleep.

He began to review his discussion with Brendan Moore and to tick off the points that the prosecutors had assembled. The more he recalled all of this, the more troubled he became. However much he wanted to believe in Steven's innocence, the facts simply didn't support that conclusion.

For a time, Mulvey wasn't sure whether he had fallen asleep or was deep in reverie, but in any event he was transported back in time to when Steven was very young, back to a dusty sandlot with patches of rich dark green grass. The sun was blistering hot, and Mulvey, sitting in the grandstands, wrapped a water-soaked towel around his neck seeking relief. His sole distraction was watching Steven, then about eighteen years of age, gracefully maneuvering around first base. He was a natural, and each time he executed a play it was done flawlessly, after which Steven would glance over to his uncle for approval. When Robert nodded or gave the youngster a thumbs-up, Steven smiled broadly. What Mulvey remembered most was Steven's sheer adulation, a love that transcended the normal relation of older brother or best friend. Steven made no decision without first asking for Uncle Robert's advice. Although he possessed the skill necessary to give serious consideration to playing baseball professionally or at least applying for a college scholarship, his admiration for his uncle was sending him off on another path.

As they walked toward Mulvey's car, sipping Cokes, suddenly Steven stopped and said, "Uncle Robert, I want to be a police officer. I've wanted that for a very long time."

Suddenly a wave of sadness and guilt engulfed Mulvey. Now fully conscious, he nearly shouted to Shannon, "Honey, pull over."

"What's wrong with you?

"Please, Shannon, pull over. Don't you see? Steven is guilty!"

Shannon exclaimed, "What are you talking about?" She guided the car from the right side of the Long Island Expressway to the wide shoulder within sight of the next exit, where she brought it to a stop. It was now quite dark, so Shannon turned on the hazard lights.

"You don't understand," he insisted. "Had he known the truth about me, he wouldn't be facing life imprisonment. I've got to go see him before it's too late." Robert leaned over and tenderly kissed Shannon on the forehead. "After Steven came to see us, I didn't tell you everything because I knew it would upset you. I told Steven about my assignment to Washington Heights and how my undercover role led to the takedown of the Corporation and the arrest of all those corrupt cops in the 13th Division. But when I began to tell him what happened to me, he cut me off. He just wouldn't listen. He said he didn't care to listen to any of it because his inspector said I was screwed by the job."

Now it was Shannon's turn to speak. "Look, Robert, I don't know where you're going with all this, but I won't let you demean yourself by telling Steven the rest of the story. The fact is, what you did was nothing short of heroic, and the department had an obligation to give you every last bit of support you desperately needed.

Instead they walked away from you. But nothing that happened to you can ever take away your dedication to the people of this city and the risks you took for police officers everywhere." Shannon's face turned crimson with anger, and she shouted, "I will not let you disillusion that kid. You were a hero and you remain a hero and even the department finally came to that recognition. No, you are Steven's idol, and whatever else may be taken from him, let him at least keep that."

"But, Shannon," Mulvey said firmly, "had he known the truth about me, he wouldn't be facing life imprisonment. I've got to see him before it's too late. Maybe if he knows what I did he'll let Green cut him a deal. Let's find a motel, and tomorrow you can drive me over to the Suffollk County jail."

Nothing Shannon could say could convince her husband that he was making a mistake, but then her heart wasn't in it. The fact was that she was beginning to believe that Steven was a murderer. In any event, Shannon agreed that Robert had to go and speak to his nephew, if only to save him from spending the rest of his life in prison.

"Steven, there is something you must know." As Mulvey began his tale, Steven sat on the chair in front of his desk, crossed his legs, and listened intently.

# 29

Suffolk County Jail,
Late Summer 1992: Mulvey's Story

Mulvey knew that Steven Holt had worshipped him for most of the younger man's life, so he knew that the story of his self-destruction had to be clearly understood. It was critical, Mulvey believed, that he wasn't excusing his conduct but rather placing the blame solely at his own door. He explained first that his six-month assignment at the 34th Precinct played havoc with his personal life. He began to drink heavily, first after work, particularly after a payoff from D'Ario Santiago, the cockfight thug. The alcohol made him nasty to anyone around him, although he did manage to conceal his growing problem from Shannon Kelly.

All through the period of Mulvey's assignment to the 34th Precinct, he had no contact with Inspector Connolly, who was receiving brief but positive reports from Lieutenant Moore. Moore's information, of course, was limited to the report he got from his undercover cop, which was limited to the quick transfer of the vouchered money given to him by Officer Mulvey.

During the first two months of his assignment to the 13th Division, there was no sign that the young police officer was experiencing any problems. Through it all he kept his drinking a secret, right up through the arrest of the Corporation members.

When Inspector Connolly met with Mulvey after the massive arrests of the corrupt cops of the 13th Division, they had a brief exchange. Connolly congratulated Robert for a superb job. "Now that you have been promoted to sergeant, where would you like to be assigned, Robert?" Perhaps the inspector should have noticed that Mulvey's eyes had a strange gaze and that he stared straight ahead at all times, or that his answer, "Your choice, Boss," was particularly flat, but Connolly didn't notice anything out of the ordinary. Mulvey was, after all, always overly deferential in the inspector's presence. Inspector Connolly decided to recommend that Robert be assigned to a prestigious police precinct located near Chinatown in lower Manhattan. When he said this to Mulvey, the young sergeant nodded obediently. Perhaps, given time, Connolly would have detected symptoms of the demons that were slowly consuming a dedicated young police officer and would soon bring him to the brink of despair—but Connolly would not get that chance.

Much of Mulvey's problem stemmed from the fact that for all of the glory he was given by the mayor and the police commissioner and the media, he was shunned by other cops. The grand predictions that Mulvey would be regarded a hero by other cops didn't come true. Soon after his reassignment, his new comrades treated him as nothing more than an informer. Not that it was ever said. He noticed that they often whispered when they were near him, or he was simply ignored, or when he entered the locker room other police officers, sometimes engaged in animated conversation, would leave immediately. This rejection and the images haunting him from his dealings with the scum of Washington Heights who thought they had a cop on the payroll caused him to become more and more isolated and at times reclusive.

The one relationship he clung to was with Shannon Kelly. Unfortunately, a particularly important and sensitive political corruption investigation involving a powerful and influential assemblyman led to her working late hours at the bureau and left little time for anything other than a few hours' sleep. As the investigation intensified, except for a few brief telephone conversations with Robert, the separation ran into several weeks. Alone in his tiny apartment, Mulvey soon began to increase his drinking, which led to weekend binge drinking. Shannon noticed a few times in their telephone conversations that his speech was slurred, but she thought little of it. These calls were late in the evening and brief. So what if Robert had a little too much at some beer racket. She had no way of knowing that the drink was vodka and not beer, or that it had begun to possess him.

Early in 1975, Inspector Connolly was promoted to one-star deputy chief and assigned to head up training at the Police Academy. Soon after, he was approaching a bank on East 21st Street in Manhattan, not far from the academy, when he spotted someone attempting to rob an elderly woman who was using an ATM in the lobby of the bank. Chief Connolly immediately ordered his driver to bring the car to the curb. Leaping from the vehicle with his gun drawn, he shouted at the gunman, "Police, freeze." The man immediately turned and emptied his MAC-9 automatic into Chief Connolly's chest. Minutes later the chief died on the sidewalk where he fell.

It was a devastating blow to Robert Mulvey, tearing him apart.

For weeks after Connolly's funeral, Mulvey spoke with no one. He took a few weeks of vacation and remained in seclusion. He repeatedly rejected his nephew Steven's attempts to visit him. He sat mostly in his darkened bedroom, drinking from a bottle of vodka until he passed out.

Late one evening the phone in Mulvey's apartment began to ring. At first he didn't move but rather sat rocking in his chair with an empty vodka bottle at his feet. Finally, as the phone rang incessantly, he stumbled out of his chair and, taking the telephone from its cradle, barely mumbled, "Hello."

"I'm so sorry, honey, did I wake you?" Shannon said hurriedly. Before he could answer, she added, "I have some great news." Mulvey didn't answer, because he couldn't. He fell to the floor in a stupor, sending the telephone crashing down next to him. Shannon looked at her watch, which said ten past seven. She'd speak to Robert about it tomorrow.

Yet the following day when Mulvey called Shannon, she decided not to mention her strange experience with him the night before but instead launched into her good news.

"Yesterday afternoon we arrested Harry Manion, the deputy speaker of the New York State Assembly. We got him accepting eighteen thousand dollars in marked money, the down payment for assuring that our undercover agent would get a judgeship on the New York State Supreme Court."

"Wow, that's fantastic."

"What's really great is that the bum makes it clear on tape that the balance of thirty-two thousand was due in two weeks."

"Unbelievable" was all Mulvey could say at first, but then he went on, "And most people believe that only cops go wrong. What can they expect a corrupt lawyer who pays fifty grand for a judgeship will do to get the money back?" Then he added, "Sounds like we should celebrate. How about dinner at Forlini's?" He suggested this because his current assignment in a downtown Manhattan police precinct was just a few blocks away from the restaurant and it was convenient to Shannon's FBI office at 26 Federal Plaza. Mulvey ended the conversation cheerfully, saying, "And I've got a little surprise for you. I'll pick you up at eight."

"Eight it is," Shannon happily responded. As she hung up, the incident of the night before was forgotten and she looked forward to her surprise.

After Mulvey hung up, he hurriedly walked to his night table, opened the top drawer and looked admiringly at a gleaming half-carat diamond engagement ring. He began to smile with anticipation, but almost immediately he wondered if she'd accept. Suddenly he noticed a slight tremor in the hand holding the ring. In recent weeks it had recurred often. He dealt with it the way he had learned to do in the past. He went to the kitchen and retrieved a bottle of vodka from the cabinet above the sink. He grabbed a glass, filled it halfway, and gulped it down. It was warm, almost hot, at first and then instantly brought a calming effect. The tremor passed and he felt good. Of course she'd say yes!

Mulvey suggested to Shannon that they get engaged immediately after he entered her apartment. She noticed right away that there was a problem—his proposal came after he'd consumed nearly half a quart of vodka only an hour before. His speech was slurred, and his bloodshot eyes frightened Shannon.

"Robert, what's happening to you?" she said, rather than responding to his offer.

Pathetically, Mulvey could hardly stand. Outraged that Shannon had ducked his proposal, he shouted, "You just made a big mistake, sweetie." Then, slamming the door to her apartment, he disappeared up the street, heading for the nearest bar.

Heartbroken, Shannon watched out her window as Mulvey stumbled from side to side out of the walkway of her apartment house. Then she closed her drapes and wondered sadly if she'd ever want to see him again.

The next day Mulvey woke up with a horrible hangover. He made an appointment at the Medical Division, and when he confessed his problem he was granted a leave. The department psychiatrist suggested that Mulvey should apply for an inpatient thirty-day program. Unfortunately, no beds were available, and in the weeks that followed, his drinking was worse than ever before.

No one knows for sure what happened. Maybe it was the miracle from his daily attendance at Mass, which he stubbornly refused to give up, but suddenly he snapped out of his depression and stopped drinking. After several weeks he requested that he be returned to duty. Following a complete physical and psychological examination, Robert was restored to duty. His superiors decided that he should be given a low-stress assignment. He was ordered to become the supervisor of the automobile pound on Fountain Avenue in a desolate section of East New York in Brooklyn.

At first Steven sat transfixed, but when his uncle had finished describing the uncontrollable binge drinking and then his redemption, he seemed puzzled. He stood and walked toward his bed, stretching his legs. As he sat down on the bed he said, "How did it all unravel again?"

"It didn't take too long, and then it became really ugly," Mulvey replied. Holt sat down on his bed and listened intently as his uncle discussed his next assignment.

The NYPD automobile pound is a vast storage lot for vehicles from Brooklyn and the adjoining county of Queens that are recovered and held for evidence in connection with pending criminal cases or during the investigation of the theft of these cars. The police officers assigned to the auto pound were, with few exceptions, miscreants who had been disciplined repeatedly for their alcoholism, cops awaiting the disposition of charges brought against them at the police department's administrative trial room, and any number of troublemakers who had connections with the PBA and had been placed in limbo to save their pension. One of these, Officer Michael O'Leary, was in particular a problem cop.

The brass at headquarters thought that this was an ideal assignment for Sergeant Mulvey. The job required his leadership skills and his ability to motivate. They actually thought he would inspire some of these misfits and restore them to full duty. But no one understood the devastating effects on Mulvey of his separation from his beloved Shannon or the desperation and profound sadness he felt following the murder of his mentor and idol, James Patrick Connolly. While he had stopped drinking, he was still moody and at times sullen. But the real problem for Mulvey lay ahead, and no one could gauge the powerful hold Mike O'Leary would soon have on him.

Forty-six-year-old Michael O'Leary spent two tours of duty in Vietnam as a sergeant assigned to a Marine Corps rifle company. In order to get a second tour in Nam one had to volunteer. O'Leary asked to return, although he didn't disclose that his reason was that he liked combat. By his count he took out sixteen Viet Cong soldiers. Even more than killing Viet Cong, O'Leary loved cocaine. In Nam, he became a serious abuser, snorting the drug as often as he could.

During his second tour and while on a cocaine binge, O'Leary rescued a trapped Marine rifle squad, and for his heroism he was awarded the Silver Star, the country's third highest military award. That award added luster to an imposing figure of a man, an even six feet tall, with a broad, powerfully constructed face, which was topped by golden blond hair. His hazel eyes bulged, in part because of his addiction, and his large nose had been flattened during several years of street brawls as a child. He had wide shoulders that were attached to muscular arms and massively large hands, weapons he used frequently with little or no provocation.

O'Leary constantly displayed the Silver Star, wearing the ribbon on all of his civilian dress and later on his police uniform. He used it frequently as a conversation ice breaker. The award also led to his election as a delegate of the PBA for the 5th Precinct in lower Manhattan when he refused an order by a young lieutenant to remove his combat ribbon. It did not help the lieutenant's case when it was discovered that he had avoided the draft through a college deferment. No charges were ever brought against O'Leary, who in short order became the hero of those police officers assigned to the 5th Precinct.

"Good morning, Sarge," said O'Leary, snapping sharply to attention with a crisp hand salute. It caught Mulvey off guard. He was not used to that kind of military courtesy from a veteran cop, a formality that often disappeared a few years after a police officer graduated from the Police Academy.

The headquarters for the Fountain Avenue automobile pound was a dingy trailer with a desk, partially illuminated by a single table lamp. Two police officers, O'Leary and a not very successful recovering drunk from a precinct in Queens, were supervised by one sergeant. Their shift was 4:00 P.M. to midnight. The tiny unit maintained contact with the outside world with two telephones, although most of the time only one of the phones was operable. While the command was small, the responsibilities for vouchering and safeguarding hundreds of recovered stolen vehicles was no easy task. Added to the mountain of backbreaking paperwork was the reality that no citizen arriving or leaving the pound was ever happy. O'Leary's charm and streetwise diplomacy made an otherwise unpleasant assignment for a boss like Mulvey bearable. Sergeant Mulvey was grateful for the way O'Leary shielded him from the often irate public, demanding to know why their automobile couldn't be promptly released or why it had been damaged while in police custody. Of course, Mulvey didn't know that O'Leary's method of calming the angry automobile owners included a price! For a hundred dollars he could arrange a swift release from the clerk's office—so long as cash came with the request. The property clerk thief was told by O'Leary that the bribe was only fifty dollars, so his twenty-five-dollar portion seemed generous.

"Don't you understand, I desperately need this car," the woman pleaded as she pointed toward her very used Plymouth station wagon. "It's the only way I can get my three kids to school in time for me to go to work. Please do something!"

"I know, miss, but those damned bureaucrats at the police property clerk's office really don't care," O'Leary replied, "unless I'm able to show that this is a special case."

"Well, how do you do that?"

Now O'Leary played the hand he used so often. "The fact is that the guy I deal with down there is a greedy SOB who won't do nothin' for nothin'." It wasn't long before the poor woman forked over a hundred dollars.

O'Leary was trouble from the day he graduated from the Police Academy, and if Mulvey's supervisors had bothered to tell him anything about O'Leary's history, the young sergeant would have demanded an immediate transfer.

O'Leary was first assigned to the 114th Precinct in Queens

County. There he had an argument with an assistant district attorney and a sergeant over the way he seized drugs from a local pusher. O'Leary didn't care much about their concern that the junk was illegally seized and that the case had to be dismissed. The argument took place on the steps of the courthouse in front of a crowd of people on their lunch hour and escalated to the point where O'Leary punched both men, knocking the prosecutor out cold. That time, his war record and his Silver Star got him off with an apology.

Now, O'Leary had an Uncle Frank, a retired narcotics detective, who while on the job supplemented his income by selling illegally seized narcotics. "I just recycle the junk for the mutts and make a few dollars on the side," he would boast to a very impressed young Officer O'Leary, who was not only his nephew but his godson.

When the story of his nephew's behavior in front of the courthouse in Queens got around to the beer rackets, Uncle Frank felt some counseling was necessary. "Now, why do you care whether two assholes second-guess you? The important thing is you know what you're doing and they don't. You better lay low for a while because unless you're careful, even those losers from IAD will nail you." Frank explained how two black narco detectives were set up by Internal Affairs and detectives from the office of the Manhattan district attorney. They were sent to state prison for five years. Frank told O'Leary that if he played his cards right, by the time the police department's Internal Affairs Division got around to taking a look at him, he could be promoted from precinct delegate to PBA trustee, granting him virtual if not complete immunity from arrest or administrative discipline.

But O'Leary would not be careful. During one of his frequent visits to the Dublin Celtic Cross pub in the Woodside section of Queens County, which had become a gathering place for the stream of Irish illegals who landed in New York, he discovered that many of them had as strong a taste for cocaine as they did for Guinness stout. Most had come from the depressed areas of northeast Ireland, where unemployment for Catholics in the Protestant-dominated province was as much as 80 percent. Booze and, increasingly, drugs were the common way to escape, but here in the States, in Woodside, Queens, they had trouble making a drug connection.

O'Leary saw immediately an opportunity to supplement his income. The recklessness that saved the lives of his buddies in Nam and got him his Silver Star would soon threaten his freedom. Overheard on a court-authorized wiretap on the pay phone at the Celtic Cross was some reference to an Irish cop and cocaine. The wiretap, placed on the telephone by detectives from the office of the Queens County district attorney, was gathering evidence about an illegal sports betting group operating out of the bar.

When the overheard information about an Irish cop was reported to the chief assistant district attorney, she did what the law required and prepared an amendment to the original wiretap order for the district attorney's signature, to permit his detectives to collect evidence of an additional crime, the possession and/or sale of cocaine. However carefully these investigations are conducted, the more people involved, the greater the possibility of breached confidentiality.

So, once again, along came Uncle Frank to the rescue. O'Leary, whose on-duty alcohol abuse was becoming a serious problem, was sent to an alcohol treatment center in upstate New York. While there remained casual references to the Irish cop and cocaine on the wiretap, the investigation, at least of that particular crime, was over.

Nonetheless, it was clear to Internal Affairs that O'Leary's fingerprints were all over trouble brewing at the Dublin Celtic Cross. An outraged Queens County district attorney demanded a department investigation of the leak that ruined the potential drug case. While the strong suspicion pointed to the rogue cop, there was no evidence.

After O'Leary finished his rehab, a decision was made to assign him to the Fountain Avenue pound until the bosses could figure out what next to do with him.

After several weeks, the combination of Mulvey's painful loneliness and O'Leary's feigned solicitude was having its planned effect.

"Hey, Boss, how about a beer after our tour?"

Mulvey, shy to begin with and becoming more and more reclusive, at first hesitated, but before he could answer, O'Leary pressed on. "Come on, Boss, it'll do you good."

A few shots of vodka followed by beer chasers and Mulvey began to loosen up, perhaps for the first time he could remember in nearly a year. Through the gathering haze produced by the booze, O'Leary's questions didn't seem so pointed or presumptuous.

"Boy, that stuff at the 13th Division must have been somethin', Boss. I guess you got there just before the shit hit the fan!" Before Mulvey could answer, O'Leary continued, "What a bunch of two-bit cowboys, riskin' everything for a few grand a year."

Mulvey's speech began to slur, and he started to see an O'Leary and a half, but he still understood and could reply. "Well, it was actually a lot more money for each thieving cop."

"But Boss, that's chicken feed. It just wasn't worth the risk."

"Well, maybe so," said Mulvey, draining the tumbler of vodka, which he quickly washed down with a glass of beer. Getting up to leave, he said, "Nothing's worth the risk, Michael."

"Maybe so, Boss, maybe so," replied O'Leary with a strange look in his eye, which Mulvey ignored.

As time passed, it didn't take O'Leary very long to introduce his increasingly vulnerable supervisor to wider substance abuse. First it was a high grade of marijuana, which when combined with the vodka and beer gave Mulvey a delectable rush and then a feeling of quiet ease and self-confidence he had rarely experienced. The problem for him was he lapsed too quickly into a stupor, which he could not control. It was followed by violent headaches when he woke up. O'Leary next introduced Mulvey to cocaine. It provided Mulvey all the relaxing joy, without the horrible side effects, but it, too, soon took hold of the young sergeant. His desire for it grew stronger by the week.

O'Leary also introduced Mulvey to a group of other cops, most of them his contemporaries in age, two of the same rank. First they drank together in the Irish bars on Second Avenue in Manhattan, then went to an after-hours topless joint where crack cocaine smoked in a pipe gave Mulvey and the others a succession of high rushes. The group began to meet regularly to discuss how they could make some money to support their habit and to put some money on the side, as one said, for retirement. Mulvey by this time was a hooked follower—hooked on drugs—but since he was often in a haze, he didn't catch on when the group discussed corruption. Nevertheless, his descent into hell was nearly complete. That phase of Mulvey's tragedy would occur shortly after O'Leary was asked by Junior Garofolo for some desperately needed help.

By the early 1970s, the neighborhood in Brooklyn known as East New York resembled Berlin in the days following World War II. Many of the single-family and two-family homes that remained standing were burned out or were otherwise empty shells. The rental income from these homes often didn't produce enough to cover the costs of ordinary maintenance care, and that led to their deteriorating conditions. Some unscrupulous landlords deliberately allowed the properties to fall into a disrepair that ultimately made them uninhabitable. Those forced out by these conditions were replaced by others who were forced to pay even higher rents. Many of these new arrivals could not afford the rent, and then they were evicted. After the cycle was repeated several times, what was left of East New York was mostly a huge slum.

With so many vacant houses and the debris-strewn lots, no one could have guessed that East New York was once a vibrant and flourishing section of Brooklyn. Nevertheless, there did remain perhaps a hundred homes and a few churches, including an African Methodist Episcopal church and a Baptist church, to provide spiritual support for those who refused to leave.

The neighborhood also included one block with beautiful brick and oak-frame homes fronted by manicured lawns and protected by wrought-iron fencing. The block included a tiny bar, a social club, and an Italian grocery store. This block on New Lots Avenue was headquarters for the Garofolo crew of the Lucchese organized crime family, led by Carmine "the Nose" Garofolo.

Carmine "the Nose" got his nickname not only for his amply sized proboscis but because he used it so often to snort cocaine that he destroyed all its membranes. The result was that his nose was constantly red and dripping, and Carmine aggravated the condition by repeatedly blowing it, producing a honking noise, which could be heard half a block away. Carmine, who was in his midsixties, was a short, fat man, perhaps five foot three, with no neck visible to the naked eye and a melon-shaped face with bulging dark eyes. He had no hair other than a wisp of black growth just above each of his tiny ears. He wore tailored Italian suits, all of them dark. He never removed his jacket, which covered expensive and gaudy silk white-on-white shirts, because he needed to conceal a huge .357 Magnum automatic handgun. His massive hands were more like ham hocks, and their knuckles carried large, ugly scars from the days when he was an enforcer before he became a boss. When he walked, he waddled on short stumps for legs, and his feet were jammed into imported Ferragamo loafers. When he spoke, mostly in a guttural, barely audible voice, he had an annoying habit of using the phrase "Who da fuck knows?" This was accompanied by a strange gesture, his hands outstretched, palms up, all the while staring at the sky. "How are you, Carmine?" was answered with his signature gesture and "Who da fuck knows?" Or "I gotta go, Boss, okay?" left the supplicant confused by the response, "Who da fuck knows?" When people got to know Carmine a little better, they got used to the fact that the phrase meant nothing, and they ignored it.

The Garofolo crew was the Lucchese crew most feared by the other four organized crime families of New York City, which controlled everything from bookmaking to hijacking to drugs. They earned and needed this reputation because they controlled and franchised the cocaine importation and distribution network in the metropolitan New York area. They dealt with the Colombian drug cartels that were known internationally for their brutal attacks on family members to exact complete submission from rivals, and even from their customers. Children would disappear and their body parts would be returned to their families wrapped in plastic bags and packed in corrugated boxes. The Garofolos also worked effectively with similarly violent Jamaican and Latino drug gangs.

Carmine the Nose and his thugs took complete control over the drug trade in New York City through a series of vicious strikes. A beheaded Jamaican and a castrated Colombian who had his hands chopped off at his wrists and then stuffed into his jacket pockets gave reason enough for these members of the drug-dealing food chain to understand who was in charge.

The cartels were permitted to export their cocaine only if it was sold to the Garofolos, who in turn would sell the drugs to the various gangs, after inflating the price to include a handsome profit. The Nose also set up geographic franchise areas guaranteeing exclusivity. The franchisees paid for the uncut cocaine, which was either sold in pure form to snorting yuppies or cut up and mixed to make crack cocaine for street junkies. To sweeten the Garofolos' profit, the franchised areas of operation for the drug dealers were leased weekly from the crew for an average of a thousand dollars.

O'Leary and Junior Garofolo, the oldest of Carmine's three sons, began their friendship some ten years before O'Leary was banished to Fountain Avenue. They met one evening, quite fortuitously for both, when O'Leary and his partner were working the late shift in a patrol car assigned to the 71st Police Precinct, which covered parts of East New York and Crown Heights. While on patrol making the streets safe for the people of Brooklyn, as they would joke, they were also looking for a score, perhaps a drunk driver to arrest. For an agreed-upon fee, they would either let the driver go or, if he or she was so drunk as to be unsuitable for release, the arrest would be processed and then later the officers would testify falsely in court, which would lead to a finding of not guilty.

It had been a relatively quiet night for O'Leary and his partner, when suddenly O'Leary spotted a car roar at high speed out from Nostrand Avenue through a red signal light and onto Eastern Parkway. The dark green, brand-new convertible Jaguar sped east on the parkway, reaching at times seventy and eighty miles per hour. O'Leary, behind the wheel of the patrol car, remained in full pursuit and was finally able to bring the sports car to a stop by pulling in front of it some thirty blocks into the chase.

Junior Garofalo stumbled out of the car and fell into the street, his left hand clutching a wad of hundred-dollar bills. His speech was slurred, and he said, "Please, Officer, bring me to my father," as he offered the money to O'Leary. Junior was of average height and build, maybe five feet eight and 160 pounds. He had a long, thin, mousy kind of face with a high forehead, a long, pointed nose, and very large ears, a gift from his mother. His tightly drawn mouth made him look perpetually sad, and when he tried to smile, which was not very often, he revealed an incomplete set of rotting teeth. He wore jeans and a dark sports shirt and black sneakers. He had just bought some coke from a Jamaican connection on Nostrand Avenue.

When O'Leary learned Junior's last name, his heart jumped with delight. *Here's my score of scores,* he thought. Junior reeked of scotch, and his nose cavities were still filled with white powder—and there on the passenger seat and on the floor of the vehicle, in open view, were more than a dozen clear plastic packets with more white powder.

O'Leary took Junior to his father, but it wasn't a happy reunion. "You fuckin' asshole," shouted Carmine as he landed the meat of a baseball bat across Junior's nose, breaking the long beak. "Disgrace yourself, you disgrace me and the family, you piece of shit!"

O'Leary took Junior to a local hospital to have his nose repaired, but not before receiving a handsome reward from Carmine for himself and his partner; enough money for his partner to make a down payment on a dream house in the village of Lawrence out in Nassau County. Of course, there was no police action taken about the incident, not even a report.

Junior became one of O'Leary's closest friends and his main supplier of cocaine, at no charge. In the years that followed, Carmine increasingly turned his business over to Junior, who never forgot his friend O'Leary.

"Mikey," Junior shouted into the telephone, "I gotta see you right away." O'Leary told Sergeant Mulvey that he was feeling a stomach flu coming on and got permission to leave the auto pound immediately. As soon as he arrived at the social club on New Lots Avenue, he went straight to the guarded office in the rear.

Junior Garofolo, his face ashen and his hands shaking uncontrollably, said, "Mikey, they killed my father. They ambushed him up on Pitkin Avenue." Junior began to sob and shake his head pathetically from side to side. "Then I get a call and a guy says tomorrow I'm out of business, that he and his people will come over tomorrow morning to arrange my retirement."

O'Leary asked, "Do you know who the guy is?"

"Nah, but he had a pretty thick Jamaican accent."

"I'm so very, very sorry about your guinea father, mon," said the huge black man with the ample reddish brown dreadlocks spilling over his shoulders.

Junior could feel his face muscles tighten as he stared at Winston Jordan, whose half smile through his neatly combed handlebar mustache revealed three prominent gold teeth. Jordan's image of himself was completed with a massive diamond-inlaid gold circular earring swinging back and forth from his left earlobe with every one of his animated head movements. Jordan was the undisputed boss of the most vicious of all the Jamaican drug gangs terrorizing many sections of Brooklyn. He'd named his gang "the Jamaican Sled Team."

"Your fucking guinea father ruled my people too long, and then he had the audacity"—here he slowly pronounced each of the four syllables for emphasis—"to try and turn everything over to you. He went too far, tryin' to pass all of this off to you, little guinea, as if it was his inheritance to give!"

At this Junior leaped out of his chair so abruptly that each of the four Jordan henchmen, clad in matching black leather motorcycle jackets, instantly produced a MAC-9 automatic. Jordan slammed

Junior back in his chair so violently that the chair toppled over, sending him to the ground.

From the floor, Junior screamed, "Listen, motherfucker, you best stop calling my father a guinea. He was very good to your people."

"No, you listen, you little guinea scumbag, your guinea father was nothing but a bloodsucker who drained the very life out of my people. Now it's over, so clear out of here before I blow your balls off and stuff them in your guinea mouth!"

"On the floor and freeze, cocksuckers, and I better see empty hands right away," O'Leary commanded, as he and six other off-duty cops, with Glocks and shields waving, burst into the room. One of Jordan's top lieutenants screeched with pain as two bullets slammed into his shoulder. He had not moved fast enough for O'Leary, who shouted, "Who's next?" Everyone quickly complied. O'Leary leaned over the rigidly prone Jordan and said quietly, "You got a big fuckin' mouth for a rum-headed junkie." Jordan wailed in horror as O'Leary reached down and in one motion ripped away his earring, tearing his lobe off, splattering blood everywhere. He then began to bludgeon Jordan with repeated blows from his Glock until the Jamaican passed out.

The six other cops began systematically pistol-whipping Jordan's men until their screams were silenced by unconsciousness. Now O'Leary filled a wastebasket with water and poured it over Jordan's head until he twitched back to reality. When the other cops saw this, each got a similar container. The cold water quickly revived the Jamaicans, and now Jordan and his men listened very carefully as O'Leary lowered his voice to a measured level and said, "Listen up, the next time you mutts are seen anywhere in New York you die—and you die slowly. You understand, dickhead?"

O'Leary had his boot against Jordan's neck, limiting his breathing so much that all Jordan could do was grunt his answer, showing he understood very clearly. The cops confiscated the Jamaicans' guns and then released the men through the back door of the social club at ten-minute intervals.

What neither the cops nor the Jamaicans knew was that as each one exited, he was blown away by one of Junior's people, waiting in the backyard and using an automatic pistol equipped with a silencer. The bodies were then stacked inside a stolen van and dumped on the sidewalk in front of the Carib-reggae club on Clarkson Avenue in Brooklyn that served as the meeting place for the feared Jamaican Sled Team.

"Mikey," pleaded a still shaken Junior, who never got used to the violence and instead concentrated his efforts on expanding the drug business, leaving the enforcement part to his people, "what happens to me if their friends come back?"

O'Leary stared hard and with disgust at this pampered wimp, who had none of the strength, leadership, or balls of Carmine the Nose, and said matter-of-factly, "Then we will kill them. And in the meantime, we'll give you all the protection you need."

At this point in his uncle's story Holt felt a wave of disgust come over him. He wondered what possessed Mulvey to remain involved with this murderous crew of rogue cops led by a sociopath. Yet Steven said nothing and continued to listen, confused but quite fascinated.

# 30

*People v. Holt,*
November 1992

Brendan Moore's prediction that Green would easily destroy the credibility of the forensic experts was not off the mark.

The ballistics expert, Detective Edmund Thatcher, had testified confidently enough about the peculiar markings the barrel of a gun makes on a bullet as it passes through on the way to a target. These markings, or grooves, were, he said, as reliable as fingerprints.

"Now, based on your experience with the science of ballistics identification," inquired Goss, "do you have an expert opinion about the origin of the bullets that were found in the skull section of Hiram Rodriguez, Ramon Rodriguez, and Scott Ruben, and the bullets you recovered after you test-fired Sergeant Holt's weapon at the police crime laboratory here in Suffolk County?"

"Yes, I do," replied Thatcher. "They were fired from an NYPD service revolver registered to Sergeant Steven Robert Holt."

Goss turned to Green with comic disdain and said, "You may inquire."

Just before Green began his cross-examination, Holt took a deep breath and turned to Lee Moran. She smiled reassuringly. He then looked over to where Sergeant Kurland sat each day. Kurland quickly gave the young officer a thumbs-up.

In minutes, Green established that Thatcher was not familiar with the works of several leading authorities on forensic science, in particular those who specialized in the science of ballistics identification. He conceded that he had not had a refresher course on the subject in at least three years, and he did not know that during that time these authorities, as well as FBI ballistics experts and experts from the New York State crime laboratory, all agreed that factors such as grit and rust can alter the markings Thatcher had compared in accuracy to fingerprints. Nor did he consider expert findings that corrosion of a bullet's shell or a weapon's barrel might lead to an inconclusive finding by a ballistics examiner.

Green pressed on. "Detective, isn't it true that in part your conclusions are based on the assumption that the gun surrendered by Sergeant Holt was used sometime in December of 1990, the same time that the bodies of the Rodriguez brothers were found?"

"Yes, sir."

"And isn't it also true that this weapon was surrendered to detectives from the Suffolk County Police Department in April of 1991?"

"Yes, sir."

"And you testified before a Suffolk County grand jury in late May of the same year? And you conducted your ballistic tests sometime between April of 1991 and May of 1991, correct?"

"Yes, sir, and if you give me a moment, I'll find the exact date."

Green quickly brushed aside the offer with a surly "It's a little late for precision, don't you think, Detective Thatcher?"

"I don't understand."

"Well, let me help you. Where was that weapon kept before your ballistics test?"

"In the office of the Suffolk County police property clerk, where I retrieved it just before conducting my test."

"And did you consider whether Sergeant Holt had properly maintained his weapon before its surrender?" Thatcher hesitated, and Green continued. "Did you check that weapon for rust or grit? Oh, that's right, you are not familiar with the technology that suggests that those factors can alter your findings, correct?"

"I did not check the weapon in any detail, but it looked clean."

Now Green shouted, "It looked clean, and that's it! It didn't occur to you to make a thorough inspection, Detective, because you have not kept up to date with these new findings, correct? In fact, since you did nothing more than a cursory inspection of a weapon which is offered for the sole purpose of sending this man to prison for the rest of his life, you have no way of knowing whether the barrel of that weapon was affected in any way by corrosion, correct?"

Goss rose and said, "Your Honor, we could check the weapon now for rust, grit, or corrosion."

"Oh, sit down, Mr. Goss," replied Judge McGowan in disgust.

Green turned to the jury. "Madam Forewoman and ladies and gentlemen, it may be lost on young Mr. Goss, but I assume not on you, that it might be rather a bit late to trust whether the authorities did anything to this weapon, such as cleaning it, after Detective Thatcher conducted his less than satisfactory ballistics test!" Green then said, "Your Honor, I have nothing more to say to this . . . expert." He carefully pronounced the two syllables.

When Green had finished, Thatcher left the witness stand. The color had drained from his face, and he looked sadly befuddled. Goss said, "Thank you, Detective, you did fine."

Flashing instant anger, Thatcher said in a loud voice, for all to hear, especially the jury, "It would have been helpful if you had spent some fucking time preparing me to testify."

Green, rarely gracious to his adversaries, except when he had a design in mind, rose to Goss's defense. Speaking directly to the disgruntled police officer, he said, "Now, now, Detective Thatcher, why must you blame young Mr. Goss here for your shortcomings? Perhaps the time has come for you to return to your previous assignment for the Suffolk County Police Department, writing tickets for parking violations!"

The detective, his face beet red with fury, wheeled around and shouted, "Fuck you, you Jew cocksucker!"

Green could not have dreamed for more, especially in the presence of the jury. By the look on the face of juror number seven, Mrs. Steinberg, he knew she was not at all happy about the remark.

Judge McGowan was infuriated. He stood and pointed a sharp

finger at Detective Thatcher, who quickly understood the impact of his stupidity and tried to apologize. The judge cut him off immediately and commanded, "Show cause by nine o'clock tomorrow morning why this court should not hold you in contempt. Now get out of my courtroom."

As Goss rose, presumably to complain or perhaps to explain Thatcher's conduct, Judge McGowan roared, "You sit down." Now he spoke to the jury, "Madam Forewoman, ladies and gentlemen, I deeply regret that ugly outburst, that filthy display. I shall deal with this police officer tomorrow morning, but I must charge you that you may not be influenced by any of this in reaching a verdict, because none of it, however repulsive, has any bearing on the evidence in this case. Now, I believe we could all use the rest of the afternoon off." Motioning to the court officers to escort the jury out of the courtroom, he said, "Please enjoy the rest of the day. We will resume at eleven o'clock tomorrow morning."

When the door had closed behind the last juror, Judge McGowan, still standing, spoke directly to Green. "Counselor, I admire your ability as a trial lawyer in every respect, but you and I both know that you goaded that police officer and intended the result to influence the jury. I warn you, if you try similar tactics during the remainder of this trial, you will do so at your own peril. The trial is adjourned until eleven o'clock tomorrow morning."

Judge McGowan did not wait for a response from Larry Green, nor was Green intending to give one. His ploy had worked, and of course he would not use any more like it in front of this judge. Instead, he had other plans to unnerve young Mr. Goss.

When Judge McGowan left the courtroom, Kurland walked up to the rail separating the spectators from the well, where Steven remained seated. Kurland leaned over and whispered, "Hey, kid, we had a great day." Holt beamed and then stood to be led back to his cell. Before he left he looked at Lee Moran, smiled, and winked.

At nine o'clock the following morning, Thatcher apologized to the judge in a way that confirmed for Green that the officer was just a run-of-the-mill anti-Semite. McGowan ordered Thatcher to apologize to Green, imposed a thousand-dollar fine, and directed an inquiry by the Suffolk County Police Department to determine whether Thatcher was fit for continued service as a police officer.

Judge McGowan had one remaining piece of business. "Mr. Goss, I will not warn you again about your refusal or inability to control your witnesses. Do you understand?"

"Yes, Your Honor." Goss slumped to his chair as Judge McGowan left the courtroom to wait for the jury to be brought in.

Moments later, things got better for Goss. He was summoned from the courtroom by a call from the Suffolk County chief of detectives, Phil Pitelli.

"Wally, I think we have the witness we have all been waiting for. I'll see you tonight." Despite Goss's pleas for more information, Pitelli wouldn't budge. "Just be patient" was all he would say before he hung up.

Later the same day, the trial of Steven Robert Holt reached that stage of every murder case where the jury is given the testimony as to the cause of death. It is generally a pedestrian exercise conducted by a deputy medical examiner of the county where a dead body is found. The prosecutor in grand style leads the ME through a series of detailed questions eliciting information beginning with the doctor's professional experience, including the number of autopsies performed since the doctor became an ME. Next, the testimony turns to the condition of the body and a description, mostly a gory one, of the wounds. In cases such as this one, involving multiple victims, the jury is given a description of the kind of wounds inflicted on each victim. Finally, with great drama, the prosecutor, in this case Assistant District Attorney Wally Goss, steps back a bit and looks at the jury for effect and then to the physician. "Now, Doctor, based on your professional experience and your examination of the body of Officer Scott Ruben, do you have an opinion within a reasonable medical certainty about his cause of death?"

Throughout this last question, quiet sobs could be heard from the section where Scott Ruben's relatives were sitting, including those of his mother and of his young wife.

After the answer—"a gunshot wound to the head"—Goss would repeat the exercise concerning the autopsy and the cause of death of Ramon and then Hiram Rodriguez. Larry Green had nothing but contempt for this part of a murder trial, but then, he had nothing but contempt for those in his profession who proudly proclaimed that they were homicide lawyers. For Green, whose trial skills went beyond pigeonholing specialties, a homicide case was a case with one less lousy witness. Green always believed that the testimony of the ME, particularly the cause of death, should be stipulated, or agreed to by the parties, because the testimony in his opinion was a sham and a ploy to wrench sympathy from the jurors. As a result, Green developed a style of cross-examination that was unsettling for homicide prosecutors.

When Goss had completed his direct examination of Suffolk County Deputy Medical Examiner Ronald Farnsworth, MD, he turned to Larry Green and said, "You may inquire."

Larry Green rose slowly and, with a sort of amble, walked toward the witness and asked just three questions.

"Dr. Farnsworth, does your autopsy tell you who caused the death of a victim?"

Farnsworth, who had been warned about Green's penchant for confrontation, shot back, "Of course not."

"It doesn't?" mocked Green, shaking his head from side to side in feigned disbelief. "And you are employed by Suffolk County, correct?"

Farnsworth cautiously responded, "Yes."

Now Green asked, in a booming voice, "So you get your paycheck from the same people who pay the salary of young Mr. Goss, correct?"

Goss rose to object, and Judge McGowan ordered, "Sit down."

When Farnsworth hesitated, Green said in a measured voice, "Do you have an answer?"

Farnsworth angrily responded, "My answer, sir, is yes."

"Good," said Green. "Then I have no more questions."

Larry Green had learned over the years, speaking to jurors about his approach, that they agreed with him that the testimony of the ME was indeed nothing more than a prosecutor's charade.

Holt was impressed with the job his lawyer was doing, yet he could not stop being distracted. He would from time to time glance over to where his Uncle Robert was sitting and think of all the awful things that his hero had been made to endure. Now he was in the same boat.

Goss rose and confidently announced, "That, Your Honor, subject to my application to reopen, is the case on behalf of the People of—"

Green didn't allow Goss to continue, jumping to his feet, but before he could speak, McGowan said sternly, "What are you pulling, Mr. Goss? Either rest your case or call your next witness, now!"

"But, Your Honor," Goss whined, "may we approach the bench?"

"No," bellowed the red-faced jurist. "Inside!" He waved angrily toward his chambers.

"First, of all, Goss," Judge McGowan thundered, "don't you ever again appear in my courtroom. Do you understand?"

"Your Honor, I don't know what I did to make you so angry."

"Well, for openers, you are rarely prepared, you have no sense of decorum, and you are a slick practitioner full of yourself with nothing of substance to support that conclusion. And finally you are not owed, nor do you deserve, any further explanation. So make a decision, without further delay. Rest your case or tell me and Mr. Green whom you will call." McGowan remained standing throughout and did not lower his voice. "Announce your decision tomorrow morning at nine thirty."

McGowan walked briskly from chambers, entered the courtroom, and recessed the trial, without either lawyer present.

# 31

Suffolk County Jail,
Late Summer 1992: Mulvey's Story

"By this time, Steven," Mulvey continued, "I was lost in alcohol and cocaine. I was in and out of reality, and in any event O'Leary made no effort to tell me about his grand scam."

Steven said nothing but shook his head in disgust.

Police Officer Michael O'Leary was already formulating a plan for a lucrative retirement package for himself and the others, who would include Robert Mulvey. O'Leary in his own perverse way had grown to admire and respect Mulvey and withheld his plan from him. Nevertheless, O'Leary could not help being pleased with himself. This would be his last and greatest score.

O'Leary and his group, including Robert Mulvey, began guarding Garofolo's interests immediately. Mulvey was told as little as possible. While he had crossed the line and done things that in the past he would have rejected out of hand, his need for cocaine had grown so great that he had to supplement his income. So he did not object to receiving his end of a payment from a desperate automobile owner willing to pay for the quick return of his car. Of course, he refused to deal directly with the citizen, but he did sign the release outside the presence of the motorist.

This relieved O'Leary from the task of forging Mulvey's name on the document as he had with Mulvey's predecessor. O'Leary always thought this was dangerous for him and made him more vulnerable to discovery and perhaps prosecution.

Having taken the small steps of corruption at the pound, it did not bother Sergeant Mulvey to perform guard duty for Junior Garofolo for a price. O'Leary told Mulvey that a mob hit had been ordered on Junior by the successors to the Jamaican Sled Team. Mulvey had followed the explosive media coverage about the executed Jamaican drug dealers and assumed that the Garofolo crew was involved. Through a haze of booze and drugs Mulvey justified guarding someone marked for execution as an appropriate part of police work.

The arrangement fully benefited O'Leary because it got both Mulvey and Junior Garofolo out of his hair to allow him to implement his grand score. It also gave O'Leary the chance to work closely with Joey Banfanti, known everywhere as Joey the Snake.

Joey was Carmine Garofolo's true second in command even though the bloodline went directly to Junior. Had Banfanti been asked by the drug-dealing Winston Jordan if it was fair that Junior should inherit the business from his father, Joey would have answered unequivocally no. Of course, Joey believed that he was the natural heir. He shared O'Leary's contempt for Junior and the new boss's revulsion toward violence. It was Joey the Snake who ordered the methodical execution of Jordan and his men. O'Leary and he would work well together. Of course, Banfanti had planned to use "that Mick cop," as he called him, to retire Junior permanently. For O'Leary's part, he knew exactly what he was doing with Joey the Snake. O'Leary told a few of his guys over several pints at Kilday's Shamrock Castle in Woodside, "That murderous little guinea Banfanti is gonna make us rich. Once he lets us know where the money is, we go, we take it, and we leave the planet."

The drug trade was not all that complicated to understand, nor was it difficult to uncover. It was nevertheless very difficult to stop because most of the law enforcement resources were spent on detection, interdiction, arrest, and prosecution, and very little of what was left on reducing the bottomless pit caused by the demand for drugs.

O'Leary learned about the way the Garofolos operated their drug business from Joey Banfanti. He told Banfanti that he needed the information in order to protect the business. Joey was too concerned about keeping the business profitable until he could figure out a way to get rid of Junior to be cautious about some of the questions asked by O'Leary. What O'Leary discovered was literally beyond his wildest expectations. If things worked out, he and his small band of thieves would never worry about money again.

Mulvey had paused for a moment to get a glass of water before continuing. He looked carefully at Steven, but he couldn't figure out whether he was getting through.

It took O'Leary virtually no time to figure out the chain of distribution once the drugs came under the control of the Garofolos. Their crew was importing hundreds of kilos on a regular basis, selling these kilos to the various drug dealers throughout New York City, and receiving the income from each franchise they controlled. As a result of this tightly supervised business, the Garofolo crew was accumulating an astounding profit of between ten and twelve million dollars a month. The crew set up a series of stash houses where the money was taken on a weekly basis until it was distributed to the various members of the crew at the end of each month. Junior Garofolo's monthly draw was a minimum of one million dollars.

From time to time law enforcement from federal, state, and local agencies would disrupt these operations and seize substantial sums of money and a large quantity of drugs. The drugs would be destroyed by burning the product in a huge furnace. The money would be divided up and distributed to cooperating state, local, and federal agencies. But the amount of money generated by the drug trade throughout the United States amounts to billions of dollars a year, and so the seizure of even a few million dollars by law enforcement agents is considered, at worst, an annoyance and a minor cost of doing business.

At first O'Leary and his gang guarded the transfer of the cash from pickup locations to the various stash houses, which were protected by Garofolo's soldiers. The dangerous part of the operation was the street transfer of the cash, so O'Leary's couriers traveled in well-armed threesomes. The maximum found in any one stash house was limited by order of Junior Garofolo to two million dollars. The details of the operation that began in Colombia and led to the exportation of the cocaine, and of the last step, the money laundering back through Colombia, did not interest Michael O'Leary in the least. His all-consuming interest was the money placed in the stash houses.

O'Leary's plan included pitting Joey "the Snake" Banfanti's greed and ambition against Junior Garofolo's cowardice and paranoia. He soon decided to create a fictitious story that DEA friends of his had overheard on a federal wiretap: a threat made by one of the Gambino crime family's crews to hijack the cash from one or more of the stash houses. O'Leary would convince Garofolo and Banfanti that all the cash accumulated in four separate stash houses had to be moved to a different location, a place that O'Leary would find, and held for two weeks until the threat had passed.

To make the threat seem real, O'Leary showed the two hoodlums, separately, copies of what he said were transcripts of a conversation in a social club in the Bensonhurst section of Brooklyn, headquarters for the Maroni crew from the Gambinos, which had in the past threatened to compete with the Garofolos. The transcript included a reference to Billy D'Agusta, the youngest member of the Garofolo crew, who revealed the stash house locations for an undisclosed amount of money.

Of course, before the purported transcripts were given to Banfanti and Garofolo, the body of Billy D'Agusta was found in the trunk of his late-model Cadillac not far from New Lots Avenue in Bensonhurst. D'Agusta had two bullet holes in the back of his head, an organized crime signature for execution. No one knew or suspected that the executioner was Police Officer Michael O'Leary.

The preliminaries of his plan now completed, all that was necessary was to find a house in a suitable location, have all the cash from the four Garofolo stash houses delivered there, and then complete his score by stealing every dollar. O'Leary estimated that the total amount would be at least eight million dollars, which had been converted from smaller denominations to hundred-dollar bills and larger by two bank officers currently on the Garofolo payroll. The last step for O'Leary was to figure out how he and his gang would leave the country with that huge amount of money and where to go.

One of Scotland's greatest poets, Robert Burns, once wrote something about how the "best-laid schemes of mice and men gang aft a-gley"—they go awry! He could not, of course, have been thinking of an Irish American police officer, born many years later, whose Scottish-born mother, whose married name was Burns, christened her son Robert.

Officer Robert Burns, a member of O'Leary's mob, had no trouble deciding where he would go after the big score. He would go to Ireland and help the Irish Republican Army liberate his sacred ancestral homeland. Unfortunately for O'Leary and the grand scheme for his last great score, Burns couldn't keep his mouth shut—particularly when drinking shots of Irish whiskey, chased by Guinness stout, all the while holding court in Fitzgerald's Pub in Woodside. Fitzgerald's was closely monitored by agents of the FBI.

It wasn't very long before Special Agent Shannon Kelly and her partner began to hear clear conversations about the unthinkable—a scheme devised by several New York City police officers to rip off millions of dollars of drug money and leave the country. One cop in particular, Police Officer Robert Burns, was planning to go to Northern Ireland and use his newfound wealth to fund terrorism and make Ireland united and free.

Neither Agent Kelly nor anyone else listening could know from the preliminary conversations the number of cops involved. Certainly Shannon Kelly could not have known that her former boyfriend Robert Mulvey was one of them.

The stash house to be selected by O'Leary would be carefully chosen not only to be secure but to be isolated from both residential neighborhoods and business districts. It would require access to a parkway system to permit each member of the gang a different route to exit New York City quickly. The scheme was designed to provide a separate escape plan for O'Leary, each of his six gangster cops, and Sergeant Mulvey, although O'Leary eventually decided that Mulvey was too vulnerable to be left alone and that he and the sergeant should travel together.

As to the distribution of the money, the six agreed that since O'Leary was the brains behind this great score, he was entitled to a larger share of the loot. If, as they suspected, there were at least eight million dollars, O'Leary would take two million and the six would get one million each. Anything above eight million would be evenly divided. O'Leary decided to give Mulvey a hundred thousand dollars of the first batch and a small percentage of the excess above the eight million. Initially Mulvey was told none of this because his drug addiction had completely taken hold of him and made him at times erratic. O'Leary decided that he would wait until the last minute before he and his men executed their plan. Then he would inform Mulvey, and they would leave New York together.

While poor Mulvey knew nothing and was left in the dark, Agent Kelly and the rest of the FBI squad knew everything about the plan down to the very last detail.

Even though he had not objected to it, Police Officer Burns did not think that the split that O'Leary suggested was at all fair, nor did he believe that Mulvey should receive any money. He complained bitterly to the "boyos," as the Irish illegals called themselves, as he addressed them in the rear room of Fitzgerald's. "Why," he rhetorically demanded, "should we share any of our money with that cokehead Mulvey? Why the fuck should he get a nickel? Half the time, he has no idea where he is." Burns's words were like daggers, inflicting excruciating pain on Shannon Kelly as she listened to the wiretapped conversation with a heavy heart. Burns continued, reasoning that while the money for Mulvey, at least in the first instance, came from O'Leary's share, it had the effect of reducing everyone else's.

Mulvey was now very near the end of his story.

"What you will see, Steven, is that I fell into the gutter." He said this earnestly. "And I did it by myself, making lame excuses for suffocating myself in booze and hard drugs. It was the police department that saved me."

# 32

Suffolk County Jail,
Late Summer 1992: Mulvey's Story

Mulvey woke suddenly. It was 4:15 in the morning. The date was June 11, 1976. The place was an office inside the federal courthouse at Foley Square in Manhattan. He rose from his chair and looked around, trying to remember how he got here. The gray walls of the room seemed to close in on him. He thought that he must have dozed off after he was placed in the tiny room. He sat back down, bewildered. Slumped in the worn leather chair in the windowless room, he became aware of stacks of files on the floor. Mulvey brought himself to his feet omce more and walked over to the files to read the words stenciled across one of them. The words sent a chill throughout his body.

UNITED STATES ATTORNEY, SOUTHERN DISTRICT OF NEW YORK, CRIMINAL DIVISION.

He felt a cold sweat; he was having trouble breathing. He sat back in the chair heavily, trying to understand it all. Slowly the words began to form on his lips.

"I'm a crook."

He repeated the words. Then he shouted them as he began to cry convulsively. The door opened quickly. Sergeant Bernie Pressler walked over to Mulvey and put his arms around the distraught young police officer.

"Take it easy, Robert," he said gently. "It's all over. It's goin' to get better now."

Mulvey's face looked too old for his years. The tears still streamed down his cheeks as he looked helplessly at Pressler.

"Robert, relax here for another fifteen minutes or so," said the sergeant. "Then we'll be ready to talk to you."

Robert stood up, although his knees were so wobbly that he nearly fell back into the chair. He braced himself and managed to say softly, "Thank you, sir."

Pressler headed out the door, leaving this pathetic young man standing there with his shoulders drooping pitiably. Once outside, with the door shut behind him, the sturdily built Pressler, with his military-style crew-cut hair, swept past several police officers of the elite Public Morals Administrative Division standing outside the room and muttered, "Another fucking tragedy for this goddamned job." None of the officers of this special anticorruption unit dared to say a word.

Mulvey's fifteen minutes in the holding room seemed an eternity. When Pressler returned to the room, he was joined by an assistant United States attorney, Bill McKecknie, who was the chief of the Criminal Division, FBI Supervising Agent Fred Goldman, and Chief Virgil Sampson, formerly of PMAD. As a result of the success of the 13th Division investigation, Sampson had been promoted by the commissioner to chief of a reconstituted and beefed-up Internal Affairs Division, with the three-star rank of supervising assistant chief.

Chief Sampson spoke first. "How are you doing, Robert?" Mulvey had jumped up to attention as the chief entered the room, so Sampson quickly said, "Stand easy, son."

After several hours of debriefing, it was clear to everyone that Mulvey's cocaine problem, combined with O'Leary's manipulation, had left the young sergeant not much more than an empty shell, a dupe who really had no firsthand knowledge of what O'Leary and the other corrupt cops in his crew had done.

The question remained: What could or should be done for Robert Mulvey? Later that day, after an evaluation by the substance abuse unit of the police department's Medical Division and a consultation with a drug rehabilitation center's executive director, Mulvey was admitted to Northern Hope, an internationally known drug and alcohol counseling agency located in Clinton County, New York, just a few miles south of the Canadian border.

At this point Mulvey interrupted his narrative. "I didn't want to let you know how screwed up I was, so that's why I told you I was going into a deep cover assignment for the commissioner. Of course, I didn't realize how long the rehab would take, and that was the reason I called you a few times. I knew you'd be worried."

Steven didn't react. He wanted to know the rest of the story.

The farm where Robert was sent was part of the Northern Hope complex and was called Blue Valley. It provided a multidisciplinary approach to recovery, which addressed physical and mental needs. Robert's weight had dropped to a dangerous level, under 140 pounds, as he took in less and less solid food and more and more vodka. It would take Blue Valley nearly eleven months to restore his health to an acceptable level for him to be considered at the stage in life that therapists call "in recovery": Drug addicts or alcoholics are never cured; rather, according to the treatment community, they are recovering for the rest of their lives. Shortly after his discharge from Blue Valley, Robert received department orders directing him to meet with the newly appointed police commissioner, Virgil Sampson.

Chief Sampson was just about everyone's first choice to be commissioner, and so it was that he would become the first African

American to hold that job. The announcement drew rave reviews from every quarter, with the exception of at least one police officer and a local prosecutor. Brooklyn's rackets chief, Kenny Rattigan, and Sergeant Bernard Pressler had great respect for Commissioner Sampson's ability, his intellect, and his sound judgment, but they were worried about his inflexibility. They remembered his opposition to the plan that led to the dismantling of the corrupt 13th Division. While he begrudgingly gave in, he could not wait until he made it so unpleasant for Detective Bosco that this "thief," as Sampson called him, filed for retirement. And neither Rattigan nor Pressler ever forgot Sampson's fury that Bosco was granted a line-of-duty disability pension, for psychiatric reasons that a panel of physicians determined were job related, giving him three-quarters of his salary tax free for the rest of his life. Bosco and his family moved on to an undisclosed warmer climate together with his fat pension. In a rare display of foul language, the courtly chief was heard to rail, "That corrupt son of a bitch beat the system after he disgraced this department. I will make sure that this injustice is never repeated!"

As Rattigan and Pressler considered what should be done for Mulvey, both the attitude of the new commissioner and the police department's policy on drug abuse were of great concern. The department's policy was, without any exception, a mandated dismissal. Zero tolerance had to be observed so order could be maintained. That was held as the standard even as society became more and more permissive about the use of so-called recreational drugs.

Rattigan and Pressler believed that there had to be an exception for Sergeant Robert Mulvey. When they learned that Mulvey had been ordered to report to the police commissioner's office, Rattigan called Commissioner Sampson and asked for a meeting in advance of Mulvey's appointment. He asked the commissioner for permission to bring Sergeant Pressler. His telephone call to Sampson ended on an ominous note with the words, "Kenneth, don't let us waste one another's time. Is that clear?" Rattigan answered, somewhat lamely, "Yes, sir." He warned Pressler that their mission would not be pleasant.

"No, goddammit, I will not permit this department to be stuck with a fucking cokehead junkie, and a corrupt one to boot." Commissioner Sampson's booming voice could be heard in nearly every corridor of the fourteenth floor of One Police Plaza, where his suite was located.

"Now, Virgil, calm down, because I don't plan to raise my voice," replied Kenny Rattigan, acting unusually conciliatory.

"Well, I'm not gonna keep my voice down, because what you are suggesting is just plain wrong, dammit," shouted Pressler, standing near the commissioner's desk, his face beet red.

"Now wait a minute, Sergeant—"

Before Sampson could get in another word, Pressler leaned across the desk, slammed his sergeant's shield to the floor, and with a menacing look, lowering his voice to a guttural growl, shouted, "Don't you fucking pull rank on me. You've no right to do that, so take this tin and stick it up your ass!"

The room fell to a deadly silence. Commissioner Sampson had leaped to his feet, staring at Pressler in disbelief.

"Hey, guys, we've been through too much together," pleaded Rattigan, "so can't we discuss this in a rational way?" Turning to Pressler, he commanded firmly, "Bernie, shut the fuck up and pick up your badge." Then he said very quietly to Commissioner Sampson, "Virgil, you're the boss, and whatever you decide, it's your department, we both know that, so hear us out, or at least hear me out."

Now a chastened Sergeant Pressler said quietly, "Commissioner, I am very sorry, I got a big fuckin' mouth, I didn't intend to disrespect you, so please, let me pick up my badge."

"It's alright, Bernie." With a half smile, Sampson continued. "What would we do without your big fucking mouth?"

The storm subsided, and Commissioner Sampson stated his case. "This department has had for decades, if not forever, two invariable policies: Corrupt cops could not retain their jobs and secure their pensions, and the department would not retain substance abusers, particularly drug addicts. And look what happened, we kept that mutt Bosco on the job, and not only does he take his salary for doing shit—"

The commissioner's rage level was beginning to rise, so Rattigan interrupted, gently saying, "You're right, Commissioner, completely right, but please remember that Mulvey is very different from Bosco."

"But Kenneth," Commissioner Sampson said earnestly, "it begins with the erosion of policy, and look what that piece of garbage Bosco was able to get, the fucking heart bill!"

This was a reference to a bill passed by the New York State legislature years before that granted disability pension payments, generally to police officers injured in the line of duty or those who had suffered ailments such as heart disease. It became known as the "heart bill." Since the disability payment was tax free, it created a windfall for those officers who received it. It appeared to many police officers that this retirement benefit was often abused, being granted to a disproportionate number of chiefs. One chief was denied the benefits of the heart bill but was nevertheless given a disability-related retirement pension for a hearing loss he claimed he sustained at a rock concert two years before he filed for retirement. Rattigan wondered why the commissioner was so exercised about Bosco's pension when so many of Sampson's former colleagues received such benefits routinely.

"He waltzed out of here with three-quarters tax free for life, all the while sticking his middle finger at every one of us. And just look what happened when we allowed a juicebag like O'Leary to go to rehab for his booze problem," Sampson continued, "who I should remind you has recently been convicted of murder for the killing of that young hood D'Agusta and for dozens of related felonies. How long will it take this department to live down that disgrace?"

Pressler, who had remained uncharacteristically silent, said, "But Boss, this department nearly destroyed Sergeant Mulvey. Don't you think we have a responsibility to help him?"

Pressler and Rattigan argued on into the late afternoon, taking turns trying to convince the commissioner that by placing a "Boy Scout"—Pressler's description for Mulvey—first in Washington Heights, then at the corruption meeting of the Corporation at the

13th Division, the department put him in such a stressful and dangerous assignment that he was emotionally unable to cope. Pressler argued forcefully that the police department should have known that someone as straight as Mulvey could not handle that kind of assignment.

Rattigan appealed to the commissioner on emotional grounds: The murder of Chief Connolly and Mulvey's breakup with Shannon Kelly had left him devastated and vunerable. Sampson would not be moved.

Brendan Moore, recently promoted to first to deputy inspector, then to full inspector after passing the captain's test, and now in charge of the police commissioner's headquarters staff, joined the meeting in midafternoon and, typically, just listened.

When the meeting concluded, there appeared to be no hope for Mulvey, who was scheduled to meet with the police commissioner the following morning. Both Rattigan and Pressler thanked the commissioner for his time and left police headquarters, angry and dejected. They could understand that Sampson was committed to restoring principle to a department in desperate need of values, but Kenny Rattigan kept thinking of the words of William Shakespeare from *The Merchant of Venice*: "The quality of mercy is not strained. It droppeth as the gentle rain from heaven upon the place beneath: It is twice blessed; it blesseth him that gives and him that takes." Rattigan was lost in these thoughts as he and Pressler parted company, and they were repeated in his head over and over until he arrived home.

Alone now with Inspector Moore, Commissioner Sampson felt utterly drained by the meeting. He was very fond of Kenny Rattigan and had grown to have deep affection for Pressler, the kind of love men can have for each other because they share a job filled with danger that could only be understood by those willing to risk their lives.

"Well, Brendan, you didn't say anything, but I know you've got an opinion. What is it?"

"Boss," Moore said slowly but firmly, "you have no choice. You must respect and pay proper honor to a brave cop, a dead chief, Jim Connolly, who cannot be at peace knowing that he died before he had a chance to help this poor, fucked-up kid."

Moore's foul language shocked the commissioner because not only did he refrain from its use, he would angrily confront anyone, regardless of rank, who dared to use it in his presence. During all the years that Sampson had known Moore, his protégé had never used that language. Moore himself was shocked and shaken as he left the room, not waiting for the commissioner's reaction. He was disgusted with himself. He took the elevator down the fourteen floors to the building's lobby and then walked a half block away to St. Andrew's Roman Catholic Church, in the plaza named for it. He spent a few moments in the last pew of the church, looking at the statue of the Blessed Virgin Mary, and wondering to himself, "Is this job finally getting to me?" It was the first time in Brendan Moore's career that he thought seriously about getting out. And he made a personal decision that if Mulvey was not reinstated he would submit his application for retirement.

On May 27, 1977, New York City Police Sergeant Robert Mulvey nervously tore open the envelope addressed to him from the office of the police commissioner of the City of New York and anxiously read the order: "Effective 0800 hours, 28 May 1977, report to the Internal Affairs Division for immediate assignment."

It was signed Brendan A. Moore, Inspector and Commanding Officer, Office of the Police Commissioner.

Scrawled across the bottom of the order were these words: "I know that you will make Chief Connolly and me very proud. Good luck, Robert. Sincerely, Virgil Sampson."

When Mulvey had finished telling the story, he waited for Steven to react. His nephew remained silent.

Mulvey continued, "So you see, what I did was no one's fault, certainly not the fault of the police department. I did it to myself.

But I will never forgive myself for what I did to you. Steven, let's talk to Larry Green and see if there is any way to end this."

Steven stood slowly and advanced toward his uncle, who was sitting on Steven's bed at the opposite end of the cell. Mulvey's head was in his hands, and he was trembling.

"Uncle Robert," he said tenderly, "I love you, but nothing you have just told me changes my opinion of what that damned job did to you." Steven hugged Mulvey and said, "Uncle Robert, you must believe me. I did not kill those men. I am innocent."

After meeting with his nephew, Mulvey had arranged a meeting at Larry Green's office. Mulvey was hopeful.

"Larry, Steven insists that he is innocent, even after I told him what I did to myself."

"When he told you that, did he appear agitated?"

"No," Robert anwered guardedly.

"Well, that's just great," Green said curtly. "That little pipsqueak Goss has all the evidence, and all you can give me is a denial with nothing to support it. Robert, let me make it plain to you. Given the level of violence in this case, coupled with the abuse Steven confronted at home watching his mother repeatedly beaten, there may be another answer."

"And just what is that?"

"Your nephew may very well be a murderer."

"And if he is, what can be done about it?"

"Barring some miracle from Moore, we may have to introduce quickly, and I mean now, the defense of extreme emotional disturbance. But I can only use that defense if Steven admits to the murders and if his mental condition—and its preexistence to the murders—is confirmed by a psychiatrist. If the jury accepts that defense, Steven will avoid state prison and instead will be confined to a psychiatric hospital where he can be treated. And it is entirely possible that one day he could be released. Our alternative is to continue to roll the dice!"

Green abruptly stood, indicating that the meeting was over.

# 33

East New York, Brooklyn, the 75th Precinct,
June 1985

"Stevie, my boy, this job used to be fun. Now it's all bullshit, run by Mickey Mouse and his band of Mouseketeers," observed Police Officer William Kerner. "Used to be, you'd hit the ground runnin' every day, every tour." He was smiling as he thought back. "Make some collars, get some overtime, and put the bad guys away."

Kerner, a veteran of almost twenty years with the NYPD, was performing the senior police officer's ritual of breaking in a new cop. At five feet nine inches, he had a slight build, which seemed to be shrinking because of severe health problems. His sustained anger directed toward the department, plus a disastrous divorce followed by a separation from his children, had left him with almost no appetite for solid food. The condition, of course, had no effect on his alcohol consumption, which consisted of shots of Irish whiskey washed down by pints of draft beer at Kennedy's Bar not far from the 75th Precinct. When he would finally arrive home, he would continue to drink beer until he fell into a stuporous sleep. His complexion had an unhealthy sallow look, and his facial skin was beginning to hang. All his police uniforms were ill-fitting, much too big for his body. His dark brown eyes were beginning to sink deep into their sockets, and his sharply pointed nose appeared larger than it really was. When he took a breath he made a wheezing sound caused by years of smoking. Kerner's fingers had a rusty color and his teeth were turning from white to brown from years of the habit. The smell of tobacco hung around him like an invisible cloud of pollution at a chemical waste disposal dump. But he would soon forget his physical and mental discomforts anytime he was training a young police officer like Steven Holt. Steven, with less than four months of experience following his graduation from the Police Academy, was behind the wheel of a cruiser and hanging on to Kerner's every word. Their cruiser was assigned to the night tour in Brooklyn's 75th Precinct, located in East New York. Their tour was from 8:00 P.M. to 4:00 A.M. of the following day, known as the eight-by-four.

"Why did it change?" Steven asked in a tentative way, not sure he was supposed to speak at all.

"It's the fuckin' junkies, drugs everywhere. Junkies muggin', burglarizin', stealin' cars, stickin' up grocery stores and liquor stores. Doin' it all for a few bucks to get a fix, gettin' high and doin' it all over again."

Kerner paused for a moment, assessing the rookie's reaction. The kid was obviously impressed, which pleased the cynical veteran police officer.

"So much fuckin' drugs and crime that the system is jammed up. So, even with hundreds more cops on the streets, thousands of more jail cells, and many more fuckin' lawyers, the thing just doesn't work anymore."

Kerner was just warming up. "Then there's the ADAs. Used to be that a guy would get out of law school, join a political club, usually the Democrats, get a job as an assistant district attorney, and have a law practice on the side. He'd hustle to make a buck, didn't get nothin' without workin' for it. The guy knew how much the public wanted law and order, so he'd never break our balls. He never questioned a cop. He didn't care that we'd fuck around a little bit—nothin' serious, just enough to get the bad guys off the street. Then after a few years the ADA would graduate to a job as a judge's law secretary, sort of half an ass-kisser and half a gofer. And finally, after a while, with a few bucks placed here and there, you know . . ."

Holt didn't know, but he pretended that he did.

"He'd become a judge, and that concluded a fine career. I used to think that one of my jobs in life was helpin' a young ADA become a judge."

Now Kerner stopped, remembering wistfully the good times. "They weren't the brightest guys in the world. But shit, we were on the same side. Then that fuckin' Supreme Court in Washington started givin' the mutts all those rights which were for honest people in the first place."

Kerner appeared to be getting angry, and indeed, although he had given this speech countless times before, he got furious every time he thought of the Supreme Court and its decisions about confessions and seized evidence, shaped largely under the leadership of Chief Justice Earl Warren. Every cop knew that the Warren Court did nothing but tie their hands. Kerner told Steven about an incident in court soon after the Warren Court's historic decision on seized evidence in a case entitled *Mapp v. Ohio.*

In 1957, a woman named Dollree Mapp was arrested by police officers for possession of obscene material. The materials were seized and the arrest was made inside her apartment, despite the officers' failure to seek a court-authorized search warrant. Dollree Mapp could not have realized it at the time, but she was about to become part of judicial history. *Mapp v. Ohio* would become perhaps the most important case involving search and seizure in the history of American criminal law.

The case gave a defendant in cases involving seized evidence the right to have a hearing, known forever after as a Mapp hearing, to test whether a police officer acted reasonably under the Constitution when he or she seized evidence and arrested the defendant. If the judge presiding over such a hearing ruled that the police officer did not act reasonably, the evidence would be suppressed and the case against the defendant would be dismissed.

Kerner recalled for Steven how he was in Judge Patrick Horan's courtroom not long after the decision in *Mapp* when a lawyer named Norman J. Feldman entered. Horan was a little guy, not quite five feet tall, who had a habit of pacing back and forth behind his bench.

He didn't fully realize that the snickering and suppressed laughter in his courtroom, which came from the court officers, lawyers, complainants, victims, and spectators, was caused by the fact that each time he passed behind his large leather-upholstered chair, he would momentarily disappear! Judge Horan's little body required custom-made judicial vestments, which nevertheless could not address the reality that his tiny head always seemed to have just popped out of the top of his robe. For all of that, though, or maybe because of it, Horan did maintain a good sense of humor. When he finally realized that he was the cause for the courtroom mirth, he installed an apple crate behind his chair so he was never again out of sight. Judge Horan was a former Brooklyn assistant district attorney, and he was very popular with cops.

When Horan spotted Feldman as the lawyer entered the courtroom, he yelled out, "Whaddaya got, Feldman?"

"I got a gun case, Your Honor," replied the lawyer.

"Ya want a plea?" shouted Horan.

"I'd first like a Mapp hearing, Judge."

"Did he have the gun?" demanded Judge Horan.

"Yeah, Judge, but the cop took it illegally."

Horan, turning red-faced, shouted, "Hey, Normie, that bullshit is for those old guys in Washington. I tell you what, you take a plea and your guy walks. But if you have a Mapp hearing and I don't see any so-called illegal seizure, your guy's goin' in the can for a year." Horan stopped and looked sternly at Feldman. "You got that?"

Feldman had his client plead guilty and that was the end of it.

Kerner continued, "So at first we and the ADAs worked together. We'd fudge a little bit about where the evidence was found. The prick had the gun in his jacket pocket but, you know, a cop has instincts. So we'd say the gun was on the seat next to him in the car in open view, as the ADAs would say. What was the big fuckin' deal? He had the gun, right?" Kerner watched Holt carefully to see if he was getting the message.

Holt, sensing that a response was expected, replied nervously, "Yeah, but isn't that perjury?"

The young police officer barely finished the sentence before

Kerner exploded, "Stevie, what the fuck is wrong with you anyway? Those gun-carrying motherfuckers kill little kids. They fuckin' kill cops. Don't you get it? Pull over," he commanded.

When the patrol car had been guided to the curb, Kerner made sure he had the full attention of his young charge. "Stevie," he shouted, "it's us against the mutts. Cops are the last line of defense between citizens and chaos. Look what's happened to our streets. Don't you see what's happening in the DA's office? Now we got two types of enemies—the mutts and all of those young smart-assed ADAs, the white guys from the Ivy League schools lookin' down their noses at us."

Kerner was now seriously angry, trying to save his newest recruit from himself. "Even those fuckin' white guys from St. John's and Fordham, their fathers cops and firemen. Even they try and treat cops like fuckin' clerks. All of them lookin' for a chance to make their reputation on us. Get a promotion—lock up a cop for lyin' or for givin' some mutt a beatin' that he deserved."

Kerner's frustration was billowing over. "Then there's the fuckin' girl ADAs with their see-through blouses, showin' off their tits, wearin' skirts that look like they've been painted on them, all of them lookin' to trap you with a sexual harassment complaint. It's all bullshit, Stevie. None of them care about lockin' up mutts as much as lockin' up us! And if that's not enough, we gotta deal with those black ADAs. Oh, excuse me, the African American ADAs or whatever they fuckin' call themselves today. And the Latinos." Kerner spit out the last two syllables to emphasize his contempt. "All those fuckin' minorities hate all whites, and don't forget that, Stevie."

Kerner slammed his fist on the dashboard so hard that it scared Holt. "It's all bullshit. I got five months to go and then the mutts can have the city for all I care. For me, it'll be sayonara. But let me tell you somethin', pal, you'd better learn fast that your only friend is your brother cop—and I mean brother. Don't you ever fuckin' trust a broad with a badge. Don't get close to no cop unless he's white. And that's tellin' you straight."

Kerner was interrupted by the police radio. "Central to Sector George, there is a 10-31 at 445 Dumont Avenue, K." Central is the citywide police dispatcher, 10-31 is the code for burglary in progress, and the letter *K* indicates that a portion of the transmission has ended. Kerner snapped into action, notifying the dispatcher that their unit would respond.

The burglary location was a bodega on Dumont Avenue, not far from Pennsylvania Avenue, the main roadway through the East New York section of Brooklyn. As the police car neared the store, Holt was surprised to see that three other patrol cars had already arrived—which was the total number of cars on duty for the eight-by-four tour in the 75th Precinct. All the police officers from those cars were already in the store as Holt and Kerner approached. The sight that greeted Police Officer Holt as he reached the doorway stunned him. He was left nauseous. Several of the uniformed officers were stacking cartons of cigarettes in a large brown cardboard box. Others were gathered around a cash register taking turns dipping their hands into the machine and extracting fistfuls of cash that they stuffed into the pockets of their police-issued windbreakers. He watched as two other officers carried an empty cardboard box into the store from the street and began filling it with more cigarettes.

After some twenty minutes of silence, as Kerner drove the patrol car back to the 75th Precinct, Holt turned to Kerner and said, "Bill, how could those cops do that, takin' those cartons of cigarettes, stealin' all that cash from the register? How could they fuckin' do that?" The perspiration ran down Holt's face. He felt like crying. "And what about you?" he demanded. "Even you took a carton. But when the cops left, you threw it on the floor—and that fat fuckin' sergeant sayin' to me, 'Take some cash, kid,' like I'm a thief, too."

Kerner spoke quietly and carefully. "Stevie, take it easy. Let's go back to the house, wash up and change. You come to my apartment. It's only a half hour from the station house. We'll talk."

It was just about 5:30 later that morning when they entered Kerner's apartment, three rooms on the third floor of a four-story walk-up. The inside was dreary and badly in need of a paint job. The smell was musty, punctuated by a strong odor of stale cigarette smoke that made Steven gag. The foyer remained darkened because of a burnt-out lightbulb. A small dining room was crowded with a large table and six chairs, relics of Kerner's former home in Merrick, Long Island. On it was the faded picture of a beautiful young woman—Kerner's wife, Florence, dead of breast cancer six years before, following their divorce. On the wall was a Cop of the Month plaque awarded to Kerner by the *Daily News,* which would monthly cite the heroism of police officers and firefighters. The living room was also small and reeked of stale beer.

Holt flopped on the couch. The pillows were ripped, with little remaining padding. Kerner appeared from the kitchenette with two cans of beer.

"I don't want any, Bill," Holt protested, but he allowed the older man to shove it into his hand. He idly placed it on his right knee, holding it, staring at it as Kerner began to speak.

"Stevie, what you saw is not what cops are about. There are about 183 cops assigned to the Seven-five, and only a few dozen are like those bums."

"A few dozen!" Holt interrupted, incredulous.

"Stevie," Kerner yelled, "where the fuck did you grow up? In a goddamned cocoon? If you had two hundred lawyers or two hundred doctors, or two hundred anything, don't you think at least a few dozen of them would lie about their income taxes, be paddin' expense accounts, or takin' kickbacks? Why should cops be any different? Fact is that most of the cops come to work, bust their asses for people who don't give a shit about them, take abuse, get punched and shot at, and then go home. They never even think of takin' a fuckin' free cup of coffee. Then there's people like who we saw earlier this morning. Around the precinct they're known as Ali Baba and his Forty Thieves."

Now Holt's shock began to pass. He had heard about crooked cops before he became a police officer, and he was determined never to be in their company. Seeing so many of them at once was overwhelming, but he was beginning to recover.

Kerner continued, "For as long as I've been on the job, there's always been a few cops in every command who would steal when they would have the chance and shake down people, taking a few bucks in return for not issuing a moving violation like speeding or not arresting them for drunk driving. When I first saw it I was shocked, but I learned to ignore it and look the other way. I also did everything I could to stay away from dirty cops."

"But why did you take the carton and then leave it after the sergeant ordered us to secure the place?"

"Because I want those guys to trust me."

"Trust you—trust you! Why would you want those crooks to trust you?"

"Because, you dummy," Kerner said firmly, "one of these days you're goin' to be at a job, and you'll be surrounded by some mutts lookin' to take you out. They'll have tire irons and chains, maybe a knife or a gun. You and your partner will be in deep shit. You will radio a 10-13 for backup, and let's suppose that the guys closest to your location are those bandits you saw in the bodega, who also happen to be cops trained to fight and trained to shoot. Only they know that you're a fink. They may even think that you'd rat them out. So they'll come—only very slowly. They'll be passed by all the heroes. Only the heroes will arrive too late, too late to save you from a beatin', or maybe too late to save your life."

Now Holt's eyes were bulging, his mouth opened in disbelief.

"You think what I'm sayin' is bullshit? Well, you ever hear of Frank Serpico? Serpico got sick of seein' so many cops stealin back in the late sixties, so he went to a newspaper reporter and bingo—there was a big scandal. The police brass and their friends at the PBA and the SBA said the scandal was all bullshit. But the mayor got scared—he's got an election to worry about, so he appoints a commission to investigate cops. And guess what? There was a scandal. Cops were taking money from gamblers and drug dealers for protection. Cops were stealin' from store owners and drunk drivers. Cops were stealin' hot stoves. The PBA and SBA union guys got very quiet. Then great reforms were announced. The mayor and the police commissioner said they wouldn't tolerate crooked cops. The five district attorneys of New York City began to wake up and indict cops. But that wasn't enough for the mayor. He convinced the governor to appoint a special prosecutor. Of course, since cops vote, the mayor and the governor assured everyone that the special prosecutor was not just for cops—he'd investigate everyone, DAs, ADAs, judges. Sure, everyone. And the special prosecutor did arrest some judges, but their cases got tossed out—by other judges."

Kerner stopped to catch his breath. "Then, Stevie, Serpico, he got a gold detective shield for bein' such a great hero. He got assigned to the Narcotics Bureau. And you know what, Stevie? The first job that brand-new Detective Serpico goes on, he and his team bust into an apartment with a search warrant and Serpico gets shot in the face. One of the mutts shot Serpico as he tried to get in the door. His team leader said later that the shooting was a terrible accident that should have never happened. Only Serpico didn't think it was an accident. Now he's livin' in Switzerland. Stevie, I took that carton of cigarettes for my own protection, and I told that lowlife of a sergeant that you were a little nervous, so we'd grab some money out of the register when they left."

"You did what?" Holt demanded.

"Stevie, I did it for you. Stevie, get used to this shit or go somewhere else. Join the fire department."

"But aren't these guys afraid of Internal Affairs?"

Kerner started to laugh. "Who do you think they get to go in that rat-fink squad at IAD? Those guys can't find their ass with two hands. The bosses make sure that the good ones don't last."

"But why?" asked Holt, doubting his partner.

"Because, Stevie, the brass are terrified of scandal. So what they want IAD to do is Mickey Mouse shit, breakin' the balls of honest cops to keep them in line. Sure, if they get a crook cold, they'll serve charges and bust him out. And maybe if a DA is alert, he'll get the cop indicted. But one or two or three ain't a scandal. You got it?"

It was 6:30, and Holt was tired and disgusted. Besides, he wanted to go to the 8:00 A.M. Mass. He shook Kerner's hand.

The older man hugged him, thinking of the two sons he hadn't seen since their mother died. "Stevie, I'll be your steady partner till I get out. By that time you'll know who you can trust."

At the beginning of the next eight-by-four, after the turnout sergeant finished advising the police officers of the precinct conditions, he dismissed them from roll call. "Kerner and Holt, stand by," he ordered. "There's some fuckin' IAD captain who wants to see you. Did you guys call him?"

"Yeah," said Kerner, "We want to surrender." Kerner's stomach churned as the sergeant smiled, but as Holt began to shake, Kerner whispered, "Stevie, be cool. If it's serious we'll ask for our union delegate."

The two officers went to the locker room, where the captain was waiting. He appeared to be unthreatening as he smiled. "Did you guys take a job at Dumont Avenue yesterday?"

"Yes, Captain, why?" Kerner responded.

"Were you not told to secure the place?"

"Yes, sir."

"Were you told to remain until the owner came, or to make sure the front door was locked?"

"To lock up, sir," replied Kerner.

"Well, you didn't, dammit, and Kerner, you should certainly know better."

Kerner could hardly contain himself. Mickey Mouse was alive and well at IAD.

"It's a hell of a way to break in this rookie officer," the captain continued.

Holt spoke. "Beggin' your pardon, Captain, Officer Kerner has really taught me a lot so far. I forgot to lock up."

"Not your fault, son. This department demands accountability from our senior officers." Turning to Kerner, the captain said sternly, "Officer, we've reviewed your record to prepare for this interview. You've done pretty well. So we'll let this go with a reprimand, okay?"

Kerner snapped to attention and gave the captain a smart hand salute. "Yes, sir," he shouted.

In late December 1985, William Kerner, like many other officers who live the dream of "twenty and out," retired to Fort Lauderdale. In January 1986, he received his first police pension check. The following week, while playing tennis, Kerner suffered a massive and fatal heart attack. At the time of his death, former New York City police officer William Kerner was forty-three years of age.

# 34

East New York, Brooklyn, the 75th Precinct, New York
Fall 1987

A newly assigned young officer was driving. Holt was in the passenger seat as the recorder, the police officer who records all official activity. The youngster had graduated from the academy three months earlier and had been assigned to the 75th Precinct for the last six weeks.

"Pull over," Holt abruptly ordered. The officer quickly responded, more than a bit puzzled because it was the first time Holt had spoken since the beginning of the tour.

"Let's get one thing clear," said Holt. "I don't fuckin' steal. If you do, I'm goin' to fuckin' lock you up. If you try to stop me, I'm goin' to fuckin' shoot you."

The bewildered young cop, turning crimson, shouted, "Yes, sir."

Holt began his first tour with every new partner this way until he was promoted to the rank of sergeant on January 10, 1988.

# 35

Police Academy,
1988

After he was promoted, Sergeant Steven Holt was transferred to the academy as an instructor because his conduct had earned the notation on his official file "not suited for regular field command duty." Since the high command at the police department had little interest in controlling police corruption, something they believed was an aberration, they marked Steven as nothing more than a gadfly, and the way the brass dealt with people like Steven was to assign them to lecture probationary police officers about the dangers of corruption. Of course, over the six months of training given to these young police officers, only one hour was devoted to anticorruption awareness. In their world of doublespeak, the brass would explain that someone had to address the possibility of corruption, however remote, and that police officers like Steven Holt who worried so much about the hazards of corruption were appropriate to give that lecture.

Steven's other duties included attendance taking and the job of chauffeuring the commanding officer of the academy. During the five months Steven was assigned to this duty, the commanding officer never spoke to him beyond a perfunctory greeting at the beginning of his tour and an equally brusque good-bye at the end.

Then the 75th Precinct got a new commanding officer. Captain Jackie Desmond had built a solid reputation among police officers for carrying out the Mickey Mouse traditions of the high command at One Police Plaza. He was looking for sergeants he could trust. When someone told him of Holt's habit of breaking in a new partner, he decided that he had his man.

Soon Steven Holt was back at the 75th Precinct, this time as one of its patrol sergeants.

# 36

## The Blue Wall, NYPD,
## Late 1980s

The problem of corruption within the ranks of the NYPD continued into the late 1980s and seemed intractable. The recommendations made by the special commission back in the 1970s, just as Captain Nevins had predicted, had accomplished very little. Despite the mayor's upbeat press announcement immediately after the arrests of the crooked cops of the 13th Division, and his sincere promise to make positive changes, nothing was done institutionally to address the cyclical nature of police corruption. The Internal Affairs Division remained a place that no police officer wanted to be assigned, so it continued to be populated by gadflies or subpar cops and others who couldn't seem to fit in regular police assignments.

The special state prosecutor's office, set up as a result of one of the recommendations of the corruption commission, was abandoned after some spotty successes. It was resented throughout all the years it existed because the governor gave it the power that had until then been rested in the five elected district attorneys of New York City to investigate and prosecute police and other forms of corruption within the criminal justice system. None of the district attorneys ever forgave or forgot what the governor did, and as a result, none of them was particularly helpful.

Then in 1990, shortly after the newly elected mayor, W. Carlton Richardson, took office, he appointed Kenny Rattigan his corporation counsel.

Rattigan in turn recommended the appointment of Sean J. Nevins as the city's new police commissioner. The recommendation, adopted by Mayor Richardson, stunned most of the police brass. While the New York City Fire Department once had a lieutenant—and at another time in its history even a firefighter, who was the president of the firefighters union—vault over its chiefs, to serve as fire commissioner, nothing like that had occurred in the police department. And while it was true that a number of police commissioners came from outside the department, these were generally prominent lawyers with close contacts to whoever was serving as mayor. Never had someone with the rank of captain become chief executive officer of this tradition-bound police department.

Commissioner Virgil Sampson was a superb police officer and administrator, but he lacked the cunning and political instinct to deal with the intransigent high command of his department, nor would he suffer the bureaucratic minutiae that were the daily staples of One PP. Accordingly he increasingly ceded his authority and control to his deputies, who gleefully accepted it. Commissioner Sampson's successors over the following twelve years were more traditionalist, and it didn't take long for the department to settle back to its goal of making no waves. If there were no scandals, there would be no shake-ups. If everyone understood that crime has cyclical stages of highs and lows, not affected by any changes outside or inside the department, no problems would be presented for the chiefs to solve. Take credit for increased public safety during the good years, and blame drugs, public apathy, politicians, and district attorneys during the bad years.

Without muckraking by the media, police corruption was largely unmentioned, and with the investigation of corruption left to the dolts assigned to IAD, the chiefs of One PP had a fine life. Keep the commissioner happy, keep him in the news visiting basketball centers with local kids, provide a few photo ops with senior citizens, get as many promotions to senior chief positions as you can, and then go off to head up the security department of a major business organization. Not a bad life, at least for the chiefs.

For the public, however, it was quite a different story. New York City in 1990 was fast becoming one of the most dangerous big cities in America, and one of its boroughs, Brooklyn, had become the fifth most violent municipality in the country per capita.

Police corruption had taken hold again. Soon there were intelligence reports from federal sources and from within the police department warning of a growing cancer of corruption. These reports, unfortunately, were generally ignored.

At least one police commissioner, Michael G. Keating, a seasoned cop and a superb chief, who rose steadily through merit to the top of the police department and who was in addition a well-respected retired colonel in the United States Marine Corps, tried to do something. Unfortunately, he served briefly and was not retained after Mayor Richardson's election. Were it not for the availability of Sean J. Nevins, replacing Keating would have been a major mistake.

Over the years, Pressler and Nevins tried to stay in touch. Pressler set his sights on passing as many promotional examinations as he could, hoping that higher rank would bring him the opportunity to make changes to prevent a return to systemic corruption. In just a few short years Pressler was promoted to lieutenant, then captain. By the time Nevins was appointed police commissioner, Pressler held the rank of deputy inspector.

With each promotion, Pressler was given challenging and exciting assignments, in commands such as the Emergency Service Unit and Intel, the Police Intelligence Bureau, where he had the responsibility of designing security programs to protect foreign dignitaries. Perhaps Pressler's most challenging job was his appointment to oversee a team responsible for the creation of a long-term approach to crime reduction by mandating accountability in each police precinct's command through the use of a computer-driven statistical analysis. Pressler's innovative program, called Crime Crash, would over the next several years receive substantial credit for massive reductions in crime in New York City and would become the prototype used by police departments throughout the world.

In contrast to Pressler's command assignments, Nevins was given jobs created to break his spirit and force him to retire. But no attempt, however humiliating, could knock Sean Nevins down. He headed a unit that reviewed applications by civilians seeking pistol permits and one within the Missing Persons Bureau checking on case files closed for ten years or more; at another time he was made director of the bureau responsible for placing and removing police barriers at demonstrations and parades.

"Sean, how the fuck do you take this shit?" asked an exasperated Bernie Pressler.

Nevins, faking his favorite imitation of an Irish brogue, replied, "Inspector, dahlin', every day when those humps at One PP review the orders and see the name of Sean J. Nevins, captain, NYPD, they die a little . . . ever so slowly. So at the end of the day we shall see who remains standing."

Pressler at this broke into a smile and gave Nevins a bear hug.

Corrupt cops who were still on the job in the early 1990s had learned well from those who preceded them. In order to survive and make an adequate amount of money on the side while laying low, waiting for the big score, it was important to operate in small, well-disciplined cells, modeled after urban terrorists, Communists, and yes, as one corrupt cop said, "freedom fighters." For this cop, he and his fellow freedom fighters were liberating assets from criminal activities for their own benefit and for the benefit of their families. They had also learned never to use a telephone to talk about their business, or to speak anywhere until they had checked for listening devices in advance. Finally, no new members were permitted to join a corrupt cell unless they were family. If any police officer was transferred out of the precinct, the size of the group or cell would be reduced until a personal friend or family member could be assigned.

The night tour, as always, was fertile ground for the operation of these corrupt units, because the numbers of police personnel provided to neighborhood patrols were reduced, and supervision by patrol sergeants was virtually eliminated.

"Commissioner," Assistant Chief Moore, soon to be Nevins's first deputy police commissioner, said with a broad smile, "I do believe you know Deputy Inspector Pressler." Here were these three old friends together in the office of the commissioner at One Police Plaza, which none of them would have believed possible—particularly with one of them holding the title of PC. It was Police Commissioner Sean J. Nevins's first full day of command. Following Moore's introduction the three men laughed with wild roars.

"Well, Bernie, how does it feel to be one of the Last of the Mohicans now that all those cellar-door dancers have jumped ship?" This was Nevins's signature line and favorite metaphor for all phonies. When Nevins was growing up, his Brooklyn neighborhood had trim little one-family frame homes. On the side near the front entrance, there was a door leading to the basement portion of the home. It was known as the cellar door and was angled at forty-five degrees. So for Nevins, the phrase described people who could dance over their principles the way his boyhood friends could balance themselves while dancing on a cellar door.

Nevins's appointment led to a flurry of resignations. Virtually every police boss above the rank of captain resigned in protest. It did not faze Mayor Richardson in the least, not just because he was a maverick, but because he remembered that when another mayor chose the fire department's first African American commissioner, there was a similar reaction from the FDNY brass. When asked what he thought of the mass of resignations, Mayor Richardson's uncharacteristic response was "Fuck 'em!"

Nor did it faze Nevins, who saw it to be a real opportunity to revolutionize this moribund autocracy. "Bernie, we just got the chance of a lifetime," Nevins began, "but all we have is two, maybe three years. Yet it's still plenty of time before we move on. And I want to start the change with you."

"Com—"

Pressler did not get beyond the first syllable before Nevins, ever volatile, leaped from his chair, red-faced and shouting. "Goddammit, Bernie, don't you ever fucking call me that again!" Nevins's cigar was bouncing in his mouth.

"Well, can I call you Boss?"

Nevins thought for a moment and said, smiling, "Okay, Bernie, but only in public, not here."

# 37

The Blue Wall Smashed,
February 27, 1990

"Sean, do you remember what you said after that judge was sworn in by Mayor Hargrove to investigate police corruption?" The commissioner didn't answer, so Pressler persisted. "You said, 'None of this will stop until cops act like cops.' What the hell did you mean by that?"

Nevins replied by reminding Pressler of the extraordinary work of the Public Morals Administrative Division, which, in contrast to IAD, was so successful in locking up corrupt cops and crooked lawyers.

"They were real detectives, whose primary mission was to disrupt and jail organized crime guys. While their investigation and arrest of corrupt cops and crooked lawyers grew out of this primary mission, it never occurred to them that they should make a distinction between these criminals. So they acted like cops."

Moore had heard this analysis several times before from Nevins, but he never gave much thought to it. It certainly made sense to him, but he had not considered how it could be applied beyond a special unit like PMAD, which had been disbanded a few years before. As successive commissioners worried more about rising levels of street crime and considered the investigation of sports betting an unaffordable luxury, fewer and fewer resources were allotted, until the effort was formally abandoned.

Unfortunately, few people in the department understood that the mob used the enormous profits gained from sports betting to fund most of its other activities, from loan sharking to hijacking to the control of drug traffic. And drug traffic was, beyond any other factor, most responsible for the seemingly out-of-control street crime. Drug-craving addicts and the greed of violent drug gangs were turning the streets of New York City into a zone of terror.

The problem in law enforcement was that so few administrators understood that sports betting was the cash cow of organized crime. The last commanding officer of PMAD surely understood the clear connection, and he often said with considerable frustration, before this elite unit was abolished, "The public has got to be convinced that every time they give a hundred bucks to Joe the Bookie it will come back to their neighborhood in the form of drugs or guns that will be used to murder children and cops." He also understood that a bookie was only a franchise operator, who had to pay a regular tribute to the mob. The network of bookies, numbering in the thousands, nationally produced billions of dollars each year that provided a steady stream of funding for the crime families.

Nevertheless, the chiefs at One PP considered this opinion to be completely out of touch, because it failed to understand that all the resources available had to be allocated to attacking street crime. The prime strategy for this attack, the so-called War on Drugs, was doomed to failure because it never made an effort to reduce the demand for drugs. Drug treatment and education programs were considered social work, not law enforcement.

These same chiefs also dismissed as a nut Chief Phil Blanton of the Transit Police Department, who said that the way to reduce crime in the subways was to come down hard on the fare beaters, aka the turnstile jumpers. What that chief recognized, and the One PP chiefs could not see, was that this kind of conduct might reveal sociopathic behavior, and if you arrested these people, a good number might have prior serious criminal records and might be out of prison on parole. When they were arrested, the transit police discovered that many had failed to keep contact with their parole officer, and many others were wanted in connection with the commission of another crime. So, the chief concluded—correctly, as it turned out—if he could take them off the streets and out of the subways, the result was a sharp reduction in subway crime.

The theory of attacking quality-of-life crime as a major tool against serious crime was not something traditionalists would embrace. It ran counter to everything they ever learned, and it was also dangerous. The police brass believed that if they announced that this approach would reduce crime and it failed, they couldn't withstand the angry criticism that they had wasted valuable resources on minor crime.

"And so, Bernie, that's what I wanted to talk to you about," the commissioner continued. "We have identified one cesspool in Brooklyn, the 75th Precinct, where the majority of the police officers are young, dedicated, and honest. We've got to get to them before the half dozen or so crooks there infect them with the virus. Tell Bernie what you have, Brendan."

Even while Brendan Moore was moving up in rank, he maintained his extraordinary network of informants. There was no piece of information, no news or news source, that was not important to him. His information gathering was not just his job, it was his hobby, the goal of which was to expand his database. It also made him very much needed in the police department, and it became his power base.

"There's a sergeant, a nighttime supervisor who has been stealing since he got on the job," Moore began, "and he has very cleverly limited his corruption activities to protect himself against discovery. Over the last few years, he led a gang of perhaps four or six other cops, including one of the precinct's PBA delegates, Scott Ruben, and an alternate, Gabe Perone. They pick up extra money the usual ways with the drunk drivers, shaking them down, and the other one-shot opportunities, but their principal source of income is stealing drugs and money from a few gangs operating in East New York. Of course, there is little new to this technique, except that this crew are very disciplined. They don't ever talk anyplace where they can be overheard, and they never use telephones.

"But"—here Moore allowed himself a broad, toothy smile—"they do make mistakes. They've gotten greedy, and instead of making arrests and confiscating the money and the drugs, dividing them up at a secure location, they set up franchises and allow the drug gangs to operate for a monthly share. While this has produced much more money, it's made them vulnerable."

Moore explained that the crew would arrest gang members, take the money and the drugs, resell the drugs that same night to another gang, and then split the proceeds at the end of the tour. This recycling of the drugs was safe, but it did not produce the kind of money they wanted, so they identified a leader of each of the eight gangs operating in East New York and demanded a percentage of the gross sales for the month. To ensure an honest count they conducted random raids, counted up the money and drugs, and then extrapolated to figure the monthly take. If they concluded that they were being shortchanged, that gang would have its operation suspended for three months. Once the period of suspension had been served, the cops told the gang members that if they were found cheating again, they would lose their police protection permanently, and if gang members were caught selling drugs, they would be arrested and would face a life sentence. The sanction never had to be imposed because the gangs understood very clearly the consequences of cheating. The "Bandits of Bush Terminal," as they were known, had created a very profitable enterprise.

This crew of rogue cops got their name because the meeting place for all of their collections was an abandoned warehouse in the commercial complex of several large buildings known as Bush Terminal, located on the Brooklyn waterfront adjacent to the Gowanus Parkway. The location was chosen because it was several miles from East New York, a factor the crew believed would lower their risk of detection.

Chief Moore's people knew just about everything the Bandits were doing but could not get anyone on the inside—no one, at least, until recently, when one of the Bandits made a major mistake. Police Officer Frank Patrice had arranged to meet Domingo Sanchez, the boss of one of the smaller drug gangs, for the monthly payoff of about a thousand dollars. Sanchez pleaded with Patrice for more time, saying he could not have the money until after the weekend. Patrice located Gabe Perone, who was attending the summer conference of the PBA at the Concord Hotel in the Catskill Mountains upstate. Perone's angry reaction to the possibility of a late payment so unnerved Patrice that he found Sanchez and, holding him by the feet from the sixth floor of the warehouse scaffold, screamed at him, "You motherfucker, you have that package in twelve hours or you will fly."

Up until then, the Bandits kept the drug dealers in check by threatening them with the law, never with rough stuff, which gets people worried and makes them do crazy things like ratting you out. Patrice, who was just plain dumb, panicked, and of course he didn't dare tell the boss. Sanchez also panicked, and he reported the threat to one of Chief Brendan Moore's operatives, who promised to help—but only if the frightened drug dealer would reveal the meeting place for the next payoff.

By the time Patrice had his next meeting with Sanchez, the sixth floor of the Bush Terminal warehouse had been turned into a sound stage by Moore's people, who placed multiple listening devices and videotaping equipment throughout the warehouse. The sights and sounds of the transaction between Sanchez and Patrice were later reviewed by Commissioner Nevins, Chief Moore, and Inspector Pressler. And, of course, this regular meeting place for the Bandits remained under constant surveillance by Chief Moore's unit until a plan could be found to catch the thieves.

For Nevins, at long last the time had come to test his theory that cops could act like cops and take police action against corrupt police officers, not as part of any specialized unit but as regular patrol officers assigned to precinct duty.

"Bernie, you're the guy with the reputation and respect to make this happen. Honest cops will follow you. And if you can make it work, the way cops look at corruption will change. We will be able to assign real cops to Internal Affairs on a rotating basis, make it a career path to detective, to other better assignments, in short, to make it a respectable place to work. "We"—the police commissioner stood up for dramatic emphasis—"can smash the blue wall . . . forever!"

Pressler didn't respond, waiting to see what Nevins had in store for him.

"Bernie, some day this is going to happen, but if you can't do it, I don't know anyone else who can."

Now it was Pressler's turn to talk. "But what do we do about the PBA and the SBA? As long as they protect their members regardless of the charges, doesn't that encourage police officers to look the other way?"

Nevins smiled and said, "Bernie, you're absolutely right." Turning to Chief Moore, he said, "Ask Billy Lally to come in, and see if Sean Tobin is available."

Police Officer William Lally entered the room, cautiously but with his usual broad smile. Five foot nine and about 140 compact pounds, he had golden blond hair and clear blue eyes that seemed to sparkle when he smiled. Lally was just thirty-four years of age and single, and some thought he was the typical young ladies' man of a cop. That mistake was made by an older opponent in the race for PBA president, whom Lally crushed in the election. The race to succeed the long-serving and seemingly invincible Rusty Russo created particular interest in the rank-and-file police officers because of his sudden resignation. It angered the veteran officeholders in the PBA because it left them to scurry around for a successor. In contrast, a coalition of African Americans, Asians, Latinos, and women joined forces with young white officers to support Billy Lally. It was the right time for someone like him.

Commissioner Nevins was particularly pleased about the election results because of Lally's credentials as a progressive. Someone who could lead an increasingly diverse department of women and people of color was exactly what Nevins needed for the changes he had in mind. Since Lally's election slate included an African American, it was the first time in the history of the union that one of its trustees was other than white. Moreover, Lally immediately began grooming a twelve-year veteran policewoman, Lisa Keller, to become the first female trustee in the history of the PBA. The commissioner believed that if ever there was a union chief who would understand that the police department had reached a critical crossroad, Lally was the guy. Similarly, Sergeant Sean Tobin, the newly elected president of the SBA, was a young progressive supported by a broad coalition of young female sergeants and a growing number of blacks, Latinos, and Asians who passed the promotional exam.

"Sit down, Billy," Nevins said cordially. "We're happy you had some time to come over."

Lally's face broke out in a broad smile as he replied, "Hey, Boss, I didn't think there was an option!"

The commissioner's secretary announced that Sergeant Tobin had arrived. Lally greeted the young sergeant. "Late as usual, Sarge."

Tobin ignored Lally. "I thought this was a private meeting, Boss," he said with a smile. "I didn't expect to see this lug, but I guess an order is an order." Tobin, the longtime fullback on the football team known as the Finest, was beginning to sag around the middle and pick up some jowls, but otherwise his stocky frame of six feet and some two hundred pounds was still rock solid. With a full mane of red hair worn too long for some of the bosses, deep dimples, and a perpetual smile, he looked like an oversized leprechaun.

It was Nevins's turn to tease, with his favorite Irish brogue imitation. "Now boys, you two dahlin' young men know my reputation as an old union fighter, and you bein' the big shots and all that, I'm much obliged you could find the time to visit a sentimental old man!" After the briefest of pauses, Nevins became very serious. He stood for a moment and then sat on the front edge of the desk once used by the most famous police commissioner of New York City,

Teddy Roosevelt. The commissioner spoke softly. "Boys, I'm going to ask you to do what no other union official in law enforcement has ever done."

"And just what is that, Commissioner?" The response from Lally was flat and very direct. Tobin didn't speak.

"Before I ask you to do anything, I want you to listen to what Brendan has to say, fair enough?"

When Brendan Moore had completed his presentation, which included audio and video tapes of the Bandits of Bush Terminal, Lally shook his head and said simply, "Those mutts make it bad for all of us."

"That's right, Billy, and it's why I want you and Sean to agree that the PBA and the SBA will refuse to furnish lawyers for these criminals."

"But, Commissioner, as you know, our organization gives, as a benefit of membership, legal help to any cop in trouble. And the fact is that since legal fees are funded by membership dues, it is considered an entitlement," Lally said. Tobin didn't respond but just nodded his head vigorously in support.

Nevins walked over to where the young union leaders sat, placed a fatherly hand on their shoulders, and said earnestly, "Boys, how many cops and their families need to be destroyed before this department and your unions decide to finally tear down this fucking Blue Wall of Silence, and with it the blue wall of mindless support?" Without waiting for a reply, Nevins continued, "I promise you both that if we can pull this off Internal Affairs will no longer be a place for jackasses and flakes who waste time harassing cops with Mickey Mouse rules. It will be an honorable place to work and a positive career path because it will lock up all sorts of crooks, whether or not they're cops. The fact is, and I know you both believe this, any cop who protects a drug dealer is no longer a cop!"

Nevins now shook both union officials' hands, a signal that the meeting was over, and said, "All I ask is that you think it over. Whatever your decision is, I will understand."

Chief Moore filled out the rest of his intelligence report to the commissioner, which included patrol strength and an assessment of those who were likely to buy into Nevins's plan.

"There are 180 police officers at the 75th Precinct, including twenty-three sergeants, six lieutenants, a captain, and a deputy inspector. The nighttime supervising sergeant and six uniformed cops, five males and one female, are our Bush Terminal crowd. There are nineteen officers, including one sergeant, who are prime candidates for our team. We recommend from that list eight officers, including that young sergeant, Steven Robert Holt. His middle name is from his uncle, whom you will no doubt remember, retired sergeant Robert Mulvey." The commissioner smiled as he recalled the sincere young police officer from Nevins's days as the commanding officer at the 67th Precinct in Brooklyn. So much had happened over the years to both of them.

"Didn't Mulvey retire out of Internal Affairs and move with his wife upstate?"

"Yes, sir," Moore responded with a great deal of pride as he recalled the role he had in convincing then–Police Commissioner Sampson to restore Mulvey to duty.

"It's a small world," said Pressler, as he, too, remembered how he and Kenny Rattigan argued with Sampson to do the right thing, "but do you think Holt would be interested after what happened to his uncle?"

"We don't think he knows about that," responded Chief Moore.

"In any event," Moore continued, "the eight officers on our list are among the most active police officers since their assignment to the Seven-five and at every previous assignment. Not only has there been no hint of scandal among them, they are known in the precinct as super straight. While Holt is well respected by those police officers who have worked for him on various tours, he is despised by the Bandits of Bush Terminal."

The seven uniformed officers on Moore's list were Holt's protégés. He often chose them to team up with him on the more dangerous assignments. Pressler decided to approach Holt directly. If he could convince the young sergeant, the rest would be easy.

"With respect, Inspector, I don't want to be a damned guinea pig. I like this job too much. But as much as I despise those mutts, they are the reason Internal Affairs exists."

"But Steven," Pressler reasoned, "your arrest activity makes you one of the most productive sergeants in this job. Isn't a crime a crime?"

"Sure it is, Boss, but what do you do about other cops, the honest ones, who would treat me like a fink? What has this department ever done to change that attitude?" Of course, Steven knew, as did Pressler, that he had made a telling argument.

Pressler argued that attitudes could change if this initiative was successful and that the commissioner was committed to making sweeping changes, particularly at Internal Affairs. At the end of nearly two hours, Pressler could see that he was not getting anywhere and that Steven was becoming uncomfortable, so he decided to use what he had planned only as a last resort. He stood, as did Holt, who was relieved that this seemed to signal an end to the meeting.

"Look, son, you have every right to be skeptical about this approach and what it can mean for this job for decades to come. We've asked you to be a trailblazer in a department that does not look for new ideas. We built the Blue Wall of Silence, permitting cops to hide behind it, and we nurtured it by our inertia, and now, suddenly, with no guarantees, other than our word that we are committed to change, we place a demand on you that you have a right to reject."

Now Pressler seemed to be pleading, something very much out of character for this gruff street cop. "Steven, don't think of the potential future benefits to the department. Think of this in human terms. How many honest and dedicated police officers have been hurt because none of us did a damned thing about corruption?" Pressler sat down and continued. "Why not speak to your Uncle Robert and see what he says about this."

"Sure, but why do you think he can change my decision?" Holt was puzzled.

"Steven, just ask him. Let him tell you why."

That evening Steven flew to Albany, where he rented a car and began the journey to Delaware County and the beautiful rural village of Delhi, where Robert Mulvey and his wife and three children had moved when he retired.

The following morning, Steven left the local motel in Delhi and, using the directions supplied by a perplexed Robert Mulvey, began the last leg of his trip. Although it was late in the summer, Delaware County was beginning to feel the first hint of fall. The slight chill was offset by the majestic though blinding sun rising over the magnificent Catskill Mountains. Soon the paved road turned to a rich, dark dirt road winding up to the top of a hill overlooking a lushly green and broad valley, which disappeared only as it reached the horizon. At the crest of the hill was a raised two-level ranch-style house, looking quite new.

In the driveway was a used brown Ford station wagon. A tall, comely woman, whose jeans and sweater showed a body still firm at fifty, answered the door. Her hair, a darker shade of blond with a touch of strawberry, was worn up and back in a ponytail. With a rich tan and a sprightly smile, delicately sculpted cheekbones, and almond-shaped eyes, softly tinted green, she could have easily passed for a woman not yet past her midthirties, but that was of no consequence to her; when age was mentioned, she almost always said, "It's only a number!" Steven greeted her with a smile and a quick kiss.

"Hi, Aunt Shannon. How does it feel to look like the farmer's daughter?"

"Now, Steven, save those lines for a future conquest. You look great. Your uncle can't wait to see you."

All those years ago, while he was in rehab, Robert wrote two unanswered letters to Shannon asking her to understand that their last horrific meeting was the product of his addiction. He pledged to her that he would remain sober for the rest of his life even if she could not forgive him.

When he was released, he received one of life's few second chances. As he walked along the crushed stone pathway away from the facility that had liberated him from his drug-induced nightmare, he was lost in his thoughts. Suddenly he heard a soft, familiar voice. "Hey, Sarge, care for a lift?" Mulvey dropped his bags and ran into the waiting arms of Shannon Kelly.

Robert had gone into town to get the newspapers and something for breakfast. So Shannon Kelly Mulvey, still possessing her FBI-agent interrogation skills, though she had retired several years ago to raise their two boys and a girl, used the little time available in Robert's absence to probe the purpose of Steven's trip with a few questions.

"Now, now, Aunt Shannon," Steven teased, "you know very well that we don't cooperate with the feds."

Not deterred, Shannon persisted, "Seriously, Steven, is there something wrong?"

Steven fixed his eyes directly on his aunt and asked, "What happened to Uncle Robert? How did he get assigned to Internal Affairs?"

Shannon's eyes welled up immediately and her nose reddened. She blurted out. "Steven, for God's sake, who put you up to this? Have you come all the way up here to break his heart?"

Confused, Holt responded, "I don't know what you're talking about."

Before another word passed, the doorway was filled with Robert Mulvey, whose broad smile evaporated at the sight of Shannon. He demanded, "Steven, what the hell is going on?"

Steven walked over to his uncle and, giving him a loving hug and a kiss on his cheek, said, "Uncle Robert, I really don't understand why Aunt Shannon is upset."

Shannon recovered quickly and said simply, as if dismissing the whole thing as a mistake, "I thought Steven was angry about your transfer to that fink squad at IAD."

"No, of course not," Steven protested. "Inspector Pressler suggested I come here to get some advice. He suggested that it was important that I see you, but when I asked him why he acted all mysterious. He said that I should ask you why. When I tell you what the inspector and the department have in mind for me, and why I've decided not to be involved, I think you'll agree with me, so I don't know what the big deal is that I should come all the way up here. Is there something I should know about you and the job?"

Mulvey answered guardedly, "Well, let's see what you have going on."

As Holt laid out the extent of the corruption that ravaged the 75th Precinct, it of course reminded Mulvey immediately of the corruption that overwhelmed the 13th Division and how he had been persuaded by Inspector Connolly to go undercover. Mulvey recalled the great success of the operation and then all of the bitterness and his destructive behavior that followed. He decided not to give Steven any of the details other than to tell him that most cops disapproved of his undercover activity because it led to the arrest and imprisonment of so many other cops. He explained that it didn't matter to most police officers that those cops from the 13th were corrupt. The culture of the police department and the mentality of most police officers was that cops don't treat other cops like perps, using undercover activity, including electronic listening devices, to gather evidence against them. Most police officers believed that was the job of the feds or IAD, and it really didn't matter that the feds were at best uninterested in police corruption or that IAD was a joke.

What truly excited Mulvey was the plan that Steven described for honest cops to conduct an investigation of rogue cops and then move in and make arrests. Finally it would be legitimate for police officers outside IAD to arrest crooks who happened to be police officers. It seemed to him to be a historic opportunity for trained and dedicated police officers to clean up their own mess.

"Steven," he said passionately, "you can't let this get away. Pressler and the other bosses see in you a true leader who can convince other honest cops to follow. Our department has suffered for too long under a false sense that snitching is wrong, and I'd be the last to attempt to convince cops that it is the only way to root out corruption. But this is very different. You've got to go for it."

Mulvey saw no point to telling Steven the complete story of his fall to the very brink of oblivion and how he ended up at IAD. He would soon decide that withholding all of that was a mistake he would deeply regret.

Alright, Inspector," Holt said, "let's get on with it."

For the next several days Steven met individually with the seven young police officers suggested by Moore; they were his first choices as well. Most of them raised the same question Holt put to Pressler: How would honest cops feel about this operation? The answer was even more difficult because none of these officers had Holt's motivation—the anger and pain he felt about what had happened to his hero, Uncle Robert. He reported back to Inspector Pressler that five of the officers were in and ready to go.

On most Friday evenings, exactly at 2300 hours, or 11:00 P.M., the Bandits of Bush Terminal would gather to divide up the purse, as they called it. The routine included each of the Bandits meeting earlier with a member of each of the drug gangs and picking up a package, which contained as much as twenty-five hundred dollars and as little as a thousand. Their leader, a sergeant, would arrange to meet with one member from each of two gangs, and the six other bandits would each meet with one member from the remaining six gangs. The assignments for the pickups were rotated and chosen by lot. This would ensure a larger share for the boss, who was, after all, the senior thief. On Thursday afternoon, the sergeant drew Domingo Sanchez, head of one of the Latino gangs, and Huey Davis, head of one of the black gangs.

Building 7 was the last building in Bush Terminal. The sixth floor of Building 7 had been the meeting place for the Bandits for more than six months, a concern for some of the crew members because they believed that habit and routine could lead to discovery.

Shortly before 11:00 P.M. Police Officer Frank Patrice arrived, followed soon by three other members of the corrupt gang of cops. Each had a package from his drug pickup. By 11:45, Patrice became concerned that the sergeant, Ruben, and Perone had not shown. He and the others did not know that this was a trap, nor did they know that their boss had been tipped off earlier in the day and had ordered Ruben and Perone to stay clear of the meeting.

Instead, the three met in the backroom of Kelsey's bar, not far from the 75th Precinct, to divide up a smaller but safer share of the money.

"What the fuck is goin' down here, Boss?" asked Perone.

"Whatever it is, you can be sure that scumbag Moore is involved. He's got his finks everywhere," the sergeant replied.

When the sergeant picked up the money from Sanchez earlier at his social club, the drug dealer told him how "that asshole" Patrice threatened to kill him and how he complained to a friend of his in the Police Intelligence Bureau. Sanchez said he was approached by some captain who worked for Moore who told Sanchez that if he didn't bring him to Bush Terminal and show him where the payoffs were made, he would put Sanchez out of business. Since the payoff locations were moved regularly, the captain's information about Bush Terminal was stale. Sanchez thought he was tricking the captain by bringing him to the sixth floor of Building 7, where he had occasionally made his payoff. What Sanchez didn't know was that while the payoff spots changed regularly, the sixth-floor location remained where the Bandits split up the proceeds.

"Freeze," commanded Sergeant Holt, as Pressler and the rest of the detail surrounded Patrice and the other crooked cops. "You're under arrest."

Holt then began a familiar recitation: "You have the right to remain silent. Anything you say will . . ."—the arrest warnings. All too familiar to cops, now converted in an instant to criminals.

One of the Bandits complained that it was no treatment for a cop. Pressler shut him up immediately, shouting, "You're not a cop, you're a fucking thief." The stark realization of his new condition caused the disgraced police officer to cry, sobbing out of control.

The news of the multiple arrest of corrupt cops by honest cops from the same police precinct didn't get the attention Mayor Richardson thought it should. The more the spin doctors from his press office tried to sell the story of cops, "real cops," arresting bad cops, the more crime-beat reporters, then columnists, and finally the editorial writers turned away from the story. They just didn't get it. During a time when police corruption wasn't very unusual, the attitude of most reporters was, "More crooked cops, where's the fucking story?"

The cynicism did not affect the pride felt by Police Commissioner Nevins. He had done it! With one strategic strike he had legitimized for street cops—perhaps forevermore, he hoped—the arrest of police officers who violated the law and who had done violence to the system of justice.

The commissioner immediately issued orders directing that no police officer could advance to the Detective Bureau and be given the coveted gold police shield without a minimum of eighteen months of assignment to Internal Affairs. Internal Affairs was no longer a division but had been raised to the more prestigious level of bureau, the equal of Intelligence, Homicide, Major Frauds, and the other high-level units of the NYPD.

Moreover, in order to be eligible for promotion through the three grades of detective, from third to second to first, an additional tour of one year at IAB would be mandated. Nor would any police officer be eligible to take any promotional test offered for sergeant, lieutenant, or captain without volunteering to serve at least six months in Internal Affairs. Finally, no captain could attain the rank of inspector or the various levels of chief without at least eighteen months of duty at IAB.

Commissioner Nevins not only had succeeded in smashing the blue wall, he had removed the stigma of serving in IAB, by making service there not only tied to promotion but honorable. Within a week, the waiting list for assignment to the new bureau required the creation of a lottery.

The day after the roundup, the PBA and SBA issued this press statement: "We have reviewed the evidence against the defendants known as the Bandits of Bush Terminal. We have decided that these charges are so substantial that the defendants are not entitled to be represented by lawyers hired by the PBA or the SBA." The statement was signed by William P. Lally, President, PBA, and Sean Tobin, President, SBA.

To the surprise of no one, certainly not Commissioner Nevins or Inspector Pressler, Steven Robert Holt was the first police officer with the rank of sergeant to apply for assignment to IAB.

# 38

Junior's Restaurant, Flatbush Avenue, Brooklyn,
Early November 1992

Famous worldwide for its cheesecake, Junior's of Brooklyn was the place to be seen if you were a lawyer with political ambition. Each morning at breakfast, beginning at 6:30, every table became a power center. The Kings County political leaders, Republican and Democrat, met at separate tables, with supplicants—lawyers looking for jobs as law secretaries to the various judges, whose staffs were, for the most part, controlled by these political leaders. Of course, no one would ever admit that such blatant patronage still existed. It was also an opportunity to meet with fund-raisers, who provided the lifeblood of politics: money.

These meetings also offered opportunities for constituents to ask for favors, or, as they were referred to in the political world, "contracts." A job given to a constituent, or the relative or friend of a constituent, was a contract that was filled. Of course, just as in the commercial use of the term "contract," something was always expected in return. The payback had become far more sophisticated since so many political leaders had landed in jail for bribery. They developed what one political columnist observed was legit graft—a payback, to be sure, but accomplished in such a way as to avoid criminal prosecution: a long, fun-filled weekend in the Bahamas for the political leader and his wife or his girlfriend, paid for by the wealthy uncle of the recipient of a political appointment; a generous contribution to the election campaign of one of the political leader's chosen candidates for the state legislature, months after the contract was filled, to make the connection between the job and the political contribution impossible to prove. Politics was still lucrative for those who controlled the jobs.

There was also a section in the rear of Junior's that, by an unwritten code, would remain off-limits to any other guest if it was occupied by people conducting serious and confidential business. That was where, early one Saturday morning, a meeting about Steven Holt's case was held. It was at Brendan Moore's request, assembled in order for him to give a report about his investigation. Settled around the table were Larry Green, Shannon and Robert Mulvey, Deputy Chief Bernie Pressler, and Queens County DA Kenneth Rattigan and his longtime mentor, Brooklyn DA Buddy Cooper. Moore trusted the ability and judgment of each—with the exception of Robert Mulvey, but obviously, he couldn't be excluded.

"No one is around who can tell us anything about the murders," Moore began, "but my guys were told by the young drunks who hang out around Bush Terminal that there was a junkie who used to cop drugs, mostly crack cocaine, from them, who disappeared sometime in late December of 1990. He didn't have a name, but since he always wore battle fatigues, they called him Soldier."

Moore paused. He was actually enjoying his brief return to the intriguing world of informers. "One thing was of particular interest: Soldier only copped drugs at the beginning of the month. They remember that because they would try to sell him crack later on in the month and he would tell them that he only had a few bucks to buy Thunderbird wine."

Pressler was the first to speak, but what he said was something that the others had already guessed. "He is either dead or he still gets a pension, sent to wherever he's moved."

"Correct," said Moore, "but let's understand something. None of those mutts we spoke with said that this guy saw anything, so his disappearance may be unrelated to the murders."

"While that may be true, I sure would like to find the guy," Rattigan volunteered.

Shannon was particularly enthused about Moore's information. "I've got some friends in the postal service, and if this guy used a post office box, and he's still alive, they should be able to find out his new address."

The excitement began to get to Rattigan. "I've got a friend, a contributor to my campaign, who is the president of the check cashers association. He should be able to find out where Soldier cashed his check. He could have cashed it at a local bar not far from Bush Terminal."

Pressler followed up. "They said he had a bad limp, so I assume he didn't go very far. Hey, Kenny," he said, turning to Rattigan, "any problem with me checking that out?"

Before Rattigan could answer, Green stood and, displaying his nastiest scowl, said, "You know, you fucking law enforcement types never fail to be predictable. Does it occur to you that Holt may be guilty and that Soldier may be the missing link in Goss's case?"

Mulvey broke the long silence with a shout. "No, Larry, no, he's innocent."

"Listen to me, Robert, and all of you, the heart is never a substitute for brains." Green hoped that this band of dedicated friends and loved ones would realize the consequences of what they were saying. "What if this fucking alcoholic junkie gives Steven up? Or let's say he can provide information to exonerate him—how do you know if he is credible? And don't answer, because not one of you, other than Brendan and I, can make an objective assessment. So here's the deal, if Soldier is found, only Brendan and I will interview him."

Green waited for the reaction. Not sensing any, he continued, "So that's settled, okay?"

One of the detectives assigned to the Kings County district attorney's office detective squad entered the rear sanctuary of Junior's and quietly approached District Attorney Cooper. He whispered in the DA's ear.

Cooper excused himself. "I've got an urgent call." He said to Green, "I'll only be a minute. Wait till I get back."

The car's horn was incessant. Its crimson-faced driver was screaming racial epithets at the car in the lane directly in front of his, waiting for the traffic light to change. Gabe Perone took his shield out of its case and began to wave it wildly, shouting, "I'm a fuckin' cop, move it!" Perone hours before had been at a beer racket in another section of Brooklyn. He was quite drunk. "For chrissake, you fuckin' monkey, get outta the way!"

The light on Lincoln Road, a boulevard-sized thoroughfare with two lanes on either side, changed to green, but the automobile carrying the Reverend Cedric Lyons, pastor emeritus of Salvation AME Church in the Bedford-Stuyvesant section of Brooklyn, did not move. Reverend Lyons, revered by the African American community of Brooklyn, had ordered his driver to hold on "while I give this young man a piece of my mind." When Reverend Lyons got out, Perone leaped from his car to confront the elderly pastor. Reverend Lyon raised his right hand and said softly, with a smile, "Now, son, what has got you acting like this?" On the sidewalk, a crowd of African American neighbors began to gather.

"Get back in your car now, or I'll fuckin' drop you," Perone ranted.

The pastor's chauffeur, a huge black man who was a former heavyweight boxer, began to walk toward Perone. He warned, "Watch your language." Perone fired twice, hitting the man in the shoulder and the right leg. He fell to the pavement.

Horrified, Pastor Lyons pleaded, "For the Lord's sake, put that gun down." Perone wheeled in the direction of the minister and put two bullets into his abdomen. He also fell to the ground.

The crowd on the sidewalk began to shout angrily, but Perone waved his gun, keeping them at a distance. In minutes the police were all over the street. Several of them ordered Perone to drop his gun. One cop smashed Perone over the head, sending him crashing to the pavement. He was manacled from behind and thrown into the rear of a police cruiser. The police commander for the local precinct, a well-respected African American inspector, was able to calm the crowd. He took immediate action, ordering officers to place the injured pastor and his driver in two separate patrol cars and rush them to Kings County Hospital. He decided that waiting for ambulances to respond would be too risky. He was told by one of his police officers, an emergency medical technician, that both victims had been stabilized and would survive. Before leaving the scene, the inspector addressed the crowd, which had grown to more than a hundred: "Most of you know me and know that when I talk, I tell the truth. First of all, Reverend Lyons and his driver are okay. Secondly, this guy we arrested is a cop, and I want you to know that I'm going to make sure he never gets out of prison."

Cooper returned shortly and informed the anxious group at Junior's, "Police Officer Gabe Perone has been arrested in Brooklyn. Perone claims that he is an eyewitness to all three murders charged to Sergeant Holt and that they were committed at Bush Terminal. He wants to make a deal."

# 39

*People v. Holt,*
November 10, 1992

"May it please the Court." Goss bowed and began cautiously, with a clumsily obsequious attempt to curry favor with Judge McGowan.

It didn't work. McGowan glowered down from his lofty perch and sternly interrupted. "Now what?"

Goss quickly responded, "Your Honor, the people found a witness late last night, and I wish to call him."

"Very well," McGowan said curtly, "call him now."

"Well, Your Honor, I can't do that right away. I—"

Before Goss could proceed, McGowan shouted, "Inside."

Sergeant Kurland walked briskly from the courtroom, as bewildered as the rest of the spectators. He spotted Lieutenant Artie Morelli of the Suffolk Couty Homicide Division, whom he had met at a police fraternal organization function several years before.

"So, Lou, what's goin' on?" Kurland asked anxiously.

"A police officer named Gabe Perone got busted, somethin' about a shooting in Brooklyn. He's agreed to testify against Holt," replied Morelli. Then, pointing in Holt's direction, he added quickly, "I think we've got him!"

"Steven," Kurland began quietly, "what can Gabe Perone testify about?"

The blood had drained from Holt's face, but his answer was firm and measured. "I haven't the slightest idea except that Perone is a goddamned crook, one of several of the Bandits of Bush Terminal who didn't show up the night we arrested the others. I was always certain that he and the rest of them were tipped off to our raid. But he'd probably say anything."

When Kurland told Holt that Perone had been involved in a shooting and was offering to testify in return for a deal, Steven shrugged his shoulders and said, "Hey, Sarge, what can you expect from that mutt? But it doesn't matter, Green will tear him to pieces."

Kurland smiled and said, "So you're feelin' pretty good?" Without waiting for an answer, he continued. "But what do you think he'll say?"

Quite suddenly Holt seemed concerned as he replied in a whisper, "He shoulda been dead."

"What did you say?"

"Never mind, Sarge. Thanks for the visit. And oh, keep your ears open."

# 40

VA Hospital, Bridgeport, Connecticut,
November 12, 1992

"The good news, Larry, is I have him." Brendan Moore began, trying hard not to raise expectations.

"Yeah, so what's the bad news?" interrupted Larry Green impatiently.

"He's been in the psychiatric ward of a veterans' hospital up here in Connecticut for almost two years suffering from a post-traumatic stress disorder."

Moore explained that sometime late in December of 1990 Soldier, whose real name was Bradley Coles, was found by police officers, wandering on a pier at the Brooklyn waterfront, several blocks from Bush Terminal. He was incoherent and appeared to be in shock. When they searched him looking for identification, they found among the papers in his wallet a discharge certificate from the Marine Corps that listed his rank as major.

The officers took Coles to the United States Veterans Administration Hospital in Brooklyn, where he was admitted for observation and diagnosis. Before his transfer to the VA hospital located in a suburb of Bridgeport, Connecticut, which specialized in the treatment of this mental disorder, Coles received his regular disability check. Using the information supplied to Shannon Mulvey by her contacts in the United States Postal Inspection Service, Moore was able to trace him there.

"I'm coming up," shouted Green.

"Okay, Larry, but it won't be very helpful," Moore replied. "The major, according to his psychiatrist, is withdrawn and frequently catatonic. When he responds at all, it's limited for the most part to guttural sounds."

Earlier in the day, one of the jurors had informed Judge McGowan that her brother had died suddenly and that his funeral was set for Monday. The judge recessed the trial without objection by either side to Tuesday morning at ten.

"That gives me four days to be up there," said Green in a call later to Brendan Moore, "and get firsthand from this guy's doctor if he can be of any help."

Assistant District Attorney Wally Goss welcomed the time off from trial to permit him a chance to negotiate with Police Officer Gabe Perone's lawyer. Because of the extended conflicts created by this new development, Brooklyn District Attorney Cooper and Suffolk County District Attorney Crowley filed a joint request with the chief administrative judge of Kings County, appointing Crowley special district attorney to prosecute the case against Perone.

At first, lawyers and community activists representing Pastor Cedric Lyons were angry and concerned that Perone would not be punished for his racist violence. In order to allay those fears, Mayor Richardson invited Reverend Lyons, his family, and all his representatives and followers to Gracie Mansion for a meeting with Cooper, together with the Queens County district attorney, Kenny Rattigan, who had a particularly good rapport with Brooklyn's African American community when he was Cooper's rackets chief. They were joined by Crowley.

Crowley did not mince words. "However important it is for us to bring justice to the memory of three people who were brutally assassinated during the Christmas season of 1990, I solemnly pledge to you that no agreement will be made with that murderous, bigoted thug Perone in return for his testimony unless he accepts a substantial prison sentence. Moreover, the terms of that prison sentence will be discussed with Pastor Lyons and his attorneys and will be subject to their approval."

Later that day, Perone's attorney, Carey Bremen, and District Attorney Crowley met at Crowley's office in Suffolk County. Bremen began slowly, "According to the press reports, you didn't give us much room to negotiate."

Crowley put on his best poker face and replied, "Carey, my boy, your client didn't give himself any room! And if he didn't have something to sell, we would be here discussing one of your scholarly treatises on the rules of evidence, and not wasting any words about that dirtbag you represent."

Carey Bremen, a former senior bureau chief in Brooklyn under District Attorney Cooper, had previously served as president of the Brooklyn Bar Association and recently been voted president of the prestigious New York State Bar Association by his peers. At age fifty-four, as an associate professor at Fordham University School of Law, the author of half a dozen critically acclaimed legal textbooks, and the senior partner in one of the better-known white-collar criminal defense firms in New York City, Bremen would not ordinarily defend the likes of Perone. His practice mostly dealt with crooked financiers, an occasional corrupt union leader, or a lawyer facing prison and the loss of his license to practice law. He had only agreed to represent Perone as a favor to the PBA president, Billy Lally, who would from time to time retain Bremen's law firm when a conflict of interest precluded the PBA lawyers from representing one of the members.

Bremen was always nattily dressed in three-piece suits with hand-tied bow ties, the appropriate sartorial-splendor uniform of a Hollywood version of a trial lawyer. His jet black hair was receding on both sides of his head, leaving a sort of peak in the middle of his high forehead. Although he was blessed with a perpetual wistful smile, Professor Bremen felt quite uncomfortable representing the likes of Gabe Perone. Nevertheless, he was an advocate, so he would do his duty.

"But Jim," protested Bremen to the Suffolk County district attorney, "Gabe Perone is your case! Larry Green has destroyed all your forensic people, and your only hope is an eyewitness. Perone is the only other person present at Bush Terminal who can give you the details of what was quite simply an execution." Crowley never changed his expression as Bremen continued, "With Perone, you then set a solid foundation for motive. Holt is the only one with a motive to kill Scott Ruben. He hated Ruben because he escaped the Bush Terminal roundup. Your detectives have informed you that he planned to kill Perone if he hadn't been arrested."

"Okay." Crowley had heard enough. "Perone faces a sentence of between five years and twenty-five for each charge of attempted murder. You know Judge McGowan's reputation—he will have no problem giving Perone consecutive prison terms. So what's he looking at? If he cooperates, I'll ask the judge for twenty-five years, which, as you know, means that he will do seventeen and change. Of course, that is if the pastor and his driver agree. If he doesn't testify, I'll ask for fifty, which doesn't let him see the parole board for thirty-four years—if he's still alive."

Bremen appeared stunned, although in truth he did not expect much better. "How much time do we have?"

"I've ordered a special grand jury in Brooklyn to meet through the weekend. They will be ready to file at 5:00 P.M. on Monday, two counts of attempted murder." Crowley's office would delay the filing of the indictment until a few minutes before the clerk's office closed to minimize the possibility of a leak to the press.

Now Crowley stood and took hold of Bremen's right shoulder. "Carey, after the grand jury files on Monday, there will be no more deal."

# 41

Hospital, Bridgeport, Connecticut,
November 13, 1992

"I am afraid, Mr. Green, Major Coles can be of very little use to you or to himself," Dr. Jeanne de Lourdes, chief of psychiatric services for the Bridgeport VA hospital, began to explain.

In the eighteen months since his transfer from the hospital in Brooklyn, the diagnosis for Coles's mental health condition had remained largely speculative. Of course, his symptoms were consistent with posttraumatic stress disorder, which the psychiatrists concluded was related to his combat service in Vietnam. The thing that troubled the doctors who reviewed Coles's chart and made observations of him when he appeared to be awake was that he did not seem to respond to traditional treatment plans designed to disassociate his memories of Vietnam from present reality. His condition was worsened initially by the violent withdrawal he suffered when he was forced to abstain from drugs he regularly used on the street.

"For most patients," explained Dr. de Lourdes, "the symptoms disappear after approximately six months. But for others the symptoms are chronic, lasting for years."

She told Green and Brendan Moore that there was something perplexing about Major Coles. From time to time he would appear to be in recovery during the day, and just before he retired to bed, quite suddenly, he would revert and be subjected to violent nightmares.

"Can you be certain that the major's disorder is limited to his experience in Vietnam?" Green asked finally, after a long pause he used to reflect on Dr. de Lourdes's analysis.

"Mr. Green, our science has not reached a stage which goes beyond speculation, and without the benefit of observation during the time closest to Major Coles's discharge from the military, it's impossible to say. But hypothetically, if the major were confronted with another violent experience, it is quite possible that the symptoms of posttraumatic stress disorder could return."

Green pressed on. "What if the major was shown something which re-created the environment where that violence occurred—for example, a picture of a jungle battlefield in Vietnam, or a similar environment, where the patient witnessed something that was particularly violent. Would that cause any reaction?"

"It's entirely possible, but what are you getting at?"

Larry Green turned to Moore and said, "Brendan, show Dr. de Lourdes the photographs."

Moore's people had shot a dozen or so angles on the floor in Bush Terminal. Moore also had pictures of Holt, Ruben, Perone, and the other indicted Bush Terminal Bandits, as well as other suspects who along with Perone got away by not showing up at the time of Holt's raid at the terminal.

Major Coles was led into Dr. de Lourdes's office. Coles was just under six feet with a trim figure, kept that way through vigorous exercise during his lucid periods. His hair was a silver gray, and the deep lines in his face made him appear much older than his fifty-one years. His greeting was a silent shy smile, which together with his hospital clothing and slippers made him look very vulnerable.

The pictures were placed on two sides of the walls of Dr. de Lourdes's office and were covered at Green's request. The psychiatrist insisted that she be the only one to speak. She would ask the major first if he recognized the floor pictures of the warehouse at Bush

Terminal, and then if he recognized the men in the photographs. Larry Green selected the order in which the pictures of these men would be displayed.

The first four pictures shot inside the warehouse produced no reaction from Major Coles, but the next two, shot from what Moore's investigators surmised was Coles's makeshift loft, brought a nod and a broad smile of apparent recognition. When the floor shots were completed, Green could feel his palms become moist. The pictures of Holt and the other three were set facedown, held by Scotch tape on a piece of drafting paper: Suddenly the doctor turned the paper over to reveal the photographs. Major Coles looked down at the display, then jumped up and, pointing with a series of jabs, began screaming, "Him, him, him!"

The attendants could not restrain the distraught former Marine officer. Coles smashed one attendant across the face, opening up a nasty gash above his right eye, causing a torrent of blood. The other received a judo kick to his groin and immediately doubled over in pain. Dr. de Lourdes had pressed the panic alarm in response to Coles's first outcry, which produced six burly attendants who with great difficulty, and aided by an injection administered by Dr. de Lourdes, brought him under control.

"Oh my God, now what do we do?" asked Green a bit later.

Moore asked the psychiatrist whether there was any way the use of drugs or hypnosis would permit a limited debriefing of Major Coles.

Her answer was too quick, in Green's opinion, and too abstractly clinical for both Moore and Green.

Green shouted, "Look, Doctor, I've got a young kid on trial for three murders he did not commit, and this guy holds the key, so don't be so goddamned quick to reject a plea for help."

Dr. de Lourdes, not prepared for Green's outburst, countered, "Don't you dare raise your voice to me or I'll throw you out of my hospital. I'm a doctor, not a magician, and you should know very well, since you witnessed my patient's reaction, that there is little I can do."

Moore raised his hand, signaling Green, whose face had turned scarlet with fury, to be quiet. "Doctor, there must be something. Isn't there anything you can do to get through to him?"

Dr. de Lourdes was immediately sorry; the grandmotherly seventy-something psychiatrist did not often openly display her emotions, and certainly not anger. She looked at these two men sympathetically. Green's face was filled with anxiety, and Moore's wore a look of frustration that she couldn't recall in anyone else. "Gentlemen, I will try to help you, but you should understand that while hypnosis can remove some symptoms, a substitute symptom often arises, and we have no way of knowing how it will manifest itself. To the extent that hypnosis has been effective in treating repressed feelings, of course I'll try it, but obviously, I'll have to wait several days."

"Doctor," replied Green quietly and dejectedly, "the trial resumes on Tuesday, the day after tomorrow. We are running out of time, and this is a long shot. In any event, we've got to tape your session with him. It's our only hope."

"You're some fuckin' lawyer, Bremen. Why don't you just get me the gas chamber?" Perone screeched in the isolated waiting room in the special security wing of Rikers Island.

The Rock, as it's called, houses inmates sentenced to up to a year in jail, people who are awaiting trial and are unable to post bail, and high-profile inmates like Perone who are being held without bail and in isolation, whose lives would be at risk if they were permitted to mix with the general population. A white cop charged with attempting to kill an elderly African American minister would not last long in a jail that has a high percentage of inmates who are African American.

Bremen at first ignored the sarcasm and allowed the explosion to subside. He then said, "Look, there is no alternative for you, nor is there certainty that you'll be held for the entire term of your sentence. If you put this psychopathic killer cop away for three consecutive life prison sentences, anything is possible. There is no guarantee, but I can move to have you resentenced, after a few years."

At this Perone shouted, "After a few years? For what?"

"For what?" Now it was Bremen's turn to raise his voice. "For trying to kill one of the most respected clergymen in New York City and for trying to kill his driver, all because you didn't like the color of their skin!"

"Oh, bullshit, it was self-defense," replied Perone.

"Okay, that's it," said Bremen. He shouted, "Officer, get me out of here."

"Hey, wait a minute," Perone suddenly pleaded.

Assistant District Attorney Wallace Goss rose confidently from his chair and with just a trace of a smile announced, "Your Honor, the People call New York City Police Officer Gabriel Francis Perone."

Goss took Perone through a series of questions, setting the stage for the grand finale, the in-court identification. It is the drama-filled moment when the witness, in front of the jury, actually identifies the so-called perpetrator of a crime.

"The Boss, Ruben, and I met at the Bush Terminal to split up money we got from the local drug dealers we protected. Suddenly two Spanish guys wandered onto the floor. I guess it must have made quite a spectacle for them to see all that cash lying near our feet. One of them claimed that he had lost his wallet at a party the previous night. As we were trying to figure out what to do, someone shouted across the huge floor of the building, 'Police, freeze.' The Boss and I didn't hesitate for a moment as we ran for the fire exit. When the Boss got out the door he scampered down the stairs. I stayed at the doorway with my gun drawn and took a shooter's position. The guy who shouted came across the floor from the opposite part of the building, and although the lights were pretty dim I recognized him right away. He stooped to where Ruben had dropped his gun and raised his hands, surrendering. The guy shouted, 'You crooked piece of shit,' and then he fired two shots, taking Ruben down. The two Spanish guys dropped on their knees and began to plead. I watched as he slowly and methodically put a round in the temple of one guy, and then he kicked the other guy to the ground and picked him up by his hair and put a round in his temple as he screamed for mercy."

"And then what did you do, Officer Perone?"

"I ran away," Perone replied sheepishly.

"Now, Officer Perone, please stand and look around the courtroom. Can you identify the person you have described as the killer of Hiram and Ramon Rodriguez and Police Officer Scott Ruben?"

"I can."

"Very well, point him out and indicate for the jury a piece of clothing he is wearing."

Pointing to Steven, Perone announced, "That's the man, and he's sitting at the defense table, wearing a blue blazer."

Assistant District Attorney Goss solemnly intoned, "May it please the Court, may the record show that Police Officer Perone has identified the defendant, Steven Robert Holt, as the one who killed all three victims?"

"Yes," McGowan replied.

"That's a shock," grunted Steven to his lawyer.

Now it was Larry Green's turn to shock Justice McGowan, Goss, and the assembled press and spectators. He rose and said confidently, "Your Honor, I have no questions for this person." Green pronounced "person" carefully, separating the two syllables to show his contempt for Perone. He knew that Perone had just committed perjury.

# 42

*People v. Holt,*
November 17, 1992

Goss stood and with a fumbled attempt at flair announced, "And that, Your Honor, is the case on behalf of the People of the State of New York."

"Very well," replied McGowan. Turning to Green, expecting him to make a motion to dismiss, which is always made in the absence of the the jury, he inquired, "Do you want the jury excused, Mr. Green?"

Green stood and replied, "Oh, no, Your Honor, we are prepared to proceed."

"Very well. Do you intend to call witnesses, and how long do you expect to take?"

"Not very long, Your Honor, since I will only present one witness."

"Alright, please proceed."

"I call Bradley Coles."

On cue, the rear doors of the courtroom flew open and Bradley Coles, accompanied by Brendan Moore, began to walk up the aisle slowly, with a slight limp. He was dressed immaculately in a three-piece blue business suit with a light blue button-down shirt and a red-and-dark-blue-striped tie. Moore escorted Coles to the entrance of the well and then took his seat in the front row. Coles continued past Holt and Green, to whom he gave a respectful nod, which he repeated for the jury and Justice McGowan. He mounted the stairs to the witness box and remained standing as he had been instructed previously by Larry Green.

"Do you swear to tell the truth, the whole truth, and nothing but the truth, so help you God?" intoned the clerk of the court.

"I do," the witness replied.

"Please state your name, state of residence, and occupation."

"Bradley Coles, the state of Connecticut, major, United States Marine Corps, retired."

Green's decision minutes earlier not to cross-examine Perone had intrigued everyone in the courtroom, especially the jury. They sat transfixed, watching Coles's every gesture.

The press, which at this stage of the trial included some of the most seasoned commentators from the national scene just couldn't figure out what the hell Green was up to. There was an air of building excitement greeting the arrival of his mystery witness. Kurland had a perplexed look on his face. Across the courtroom directly opposite where Kurland was seated, Mulvey, Shannon, and Lee Moran were huddled together. They knew what to expect from Major Coles, but they also knew that his testimony was fraught with danger. They stared in anticipation as Coles sat down, and they prayed silently.

Green knew full well that what he was doing could bring his career to an abrupt end. He strode confidently to within a few feet of the witness box, and with an uncharacteristic broad smile, he began.

Earlier, Dr. de Lourdes had told Larry Green that the hypnosis therapy seemed to be holding, and while she could assign no scientific reason for its success, she was quite certain that it had a limited duration. Green decided to withhold from Judge McGowan that Coles's testimony would be the result of hypnotic inducement. The lawyer certainly knew that such testimony was inadmissible in

New York State and that if his deception was discovered, McGowan could hold him in contempt and refer his actions to the lawyers' grievance panel, which would undoubtedly recommend a sanction that might very well result in the loss of his license to practice law. Despite all of this, Green decided that he had no other choice.

Dr. de Lourdes was clear about the risk. "He could break down at any time, and since you witnessed it, I need not describe the volcanic nature of his flashbacks. Just ask your questions gently, and pray!"

"I wish I had I that in my arsenal, Doctor," sniffed Green. "I mean prayer and all that stuff!"

Dr. de Lourdes had never quite gotten used to people who volunteer their agnosticism or atheism, so she answered with a smile, "Very well, then I'll pray."

Green began in a soft but firm voice. "Do you recall where you went after your discharge? By the way, what was the nature of that military discharge?"

"I was honorably discharged for medical reasons. I headed back to Brooklyn, where I lived as a kid."

"And did you arrive at your destination?"

"No, I did not," the major answered.

Coles described how he blacked out repeatedly and found himself in a warehouse complex he came to know to be Bush Terminal. He testified about his journey into drug addiction and alcoholism, how he built himself a kind of loft high above the floor of one of the warehouses, and how he lived on his disability checks. Next Green brought him to the time of the murders, the evening of December 19 into the early morning of December 20, 1990.

"Now, Major," Green continued gently, "please describe what you observed." As Coles spoke, Green never lost control of the inquiry. It was important, he would lecture his students, that on direct examination the examiner not permit the witness to give long narrative answers, which frequently could cause jurors to lose interest. In this case that would not be a concern, but control over Major Coles's direct testimony was particularly important because of his fragile mental condition. So Green would interrupt Coles gingerly with well-rehearsed phrases such as "Please hold it there for a minute" or "Let me briefly interrupt you."

Green carefully guided Major Coles through each of the brutal executions. As Coles described the first murder, Green literally held his breath, but the Major's responses, as he recalled in vivid detail how each murder was carefully carried out, were both clear and measured.

When Major Coles had finished this portion of his testimony, Green stepped back to the rear of the jury box, which was directly across from the defense table, on the opposite side of the courtroom, and addressed Judge McGowan. "May it please the Court, may I have the defendant stand up?"

"Of course, Mr. Green," the judge replied. Green motioned to Steven, and he stood up on wobbly legs.

"Major Coles," said Green firmly and confidently, "can you point to the man whom you observed murder Hiram and Ramon Rodriguez, and later kill Police Officer Scott Ruben?"

"I can."

"Please point him out and identify him by a piece of his clothing."

As Coles stood and pointed his right hand and extended his index finger, he began to shake. For a moment, Green actually caught himself thinking of a little prayer in Hebrew he learned at yeshiva school in the Flatbush section of Brooklyn. As Green was finishing his prayer, Coles said in a strong voice, "That's him in the row reserved for police officers, the fat guy in the gray windbreaker."

Judge McGowan stood and commanded, "You, sir, identify yourself, now."

"I'm Sergeant Joseph Kurland of the NYPD."

Goss leaped to his feet and shouted, "Wait a minute. I want to cross-examine this witness."

McGowan responded, "Be quiet."

Now pandemonium broke out across the huge courtroom. The

press corps had jumped to its feet like a well-drilled military squad and headed in Kurland's direction. Some of the spectators, police officer friends of Holt, stood and began to shout at Kurland. Kurland for his part began to look for an escape route.

McGowan stood, pounding his gavel, immediately demanding order and directing the court officers to control the courtroom. Next he ordered the jury removed. When the last juror left the room, McGowan pointed to Kurland and ordered Morelli, "Lieutenant, arrest that man." Morelli quickly handcuffed Kurland from the rear and began to escort him toward a holding pen behind the courtroom.

# 43

Forlini's,
November 25, 1992

It was a Wednesday, late in the afternoon, and the Forlini brothers made a rare exception and shut off their rear room to the public to allow for Steven Holt's celebration. In addition to Steven and his fiancée, Lee Moran, the crowd included Robert and Shannon Mulvey, Larry Green, and the three district attorneys, Cooper of Brooklyn, Rattigan of Queens County, and Crowley of Suffolk County. Brendan and Peggy Moore took their seats at the midpoint of the large table that took up most of the space in Forlini's rear room. Apart from the celebration, everyone wanted to hear Brendan describe how he and his operatives found Soldier, or Major Coles, and the circumstances that led to the dramatic dismissal of the case against Steven and the arrest of Kurland.

Moore, now savoring the spotlight following his brief return from retirement, began to spin his tale. The story he told the group was pieced together from interviews conducted by Moore and his investigators with the drug gang leaders Kurland and his crew protected and with Gabe Perone. Even Kurland, in an effort to shave some time off his prison sentence, eagerly agreed to cooperate. It did not work!

"After the crackdown on the Bandits of Bush Terminal, as you will recall, Steven, your unit began systematically taking out every drug gang which had operated under the protection of Sergeant Kurland and his crew. But Kurland had a plan for the two surviving drug gang bosses."

"Hey, Domingo, look at it this way, with the other gangs out of business, you and Davis here control all of East New York. Here's what we do . . ."

As Kurland outlined his plan on the top floor of Building 1 of Bush Terminal to the two drug gang honchos, they, together with Scott Ruben and Gabe Perone, were shocked by his recklessness. Only a week after several cops in his crew were led away in handcuffs from this very same commercial complex—although on the opposite side of the terminal in Building 7—and despite the fact that Domingo Sanchez fingered those cops for the arrest, Kurland was acting as if nothing had happened. He was determined to resume full operations. He would later explain his plan to Ruben and Parone.

"Look, these two mutts are not planning anytime soon to open up a Burger King or a McDonald's. Without competition, their business is going to explode, and they will need our protection more than ever. In just the last week, Holt and his fucking Girl Scouts have been raiding every one of the spots controlled by Sanchez and Davis." Kurland allowed himself a rare smile, as he continued. "And that fucking rookie sergeant is driving up our price."

Ruben protested, "But Boss, we're all hot. They have to know we were working with the others and—"

"Scottie, me boy," Kurland interrupted, "they got shit on us, and even if the other losers try and give us up, they still got shit because we are all co-conspirators." Kurland continued with a scholarly recitation of the law: Without corroboration, or independent evidence, one co-conspirator could not be found guilty solely on the testimony of another co-conspirator. "Besides," he reasoned, "the three of us are less than two years from getting out of this job, and with the kind of increased take we'll get from our boys Sanchez and Davis, we ain't never gonna worry about money again."

Both Davis and Sanchez understood the risks involved, but they also knew that when the heat was off and they were no longer being watched so closely, they would need protection as their drug-dealing enterprise boomed. Not only did Holt's crackdown increase the cost of protection, the street price for the now scarce crack cocaine tripled.

"That fuckin' guy had balls like a brass monkey, but what other choice did we have but to deal with him?" Sanchez told one of Moore's investigators.

So the payoff meetings continued at Bush Terminal Building 1, although the days were rotated—a Thursday here, a Monday there, not because Kurland thought it a safer strategy, but rather because it made everyone else feel more secure. He would even shift the meeting to different floors of the empty warehouse, suggesting to the others that this would avoid detection by sophisticated surveillance devices.

While the decision to continue operations as usual might have allayed the fears of Ruben and Perone, it was plain stupid and was bound to blow up in Kurland's face. One reason it would fail was circumstances that Kurland could not control. Each time they gathered on the fourth floor of Building 1, they could not know of or see the pair of eyes belonging to a haunted and tired man with a constantly tear-stained face, who watched their every movement from a makeshift loft, high above the factory floor.

Those eyes of Bradley Coles would bulge on those various evenings when, among the debris, three white men would meet and count stacks and stacks of cash, more money than he had ever seen. The purse had grown with the huge increases in the drug business in East New York, now the sole monopoly of Domingo Sanchez and Huey Davis, until it averaged between fifteen and twenty thousand dollars every seven days.

The more he observed of all this, the more Coles became confused. He was too high up near the ceiling to hear anything, so all he could do was watch the routine of counting out the money and then the distribution. He could see that the fattest and oldest of the three men appeared to be the leader and got the largest share.

And one night, not long after these strange clandestine meetings began, his eyes would be transfixed with fear as he watched a gruesome and horrifying sight. It so unnerved Major Coles that he fled his sanctuary and was never seen in the neighborhood again.

Hiram Rodriguez, twenty-six, migrated to Brooklyn in the summer of 1989 from a suburb of San Juan, Puerto Rico. Hiram had a slight but muscular build and the dark good looks of the Hollywood stereotype of a Latin lover. Possessed of an infectious charm and a perpetual broad smile, Hiram was the darling of the campus at the University of Ponce, from which he graduated third in his class with a degree in electrical engineering. But his class standing, his impeccable dress, and his wit and other social skills simply didn't matter, because there were no jobs for electrical engineers anywhere in the Commonwealth of Puerto Rico.

The job market was no better in New York, so he was forced to take an apprenticeship in an electrical supply company, located in Building 3 of Bush Terminal. The pay was decent, and the prospect of getting a union card with the powerful Local 3 of the International Brotherhood of Electrical Workers was fairly certain. After several months, Hiram was able to get the promise of a laborer's job for his baby brother, Ramon, who had just turned eighteen and who appeared to be drifting with no plans for his future. This, together with Hiram's concern about increased drug use by the teenagers in his hometown, led him to convince Ramon to join him in Brooklyn. When Ramon arrived just before Thanksgiving of 1989, Hiram had already secured a job for his little brother.

Each year, Sid Leibowitz, the owner of Leib Electrical Supplies, who cooperated with Moore by giving background information about the Rodriguez brothers, would throw a party to celebrate

Christmas and Hanukkah for his employees, who numbered about twenty. The party grew to several hundred celebrants with all of Leib Electrical's customers, their spouses, and friends. The crowd also included police officers from the 72nd Precinct, who made it a habit to respond quickly to calls from any of the businesses housed at the terminal. The management and maintenance personnel of Bush Terminal were also invited, to show Sid Leibowitz's gratitude for the discount rental for the party space and for allowing the party to spread to several floors of the otherwise vacant Building 1.

The 1990 celebration was set for December 18. The invitation promised much food and drink and a six-piece band for the enjoyment of all, "from eight in the evening until two o'clock the following morning."

"Good Mother of my Lord," groaned Ramon, cradling his head with both hands.

"Well, Ramy," replied Hiram, using his affectionate nickname for his brother, "how many times did I tell you to lay off the booze?"

"Okay, okay, stop the big-brother bullshit and give me some aspirin," Ramon cried out.

"Oh, damn it," Hiram shouted, searching for the painkiller, "I can't find my wallet."

After a fruitless search in the apartment, the brothers decided to go to work. Hiram did take the time to cancel his two credit cards and call the Bush Terminal security desk to see if anyone had returned the wallet. The answer was no, but with a promise that a security officer would take a look through Building 1 later that day. Hiram recalled that he had about sixty dollars in cash, and since he was able to cancel his cards, it wasn't a big deal.

The brothers decided to go back to Bush Terminal after work to search for Hiram's wallet.

"Holy shit, will you look at that." Sergeant Joe Kurland was overwhelmed by the mound of money that poured from the sack carried by Scott Ruben. Gabe Perone, for one rare moment speechless, gasped and then produced a long, loud whistle.

"And it's not just tens and twenties. It looks like a lot of fifties and hundreds," Kurland continued. "I wonder just how much we got?"

Ruben beamed with pride and said, "Boss, I know we're not supposed to count, but I couldn't help—" Ruben was stopped in midsentence as Kurland slammed the butt of his off-duty automatic against the side of his head. He followed through with a fierce kick to Ruben's groin that sent him, wailing with pain, crumbling to the factory floor.

"Next time, show some self-discipline, you little fuckin' weasell"

Ruben, who had nearly lost consciousness, looked up at Kurland, terrified.

"Well, how much fucking money is there, or should I say was there?" asked Kurland with an angry scream.

"Boss, I swear on my dead father, I counted the cash and I left every bill. There's nineteen thousand, three hundred and fifty dollars."

"Wow," shouted Perone.

"Empty your pockets, motherfucker," commanded Kurland.

"Boss, please, don't you believe me?" Ruben pleaded. "I swear to you, I didn't keep anything. Please, don't do this to me."

Kurland put a full clip into his weapon, pulled back the slide, loading the chamber, and took the safety off as he screeched, "Turn your fuckin' pockets inside out, now."

Suddenly Perone bellowed, "What the fuck are you guys lookin' at?" Hiram and Ramon Rodriguez had appeared from a nearby stairwell. Perone ripped his gun from his ankle holster and ordered the two brothers to put their hands in the air.

The brothers couldn't prevent themselves from staring, first at all the cash on the floor, and then at Ruben's quivering body and the shock on Kurland's face. Kurland quickly recovered and demanded, "What the fuck are you doing here?"

Hiram spoke, trying to mask his terror by responding slowly. "This is my little brother. We both work at Leib Electrical Supply here in the terminal. We had a Christmas party in this building last night, and I lost my wallet."

"There was no party on this floor," Kurland interrupted," so what the fuck are you doin' here?"

Hiram felt himself reacting to Kurland's anger. His fear for Ramon and himself made his body shake involuntarily. He replied, "No, sir, the party wasn't on this floor, but I thought maybe someone found my wallet, took the money out, and threw it somewhere in this building, so we have been searching each floor." It was, of course, the truth, but in Hiram's state of panic, he thought it sounded contrived.

Kurland shouted, "Get on the floor, facedown." Hiram's protest ended quickly when Kurland pointed his gun and said, "If you are resisting arrest, I'll fuckin' blow your head off."

Above the factory floor in the sleeping loft he'd built several years before, Bradley Coles could not understand or even quite believe what was going on. Coles watched in horror, certain that Kurland was about to murder Scott Ruben. When that drama was interrupted by the intrusion of the Rodriguez brothers, his fear subsided and he took a deep swig of wine, exhaling a burp and a long sigh. The respite was, however, short-lived, ending when Kurland ordered the brothers to hit the ground. It instantly reminded Major Coles of a deadly moment he witnessed in Saigon, when soldiers from the regular army of South Vietnam surrounded two teenagers they claimed were members of the hated VC. No sooner had the youngsters hit the ground than the regulars opened fire with their United States Army–issued M16s, sending their automatic fire ripping through the bodies of their hapless victims. Soon the ground around the youngsters had turned crimson with blood pouring from countless wounds. Coles could feel his sweat flowing from every pore as he recalled that nightmare.

The brothers quickly obeyed and dropped to the ground. Kurland said to Ruben and Perone, "Don't let these guys move. I'll be right back."

Coles knew it was over—at least for now. He took another gulp from his wine bottle.

Perone yelled after Kurland, "Boss, where're you off to?"

"Never mind. Just keep those two mutts quiet, and I'll be right back," Kurland shouted over his shoulder.

Kurland knew that Holt, "that fuckin' Boy Scout," was away visiting his uncle in upstate New York. The time had come for Kurland to get even for Holt's betrayal. Using a passkey, Kurland quickly and quietly entered the basement of the 75th Precinct, through the rear entrance. It was now well after midnight, and Kurland knew that most of the house would be out on patrol. In minutes, he found himself in front of a locker marked HOLT, STEVEN ROBERT, SGT., where he easily slipped the lock and wrapped his handkerchief around Holt's .38 police special, which had been secured in a box at the bottom and to the rear of the locker. Kurland placed the weapon in a small canvas bag and was in his van headed back to Building 1 of Bush Terminal in less than forty-five minutes.

Kurland walked swiftly across the factory floor. He held Holt's gun firmly by the grip, which was still wrapped in the handkerchief to avoid finger or palm prints. He had the weapon at his side and to the rear so it could not be readily seen.

Coles saw what Kurland was doing, and his heart began to beat rapidly as he looked on, helpless to do anything.

Kurland ignored Perone's greeting, "Hey, Boss, that didn't take long, did it?"

Hiram and Ramon were lying facedown in roughly the same position as when the sergeant left the factory. Kurland walked in their direction, never taking his eyes off them.

Coles watched on in horror. When Kurland reached the two brothers, he knelt next to Hiram's head and placed the gun against his temple. The metal click of the trigger produced a sickening popping sound that reverberated across the empty floor.

"What have you done to my broth—" Ramon never finished his sentence, because Kurland kicked him in the back of the head. Quickly Kurland bent over him, placed the gun to his temple, and completed the executions. Kurland then inspected both men, each with a single hole in the left side of his temple; he seemed pleased.

Coles began to gag, then to vomit, doing all he could to suppress the noise, and quite suddenly he passed out.

"Boss, what the fuck did you do that for?" Ruben broke the silence, giving voice to the bewildering shock he and Perone felt.

"Empty out your fuckin' pockets, you piece of shit," commanded Kurland as he drew back the hammer of his gun and pointed it at Ruben. Ruben let spill from his right pants pocket three hundred-dollar bills and four fifty-dollar bills. At the same time, he fell to his knees, sobbing and pleading, "Please, boss, please let me live, I beg you." Turning to Perone, he said, "Gabe, please help me."

Kurland released the hammer, put the gun in his shoulder holster, and said flatly, "We got a job to do. Let's go."

After loading the bodies of Hiram and Ramon Rodriguez into the rear of his van, each wrapped in an oil-stained blanket, Kurland and the other two set out toward Robert Moses State Park in Suffolk County. The raging snowstorm made the driving treacherous, but it didn't matter, because the events of the evening had brought much satisfaction to Sergeant Joseph Kurland. He smiled as he thought, *But the best is yet to come!*

The men drove in silence, mostly because Ruben and Perone had no idea where they were going and were much too afraid to ask, and because Kurland was spending this quiet time reflecting . . . and planning.

On the way back to Brooklyn, at nearly 5:30 in the morning, as the van crossed over the line dividing Queens County and Brooklyn, Kurland ordered Ruben to drive back to Bush Terminal. "Let's check out the factory. I want to make sure that there's nothin' left to cause us a problem."

"Sure, Boss," Ruben responded, certain now that his crisis had passed.

The noise of the door to the fourth floor opening roused Major Coles from his deep sleep. He peered over the side of his loft as the three men walked to the center of the room. The contents of the three bags they carried were soon emptied on the floor, and they began counting and dividing. Coles was astounded by the sheer volume of the stacks of money. When Kurland and Perone had finished counting the money from their respective bags, the sergeant slowly rose from his kneeling position next to his bag of money and walked over to Scott Ruben. In a flash, Kurland took Holt's weapon, with the handle still wrapped in a handkerchief, and placed a bullet neatly behind Ruben's ear. This was followed by an eerie silence, with both Perone and Coles frozen with fear.

Finally Kurland broke the quiet with the sound of his boots, walking over to Ruben's money sack and spilling it out. He began to divide it. Then he said, without looking up, "Gabe, never trust a fuckin' thief."

Ruben's body was wrapped mummylike in sheets and then in plastic, to hold down the stench from the decay. Then it was placed in the rear of the subbasement of Building 1, in an abandoned tool shop long ago forgotten by the management of Bush Terminal.

Ruben's body would be found when Kurland was ready to spring the final phase of his trap.

When Moore had finished, no one spoke. It was too difficult for anyone to absorb the depravity, the quintessential evil created by a New York City police officer.

District Attorney Crowley described how Perone, when faced with a prison term that would have kept him behind bars for life, pled guilty to an added charge of perjury and agreed to testify against Kurland. He would be sentenced according to his original agreement. Afterward, Crowley announced to the group that he would personally try the case against Kurland.

# epilogue

It took the jury less than seven hours to convict Kurland of all three charges of murder in the second degree.

Shortly before Thanksgiving Day 1992, Judge Michael McGowan sentenced Joseph Kurland to three consecutive sentences of twenty-five years to life. Kurland was confined to Attica State Prison. Because he was a police officer, he is kept segregated from the other prisoners. His parole eligibility will not occur until he serves seventy-five years, which will keep him in prison for the rest of his life.

Gabe Perone is serving twelve and a half to twenty-five years, also at Attica State Prison. He, too, is segregated from the rest of the prison population.

Police Commissioner Nevins retired early in 1993 to Phoenix, Arizona. His reforms were embraced by successive police commissioners, and systemic corruption has not reappeared. The commissioners have been aided by a new breed of chiefs committed to preventing any return to cyclical corruption.

Brendan and Peggy Moore withdrew to the tranquility of Lookout Point.

Robert and Shannon Mulvey still live in Delhi, New York.

Kenneth J. Rattigan was reelected district attorney of Queens County in the fall of 1993.

Brooklyn District Attorney Buddy Cooper retired in 1993 and resides in Israel with his wife, Boo.

Larry Green still practices law.

In the fall election of 1994, District Attorney Jim Crowley defeated Governor David Laurel and became New York State's first Republican governor in two decades.

In June 1995, Governor Crowley elevated Judge Michael McGowan to the New York State Court of Appeals, the state's highest court.

Wally Goss resigned from the office of the Suffolk County district attorney and was named by Governor Crowley New York State's inspector general, the state's integrity watchdog, with jurisdiction to investigate every agency in New York State.

Bernard Pressler resigned in November of 1993, after Rattigan's reelection and the election of a new mayor. He sent the following letter to District Attorney Rattigan: "Kenny, it's time for me to get off the merry-go-round. I've had a good run, but it's time to go. Please watch your back. Bernie." Pressler lives in Naples, Florida, where he plays endless rounds of golf with former police commissioner Lou Guido and former chief of department Keith "Cookie" Nolan. They never discuss the job.

By the mid-1990s, serious crime had plummeted throughout New York City as Pressler's legacy of reform, Crime Crash, was institutionalized by the NYPD.

With Dominican and Jamaican families arriving in record numbers, their leadership resolved to eliminate drug dealers from their communities. Accordingly, the phrases "Dominican drug dealers" and "Jamaican drug gangs" have disappeared from the headlines. Today, Dominicans in New York City are mostly known for their player contributions to Major League Baseball, and Jamaicans are recognized for their contributing leadership to the annual Caribean Day Parade on Labor Day in Brooklyn, the largest parade in the United States.

Shortly after the dismissal of all charges against Steven Holt, Police Commissioner Nevins assigned him to the Emergency Service Unit of the New York City Police Department. "You know, Steven," he said, "if I didn't send you to ESU, your Uncle Robert would never forgive me."

On September 11, 2001, Lieutenant Steven Robert Holt, assigned to Truck 1, ESU, responded with his partner to the scene of the World Trade Center disaster. Both officers entered the lobby of World Trade Center, Tower 2, and headed up the stairwell in search of a large group of civilians trapped by smoke conditions between the fourth and fifth floors. As they reached the fourth floor, they began to shout to the people in the stairwell, "Police, police, head down in this direction."

Steven heard a woman's voice. "Thank God. We're coming, Officer."

Suddenly the police command center broadcast: "Central to all units, this is an emergency. You are to immediately evacuate from World Trade Center, Tower 2, K. I repeat"—the voice was urgent—"immediately withdraw from World Trade Center, Tower 2, K."

"10–4," Holt replied. "This is Truck 1, ESU. We are leading a group of civilians out of Tower 2, K."

That was the last transmission recorded from Lieutenant Steven Robert Holt. Neither his remains nor those of his partner were ever found. At the time of his death, Steven Holt was thirty-seven years of age. He and his wife, Lee, were the parents of three children.

# author's note

While a great deal of what is told in this story is true, particularly the systemic corruption in many parts of the New York Police Department found in the '70s and '80s, it is important that I acknowledge the vast positive changes made by the NYPD to eliminate organized police corruption and to credit those responsible.

First of all, Raymond Kelly, while serving as police commissioner under Mayor David N. Dinkins, responded aggressively to the recommendations of a police corruption investigative panel headed by retired Justice Milton Mollen. Commissioner Kelly changed the name of Internal Affairs from Division to Bureau and raised its status within the NYPD by the appointment of a hand-picked three star chief who reported directly to him. Additionally the commissioner encouraged experienced superior officers to serve in IAB and to recruit police officers of all ranks from the field and to indoctrinate and train them to root out police corruption. Commissioner Kelly took the Mollen Commission report recommendations and went far beyond them, creating a broad design that he was confident would institutionalize anti-corruption programs within his department.

With the change of the mayoral administration, Commissioner

Kelly was not retained. Fortunately his successors had the good sense to keep his blueprint for ending the cyclical police corruption which had plagued the NYPD, reoccurring roughly every twenty years for more than a century.

Once again police commissioner under Mayor Michael R. Bloomberg, Raymond Kelly continues to hold the integrity of his department as one of his highest priorities. He has been aided in this effort not only by his chiefs and other superior officers but by the police unions, particularly those with the highest number of members, the PBA and the SBA, as well as the smaller unions representing other superior officers.

The story as it relates to two scandal-ridden police units is largely true but the fictionalized portion of the story is meant to suggest how police corruption could lead to tragedy for two police officers and to murder.